# PRODUCTION WIFE
## *diaries*

Freddie Rae Rose

outskirts
press

Outskirts Press, Inc.
http://www.outskirtspress.com

ISBN: 978-1-9772-3311-0

Cover Image by Katelyn Viveiros - Rosy Made Photography

Outskirts Press and the "OP" logo are trademarks belonging to Outskirts Press, Inc.

PRINTED IN THE UNITED STATES OF AMERICA

# CONTENTS

Dedication................................................................ i

Introduction.......................................................... iii

## Season 1

Episode 1: Horse Races, Soulmates and Welcome to Hollywood..... 3

Episode 2: The Western Production Assistant SD to LA................. 34

Episode 3: The Western, Our Relationship? Miracle?............ 45

Episode 4: The Salt Water Show and Cystic Fibrosis................... 56

Episode 5: The Blues Movie and My Little Buddy........................ 71

Episode 6: Motorcyle Drama and Rolling Our Dice..................... 78

Episode 7: Vampire Show Season 2 And Expecting a Miracle #2.... 81

Episode 8: Vampire Show Season 3 and Blue Eyed Boy................ 88

Episode 9: Marriage Counseling.................................... 122

Episode 10: The Vampire Show Season 4 and the Good Life........ 125

Episode 11: The Vampire Show Season 5 Premier
and My Wild Card.................................................... 133

Episode 12: Free Falling and a Hiatus from LA...................... 137

Episode 13: The Vampire Show Season 6
and Marriage Retreat In Vegas .............................. 152

Episode 14: The Vampire Show Finale and Our Marriage?.......... 155

Episode 15: The Robot Show and Back at the Ranch ............. 167

Episode 16: The Demon Show
and North Carolina for the Summer......................... 172

Episode 17: Thriller and a 500 Mile Walk............................181
Episode 18: Transition, LA to SD and a Leap of Faith...................200
Episode 19: The Mama Drama 2 and Geographic Separation......207
Episode 20: Divorce Vows: Beginning and an End.......................217
Episode 21: Lawrence and Reese Together Again, Season 2?.......231

## Season 2

Episode 1: My Script Notes............................................239
Episode 2: His Script Notes...........................................241
Episode 3: Hiatus.......................................................245
Episode 4: The Creepy Show.............................................254
Episode 5: Jet Lag and the Deal.......................................257
Episode 6: Home Box Office and Lawrence's Angel......................268
Episode 7: From Rehab and Mehab to The Emmys......................286
Episode 8: Best Friends................................................289
Episode 9: Running to Nashville......................................291
Episode 10: Followed My Shell Home.................................295

# DEDICATION

I dedicate this book to my sister and Jay. If they didn't lose their bet at the horse races that day, I wouldn't have met my first true love. Mark, in Transpo, thank you for reminding me to follow MY dreams. And a big thank you to our many counselors, our trainer and my girlfriends/sisters that volunteered their time to help me finish this novel.

Thank you to every friend that listened to me in my hardest days.

To all the people that saved my life-Thank you.
To all the men and women who gave their lives-Thank you.
To all the men and women who protect our lives-Thank You.

Special Thanks

God
Alma
Steve
Alysha
Glenn

___

Starbucks Crew in San Diego-Ellen, Marc, Martina, and Gabby

Thank you for getting me out of bed every day in my hardest moments.

Thank you for giving me more than a cup of coffee.

"Death is actually not a scary thing. The scary thing is living a life without a passion and then realizing at the very last moment that it's over and you haven't done what you wanted to do-and that you're not proud of your life. That is much more terrifying."

Claire Wineland(15), TedxMalibu

"I'm sure you have challenges, things that you wish you could overcome, or things that you wish you could get over... Stop. Stop trying to get over it. Because if we are trying to get over all our problems in life then our entire lifetime is just going to be trying to get over problems—and you may miss things you could truly accomplish. And that is not a life to be proud of. Instead, find those challenges in your life and use them! Use them and turn them into opportunities.

Claire Wineland(15), TedxMalibu

John 3:16

# INTRODUCTION

**Many, many years ago in my twenties...**
I was the production girlfriend carried out of many Hollywood premier and wrap parties.

I was the young production wife who, in front of my husband, told the lead actor in the show he was my wild card.

I was the production wife at the talent show rehearsals that told the LA PTA moms to go f*ck themselves. They deemed my kids' stunt fighting skit as too violent to be considered talent.

I was the production wife that told my doubles partner, "I don't give a f*ck if your husband is a famous *****. And I said it in front of him and all the party guests.

I was the production wife who thought that a man could bring me happiness.

I was the production wife who once thought money could bring happiness too.

I was the drunk production wife who told an asst. director (now a huge TV and film exec) I was going to sh*t on his face to get him to stop talking about himself at a film premier. Gross. I was so drunk.

I was the production wife that fell in the bushes and lost my wedding ring at the Emmy Party...I think.

I can't say I am proud of how I handled all these

moments. I can say these moments were part of my journey and without them **I wouldn't be who I am today.**

**I am** the production wife that managed to execute a huge charity event and simultaneously support my husband as he battled a life-threatening disease.

**I am** the production wife who helped save my husband's career. Who wouldn't?

**I am** the production wife that raised hundreds of thousands of dollars for charity.

**I am** the production wife who kicks ass as a mom and raises two brilliant boys, one battling cystic fibrosis.

**I am** the production wife that supported her husband as he followed all his career dreams.

**I am** the production wife who took a look at myself and changed the program I was given.

**I am** the production wife that learned to love herself and others with all my heart.

**I am** the production wife who believes in miracles, as I have seen many first hand.

**I am** the production wife that without a doubt believes there is a God.

**Will I be the production wife that is strong enough to leave a marriage that becomes unhealthy?**

**How hard will I fight for the vows I made?**

**Am I enough?**

**Will I lose my friends? Will I lose my family? Will I lose myself?**

These next chapters/episodes are just a few pages in my journey, but without the pages, we wouldn't have the script. There will be missing pages and in time I will fill them in—when I am ready.

Let's rewind this season to the first episode.

I have spent more than a decade with my love in the

television industry and, while I have been by his side through it all, our season has had its ups and downs. This is the way I want to remember our season, so I will play for you our script. Let's say this season is inspired by a few true events with dramatization and a lot of embellishing, enhancing and editing, because it's Hollywood so why not? Let's also say that this season is part of a series. There are many seasons in my life and my time as a production wife. I am much more than that, but proud to share my production wife diaries. If I can help one more human being then I have achieved my goal here. My love is not just an amazing, hardworking TV producer, but he has produced an amazing life for me and our boys. He is a great father. Thank you, Lawrence, for making me beyond strong and for being my biggest teacher. For though we may have brought out each other's worst wounds at times, we were each other's biggest teachers and now it is our responsibility to be our own healers.

*Two of the great lessons humanity will learn in the 21$^{st}$ century will be:*

*to harm another is to harm oneself*
*when you heal yourself you heal the world*

*Yung Pueblo(Diego Perez)*

My diaries helped me accept and appreciate myself and this life. Our boys are the best part of a love story-crazy love story that takes on many roles such as lovers, friends, partners, roommates and parents, perhaps singles? However it turns out I am thankful, beyond thankful, to breathe each day, especially in the good times.

Thank you, Hollywood, for taking me on this ongoing

journey of self-discovery and healing. I am also sorry for resenting you, Hollywood. I hated you for taking him from us, but you didn't. He chose you over us as part of his journey. It had to happen that way to be where we are right now. Thank you for giving him a purpose, especially in his darkest days when the boys and I could not. Without Hollywood we wouldn't have the good memories and amazing insurance. Once again thank you for being part of our journey. Without your lessons and support we would not be the people we are today. This how I want to remember Hollywood.

# Season 1

# Episode 1

## HORSE RACES, SOULMATES AND WELCOME TO HOLLYWOOD

June 5, 2017

Soundtrack:
**Is It True**
**(Juni Ata)**

"**D**o you vow to celebrate what you have with Lawrence including your boys, your memories, family and friends?" asked the officiant as I noted Lawrence had lost twenty pounds. Did he meet someone else? If so, I needed to be happy for him. That's why we're here: to be the best for our kids and be happy for each other. They deserved this. They didn't deserve divorce, but they deserved the best case divorce and parents that got along. Parents that loved each other.

"I do," I said with confidence. I wasn't wearing white as I said these vows. My Black Orchid Denim and Free People body suit would do. I had put on my Ned lip balm and some tinted moisturizer, unlike the professional hair and make-up on my wedding day. I liked simple. It was time to find that again, especially within myself.

"Do you vow to celebrate what you have with Reese? Do you vow to celebrate your boys, your memories, family and friends?" Bryce, the divorce officiant said with a calm tone. He was a tall handsome brunette and friend to both of us for years. Who knew the man Lawrence met on a drunk golf day with his studio exec would be the officiant for our pre-divorce vow ceremony?

"I do," Lawrence agreed with soft green eyes. A piece of paper peeked out of his pocket. Did he write down his answers to the questions? Did he have something to read? We didn't write our marriage vows, why write divorce vows?

"And back to you. Do you vow to take 100% responsibility in your part of the failure of your marriage? Do you vow to forgive Lawrence for his mistakes in the marriage?" This felt surreal. I felt a different energy from Lawrence. The stressed workaholic seemed at peace. This was good for both of us. Clearly.

"And Lawrence, same to you. Do you vow to take 100% responsibility in your part in the failure of your marriage? Do you vow to forgive Reese for her mistakes in the marriage?"

"I do," I said as I looked Lawrence in the eyes. I gave it all I had. I did my best.

"I do," Lawrence agreed. We had rows of empty seats. Not one family member or friend supported us in our divorce. Well, one did: Bryce, the man reading our divorce vows to us. Our parents had 90+ years of marriage altogether. They always said to make it work. That's when you know you have clarity and peace within, when you don't care what anyone else thinks.

"We do," we said in unison.

"And this is the hardest one. Reese and Lawrence, do

you vow to be 100% happy for each other in future relation-ships, job decisions and life decisions?"

"We do," we said in sync, taking these vows as seriously as we did on our wedding day, hopefully more seriously.

"By the power invested in me I now pronounce you hap-pily capable to divorce or legally separate. Your six month waiting period can begin." This divorce vow ceremony was something we learned from one of our counselors. She wasn't always for divorce, but if a couple chose that route, these were her vows the couple had to work on before fil-ing. The focus was to keep the children the priority during the transition.

I closed my eyes. How did we get here? This was an in-teresting way to celebrate my birthday. Was I 100% sure about this? Yes. Many years of traditional marriage counsel-ing, years of non-traditional marriage counseling, individual counseling, two marriage retreats and over 200k spent in saving our marriage. Yes, I was 100% sure. How did we get to this point? We did invest almost every dollar, well after memory-making into saving our marriage. The beautiful truth was that even after all the pain, I found a way to fully love him as the father of my children.

I walked away in my wedges. I turned around and he smiled at me. I kept walking. It just didn't add up. We could have been so good, but still the trust wasn't there. We had everything but trust. He couldn't trust me and vice versa. The vows, I agreed to the vows, but the trust. I had to remind myself that this is why I am doing this, but still something just didn't add up, it never did. I had to remind myself we brought out the absolute worst in each other at times and we just couldn't take it anymore. It was time to truly forgive myself and forgive him for the faults of our marriage. I did my best. Could he say the same? That wasn't for me to answer.

## July 2003

Like so many great adventures, ours began at the horse races. The iconic Del Mar racetrack on the coast just north of San Diego, to be exact. It was the summer of 2003 and I was young, carefree, and living life to the fullest. I was fully prepared for a wild night out with my girls. Little did I know it would turn into so much more.

The doorbell rang and my younger and closest sister, Makayla, was there with our friends, Laurel and Leigh, to pick me up. Why she was ringing the doorbell, I don't know. Makayla and I lived with our parents for the summer, but she had gone to Laurel's parents to borrow clothes for herself and grabbed me some pieces too.

"You all look super-cute, like girl-next-door cute," I said, hugging them. I felt pretty spicy myself after throwing on an A-line shaped skirt from Laurel, paired with a white cotton Abercrombie tube top to bring out my summer tan. I had just run five miles and cut some fresh bangs to change up my 'do. They framed my face and gave me a little extra confidence that night. My confidence turned on and off like a light switch. Tonight, it was on.

In no time, we were on our way to the Del Mar racetrack to catch the last 4:00 p.m. Friday race of the summer season, followed by a Hoobastank concert. As we drove, we spelled out our goals for the night.

Makayla, with a Hawaiian modelesque appearance, shouted, "My goal is to find a guy to buy us all drinks." She had one year left playing division one soccer, her toned legs were proof of her athleticism.

This was not surprising to me at all since this was her M.O. pretty much every time we went out, but we weren't complaining because, hey, free drinks.

Leigh followed with her goal, "Mine is to win money!" This also was not surprising since she was pretty broke at the time, being a student at Pepperdine in Malibu. She was an athletic, shorter version of Nicole Kidman with the most gorgeous, thick, strawberry blond hair and killer six pack. She said she would buy a house on Broad Beach for all of us someday when she became a lawyer. Actually, we were all broke back then. We were rich in youth and innocence. Leigh radiated those qualities with her perfect smile and kind heart. She had it all, including a perfect family full of faith and love.

Sun-kissed and brainy, UC Santa Barbara student Laurel chimed in, "Mine is to not hook up with a stranger, but of course someday I will marry a man with a PhD that loves sports" – a noble goal for her.

We all laughed. By hook up she meant kiss. She was going to be a pharmacist and was undecided where she would continue for her doctorates. Would she find chemistry tonight?

"Reese, your goal should be to not kiss a bald guy with your beer goggles," Makayla teased.

"I am the DD later, you brat. And the bald guy was not bald. He shaved it because he was a pilot," I teased back. "Don't give me a hard time for kissing hotties that serve our country. Yours should be to limit your make outs to five guys instead of ten."

We had that banter as sisters. Even though I was eighteen months older, I felt we were raised as twins, being on most of the same teams, and at times competing for the same guys. This was an insecurity of mine. She beat me in every sport and had legs a foot longer. I spent way too many high school days longing for her legs and ability to talk to non-guy friends without being awkward. College had helped me be more confident, but I wished I had seen my worth earlier on. I ignored the fact that I was captain of the soccer team, on the A team and had tons of friends. And on top of that I had unconditionally loving parents. I was always looking for more.

"Well, mine is kind of opposite of Laurel's. I want to make out with a hot guy on the beach – because why not?" I stated with every intention of reaching my goal. "What can I say? This is our last week of summer before returning to college? I just want to have fun."

I had just one semester left of my senior year as a wildcat at University of Arizona. I was graduating early. All those extra classes had paid off.

The Makayla, Leigh and Laurel trio was the best of both worlds. They knew how to balance studies and fun. Study hard and play hard. I played too hard my first semester of college and received credit for only six units out of the registered sixteen. But I made up for it by taking extra classes and proving to my parents I wasn't wasting their hard-earned money for out of state tuition. I was good at getting back up when I fell. I was a fighter.

The Brigantine was on our right as we turned the corner toward the north parking lot entrance. We drove through the dusty parking lot laughing about our goals and wondering who would actually accomplish theirs. I took a few swigs of Laurel's mini flask that she kept in her bra. "Makayla, I'll drink a little now and sober up to drive us by the time the concert ends."

"Deal," Makayla shouted over Garth Brook's "Friends in Low Places."

As we approached the parking attendant at the racetrack, wind was blowing through our hair, but dust was getting in our mouths. We were blasting Country to get into the horsey feel even though horses were the only common denominator between Country and racing. Makayla started paying the attendant in pennies and nickels. Parking was fifteen dollars. As she counted them out slowly with a long line of cars behind us, the attendant said, "Go ahead, please," after just one dollar in change. We couldn't stop chuckling at the look on his face when Makayla counted out the coins from her ashtray one at a time. We were wild and free and living life with no worries or real responsibilities. We had no idea how stressful life would get once we grew up. I'm sure all of us wish we were still back there in that Jeep enjoying whatever came our way...aside from the dust.

Our bodies were glowing, young and wrinkle free. We were exuding the vibe of youth and we were on the prowl for a good time. Like little cougar cubs, we smiled and innocently eye-thrusted all the men as we padded into the races. We were definitely teases. We were all prancing through the crowd. That authentic innocence worked in our favor. First stop was the bar. Margaritas for everybody.

Makayla pretended to trip as she worked her way to the front of the line. When she got to the front she realized, oops, she didn't have her credit card. As she returned holding two marg shakers and a sexy stud holding a couple more, I knew this was going to be a great night.

"My goal accomplished! Free drinks!" Makayla whispered with glee as her brown locks danced around her face in celebration. We started walking away but the gullible drinks buyer chased after us.

"Where are you girls hanging out? My boys have a box at the finish line if you want to put your feet up," he offered sweetly in a navy suit with a light blue popped collar.

"Great! We may just take you up on that offer. But later.

---

We're off to check out some horses," I said as we sashayed away, drinks in our young hands. I took one sip and passed it to Laurel since I was the DD in seven hours. Those few sips of tequila would wear off by then. "Don't forget to hold the lid down when you shake."

I loved checking out the horses before the races. It was my only real strategy when it came to betting. Basically, I looked to see which jockey looked the happiest or cutest and bet on him. Makayla's strategy was to hang out with whichever guy looked like the most experienced bettor and copy from his betting book. Leigh and Laurel just picked their favorite numbers. We were real pros.

While looking at the horses, we decided to add a bet to our goals that night. Whichever girl picked the losing horse on the last race had to find a handsome group of stallions to join us at the Hoobastank concert straight after.

I don't remember how I did on my bets that day, but I know we had a blast watching the races. At the last race, Makayla's horse and Leigh's tied for last place, so they teamed up to figure out our next move for the evening. They were on a mission when a sweet whiff of tequila caught Makayla's attention.

"Ladies, want to join us on the patio overlooking the concert? My buddy just won a ton of money and wants to share it with all the beautiful women!" said a familiar voice. It was the guy from earlier. Must have been good karma. He bought us drinks and then his buddy won a ton of money and was buying him drinks...and us, it seemed. Our goals were working –Leigh had won money, Laurel was resisting men, Makayla got free drinks, and I was on my way to find a hottie to make out with.

Things became blurry as shots of tequila were passed and crowds of people swirled around us. But everything came into focus when I met Lawrence.

"Hi, I'm Reese," I greeted him as I tossed my chocolate mane to the right side of my neck, swirling the ends with my right index finger and plopping down right next to him. "Lawrence. Hey." He had deep vocals and green eyes. "I'm driving tonight and staring at all these margaritas is killing me," I said innocently, bouncing in my chair. I had a lot of energy.

"That makes two of us. Can I check your ID? My friends are betting your group is underage, and in that case, I shouldn't be talking to you," he said seriously.

"Here you go. Twenty-one!" I handed him my ID. Was he serious?

"Oh, thank God. You girls looked barely eighteen," he muttered, still acting a bit hesitant and rubbing both his hands on the back of his neck in an intense scratching motion. His hands resituated his hat three times. He then bent his arms and stretched them behind his back. I wasn't going to bite him. Was he nervous?

"Um, I think I saw a camel go by," I announced with a cute little smile. Braces paid off, along with those whitening strips.

"Pardon me?" he responded with his pillow lips.

"When you moved your bicep. I thought I saw a camel go by." I laughed trying to make him feel more relaxed and noting his lips would be perfect for a make out session. That was all I really knew how to do.

"Cute, very cute," he expressed with a returned smile.

My joke broke the ice and bonded us instantly, along with being DDs for our friends. We chatted and relaxed as the music played and the sun slowly set. I swear it was like a scene out of a Rom-Com, with the Pacific Ocean as the backdrop and Hoobastank playing the score. What a beautiful way to end the summer before I went back to college.

The concert ended, but we were determined to keep the party going. His crew was thinking the exact same thing. "Do you girls want to come to our beach house in Carlsbad?"

We grouped together and strolled through the giant parking lot. We reached Lawrence's friend's car first. Suddenly, my drunk sister and friends squeezed right into his buddy's Range Rover along with his crew, leaving me alone in the jeep to follow soberly behind.

"Reese, can you follow me? It will be fine. Where are you parked?" Lawrence said, picking up on my worried radar. My expression did not hide it. I prayed these men were decent human beings. Coincidentally, I was parked really close to them, so I pulled up to his car and some of his friends hopped in mine. I was uneasy about all this, but I hoped my instincts were wrong. Would the night end like a Rom-Com or a horror movie?

The drive wasn't too long, thank God. And I was stunned when we pulled up to a gorgeous cottage that was literally right on the beach. As my sister and friends poured out of the Rover all smiles and clearly enjoying every minute, I breathed a sigh of relief. Everyone ran around in the sand, laughing and intoxicated by the full moon. But through it all, I still had my eye on Lawrence. When he started to take a stroll down the beach, I poured myself a drink from the collection of liquor in their house and decided to make a move. I also decided we were staying at this beach cottage because there was no way I would be able to drive after these drinks.

"May I join you?" A rhetorical question as I was out of breath from trying to catch up with him, drink in hand.

"Of course," Lawrence replied.

"Are you married?" I asked without the least bit of subtlety. I was saving myself for my future husband.

"No," he answered bluntly. For some weird reason, I noticed he had really veiny forearms.

"Why not?" I pried as I gulped down my pineapple and Malibu concoction.

"Because..." he started to answer.

"Because why?" I interrupted, sipping again.

"Do you always interview strangers?" he said jokingly.

"We already met so I am not a stranger. Really, why aren't you married? You're tan and gorgeous." I was flattering him, but I was also genuinely curious how this perfect specimen of a man could be single.

"I haven't met the right girl," he said, clearly enjoying my shameless flirtation.

"I'll marry you and have your kids," I said with a grin. Of course, I wasn't serious, well, maybe a little, but looking back I must have sounded pretty desperate. Who was I, offering to marry a guy because he was insanely good looking? Twenty-one, all bronze and no brains. Did I choose men the same way I chose horses?

"Are you sure about marrying me? I am currently unemployed. I just got fired from McDonalds." He said it so convincingly that I believed him, but was totally unfazed.

"That makes two of us who are broke. Another thing we have in common, besides being designated drivers," I confidently assured him. We were clearly meant to be. He was so smoking hot I didn't care what he did as long as his part time job could be kissing my lips.

My goal that night had been to make out with a hottie on the beach and so I took advantage of the moonlight and decided to go for a swim. I charged the water with reckless abandon and felt a rush of adrenaline course through my body as the waves crashed around me. Lawrence chased after me, pulling his shirt over his head to reveal drool-worthy abs that glistened in the moonlight. Funny thing is, he rolled up his jeans and took his shirt off. Why didn't he just take off his pants? He obviously wanted to show off his abs. Well played, Lawrence. He was worried for my safety as I frolicked around in my skirt, soaking wet from head to toe. It was a magical fairy tale moment as I jumped into his arms, wrapped my legs around him and started kissing him all over. He returned the kiss with intensity. I tasted passion, sexiness and salt on my lips. My skirt was wet as the rhythm of the waves drew us even closer. The waves crashed all around us, but it didn't matter because time stopped.

"Why is God so good to me?" I yelled, instantly regretting my honesty and proof I had no game. Can I blame it on the alcohol?

Even though I joked about being his wife that night, I definitely was not looking for Mr. Right, just a hottie to make out with. I had no expectations of the evening's outcome and that allowed all of me to align with Lawrence. I had accidentally met my soul mate. Tingles took over my soul, yielding a collision of our universes. It was amazing. It was fire. I cannot fully explain the sparks that flowed, but any worry or fear dissipated as I melted into his arms. We fell asleep on the beach that night and I never wanted it to end. My head snuggled against his slick chest and my body was held by his camel biceps. He was such a man and I had only dated boys. Was he my Richard Gere–just an unemployed one? Was I his Julia Roberts-just a virgin one? Was it the alcohol talking?

But the next day it was back to reality and back to school for me. I drove five fast hours back to Arizona to finish my last semester of undergrad. Lawrence and I stayed in touch and a few weeks later I got the call I was really hoping for.

I was watching the *Bachelor* with my roommates, one being my sister in our Tucson house, when the phone rang.

"What are you doing?" he asked with that hot deep voice.

"Thinking of your abs," I flirted superficially. I talked a big game but had no real intimate experience at least from what I remembered.

"I am sitting on the beach staring at the full moon and wondering if you'll meet me in Havasu next weekend?" he asked.

"I have a soccer game, but let me see what time it starts, maybe I can swing it," I quickly responded, excited to see my soulmate.

That weekend, my game was gloriously cancelled so I jumped in the car early morning and drove to Havasu. It was my first time. There were many firsts with Lawrence.

I pulled up to the driveway and was greeted by Lawrence and two married couples. Old and boring were the two words that popped into my head even though I was offering to marry Lawrence. Was I really ready to be in that type of commitment? One day at a time. I hadn't even spent twenty-four hours with him.

Their truck was ready to go with boat in tow. I quickly threw my bag in the guest room next to Lawrence's, jumped in his 4Runner and we followed behind.

We boarded the boat with intentions of a good time.

"Hi, I am Reese," I said, shaking hands with the couples. "Where are you from?"

"Newport and Laguna," the wives answered in unison. Weird.

Lawrence had worked for years with one of the wives, Summer.

They had so much to catch up on. I learned they'd

worked five years together on a TV show. I guess he did this before McDonalds and Sears? Lawrence started as an assistant after graduating from USD, a beautiful private Catholic school in San Diego. Apparently, when people work on TV shows they become very close. Summer seemed like a sister to him, a special one. What exactly did Lawrence do? The only industry jobs I knew were actor, director and producer and still even director/producer roles were unclear to me.

"Hold onto your drinks and your tops," Summer's husband, Bernardo, yelled as he illegally sped down the channel. Lawrence sat next to me with his shirt off and of course glistening abs. He seemed distracted with Summer as they had so much to catch up on. I wanted to hang out with someone and if I was going to be ignored, I would find something fun to do. The entire group was at least thirteen years older than me. I became shy and plastered sunscreen on my body to take my mind off negative thoughts. I wish Lawrence noticed me struggling to apply sunscreen to my back. Why was I here? I took my hat off to apply sunscreen to my face and realized it was my ex's hat. The ex from Beverly Hills. Did I belong back on campus in my element with people my age—people like my ex? My confidence switched off.

The boat parked on the sand barge where many people stood and talked in shallow waters, drinks in hand. Some brave girls wore pasties. I had to ask others what they were called. I had never seen them before. I stood in the water, taking in the beauty of the lake with my windblown hair and pink polka dot ruffle bikini, when a football splashed by my toned soccer thighs. Now this is my element, football. Why did Lawrence invite me if he didn't want to hang out? I picked up the football and threw it back to the owner. Did he sense my need for attention? The attention I was wanting from Lawrence.

"Nice throw," he yelled.

"Thank you," I yelled back, smiling and motioning for him to throw it again. I was instantly transported back to my childhood days of playing football with my neighbors, the Lewis brothers and the fun lunchtime football league in middle school. I was the girl that wore a dress with sneakers, so I could play sports in it. I was an athlete and I was thrilled to hang with this guy, whoever he was. Sports put me in my comfort zone.

After thirty minutes of catch with my new friend, "Want to come to my boat and get a beer?" he invited loudly, as Lawrence and Summer looked in my direction.

"I can't," I answered awkwardly.

"Why not?" proposed Summer, pushing out her newest enhancements. Was she trying to get rid of me? And what was I supposed to say? Lawrence had been deep in convo with her for a while now and if I was just with my friends, I would have grabbed a beer with football guy. But I thought I was hanging with my soul mate and his friends. Or so I'd hoped. I stumbled for words. The best I could muster was, "I can't."

"Why can't you?" questioned the six-foot, brunette, sun-kissed Greek god.

I just looked at Lawrence trying to signal to my new friend that I was with him, but suddenly, I didn't want to be. I drove four hours to see the love of my life and was being ignored. I felt trapped and frustrated. Why didn't I just leave with football guy?

There were no hugs or kisses like the salty ocean ones I got our first night together and I couldn't wait to leave the next day. I didn't like how I felt.

Lawrence recognized my effort. "I made you a CD for the ride. Thank you for coming." The title read "Unwritten

Law." It was very sweet of him, but I was bummed. This was not the romantic weekend away I'd envisioned. I put the CD in and got lost in it. Did he know they were from my hometown area or was that a coincidence? As I listened to their entire CD I remembered when the band had knocked on my childhood friend's door. The band paid her family and gave them a ton of swag to shoot a video on her lot. "Cailin" was my favorite song.

The great CD made time pass quickly and soon I arrived back in Tucson doubting our previous soulmate title. I still couldn't stop thinking about that first night. His lips, his touch, his smell and jokes played over in my head. I wanted that. I wanted that back. I wanted that passion. I called him.

"Lawrence, how would you feel about a weekend in Vegas with me and my girls? We are flying out there for Halloween." I presented my offer and it would be my last. If I felt a connection again, I'd pursue him. If we didn't click over Halloween, I was going to be done.

"I'm working, but I can come for ten hours," he explained with phones ringing in the background. "It happens to be my buddy's thirtieth, so my group will be out there as well for a night if you don't mind us all meeting up? I originally wasn't going to make it."

"Okay, I am calling Southwest right now with my free flight voucher and booking you a round trip flight," I assured him as my sister listened to the conversation. I gave her a peppy thumbs up. This was a very generous gesture being that I could have used that voucher to fly home to SD one weekend.

"He's in. I promise if we don't have a good time I will never talk about him again," I whispered as I hung the phone back in the cradle. Makayla painted her toe nails and tried to smile. But she was dubious. My recounting of the last weekend away had not inspired confidence in our big romance. She had been furious at him for ignoring me. I had to admit, I had been too. Was I insane to give him another chance? Should I bring up my feelings or move on?

## October 30, 2003

Lawrence and his beach house roommates flew and the six of us single girls, mainly my sister's friends, drove from one desert to the next. I struggled to have tons of college friend groups like my sister. Whatever boy I was dating became my priority, putting roommates and girlfriends on the backburner. My time was spent with the flavor at the time and his friends. When I broke up with a boyfriend I would lose, not just my boyfriend, but my friends too since his friends became my friends. When I went back to my roommates after a break up they felt like second fiddle. When I needed a group of girls, my sister always pulled me in. She gave me unconditional love whether I made her my priority or not. Her friends were always so fun.

I guess my friends at home were so great it was hard to find friends that measured up to my childhood soccer teammates. Makayla was free spirited, so it made sense she would attract fun, positive friends. Jaime was a twin attending U of A without her actual sister. Belinda was a super So-Cal girl who made smoochie signs out the window to hot Vegas goers and Joy was also So-Cal but with a little church-girl thrown in. This was made very apparent by her DJ selection. Let's just say I've never listened to so much Amy Grant in my life. Not bad. My parents did bring me home a signed shirt when they went to her concert. I grew up going to church, but never had a real relationship with God. I didn't know how to let him in.

We pulled up to the Flamingo and marched to the reception desk.

"Can I help you?" the receptionist asked, as we stood holding handbags and no luggage. Inside we'd jammed swimsuits, Fredrick's of Hollywood Halloween costumes, make-up, pajamas and one extra outfit. We were good at packing light.

"Checking in. The room is under Sigars," I responded, all smiles, until I noticed a missed call from Lawrence. I checked my voicemail. I panicked. Was he cancelling? Of course, he was. Why was I such an idiot? I listened nervously.

*Hey, I am here. My boys have a table at NOBU if you and your friends want to join. Reservation at eight. Please let me know if you can't make it. If not, I will see you there.*

I breathed a sigh of relief, grabbed the room keys from the receptionist, grinned and got in the elevator with the girls in tow.

"Makayla what is NOBU? Do you guys want to go? Res at eight."

"I think it's sushi at the Hard Rock," said Belinda.

Jaime chimed in, "It's seven already so we need to get showered quick."

One shower and six girls. We swung open the door to two beds. Two beds and six girls. Who would take the floor? I didn't care too much. All I cared about was this group of girls meeting up with Lawrence. They'd set me straight if I was falling for a player. We ran around like crazy getting ready. I made sure I looked flawless.

"Leaving in five," I yelled as we scurried to add final touches – earrings, lip gloss, hair spray.

We whisked down the elevator, jumped into two cabs and made it in perfect time for eight o'clock.

"Wow," Belinda said as we entered the restaurant., "This place is fancy." Puffy, peaceful white pillowlike lanterns lined the black ceiling reminding me of moon jellies danc-ing in the ocean. I was reminded of the time I visited the Aquarium of the Pacific in Long Beach with my family in my teens. This atmosphere calmed my nervousness about see-ing Lawrence again. I was putting it all on the line. Would our hearts illuminate like the moon jellies?

"Are you joining a group of men?" the hostess asked knowingly.

"Yes," Joy answered, smudging her hot pink lipstick around.

"Follow me." The hostess adjusted her chopstick stabbed bun and led the way.

"Welcome to Vegas," a loud in-sync cheer resounded as we approached the table.

Lawrence stood up to greet me with a hug as the oth-er smoking hot Carlsbad surfers pulled out chairs for my friends. I noted the manners and was impressed. I recog-nized Eric, Lawrence's friend and roommate from the races. Makayla had her eye on him. Blond hair and blue eyes with a perfect resemblance of Taj Burrows. Could he surf like him too? Doubt it. Perhaps his future offspring.

"I hope you ladies don't mind, we just asked the chef to bring out the best dishes and to keep it coming," he said as intros took place. There was already a great chemistry in the group of twenty and thirty somethings. I grinned inwardly. Lawrence had also not let go of my hand. I fully forgave his Havasu behavior in my mind.

Hamachi, meaning yellowtail in Japanese, was placed in the center of the table. A first sushi experience for me led to a lot of stabbing with my chopsticks. I am half Asian, but Indonesian, not Japanese and had no idea what I was doing. The guys were dying laughing, "You know you are stabbing at the best sushi in town?"

"My first time," I chuckled. It felt like the scene out of *Pretty Woman,* my favorite movie, when the snail shot off Julia Roberts's plate.

The chopsticks rested gently on black stones. I picked my stone up to guess what kind of rock it was. It was smooth and heavy.

"You know why the rocks are there?" Lawrence quizzed me, touching my thigh. I wanted to extend this quiz a bit longer if I was going to feel tingles. I had these fantasies and thoughts, but never carried them out.

"Why?" I asked, wanting to draw out the touch from his huge hands, but then pulling my leg back a little.

I was feeling vulnerable when he finally answered.

"These are exfoliating rocks. If you want to rub them on your face, that's what they are there for."

I rubbed the rock on my face along with Makayla. The thirties began dying with laughter. It was a joke. I was so embarrassed I had no good comeback. Luckily for me, Belinda was not under the spell of Lawrence's thigh-stroking hand.

"Glad my friends can provide entertainment for all of you assholes," she smirked, drawing a few eyes to her cleavage. To my relief, she was never lost for words. I squinted my eyes at Lawrence, chiding him for his gag. He shrugged with a smile and touched my newly exfoliated face. Suddenly I felt like there was no one in the restaurant but the two of us. It was happening. The connection was there. I soaked up every second.

Lawrence stood up. God, he was hot.

"Are you looking for the restroom? It's right over there where that rock wall is," I said.

"Thanks," he winked and headed off.

Five seconds later he walked back out. "Funny, really funny."

"How was the tour of the kitchen?" I grinned.

The bill came and the twenties pulled a few bucks out of bras and wristlets. The guys looked at us and told us to put it away. I glanced at the bill and for ten of us it was over one thousand dollars. Nobu did not equal college girl budget. But its definition did mean *trust* and *faith* in Japanese and I hoped that was a good omen.

We continued to embrace every minute - mostly at the roulette table.

"I can't wait to teach you how to play roulette," Lawrence said as he led me out of Nobu to the roulette tables.

"Is it hard?" I asked excited to learn something new.

"Something is. Ha. No, truly it's fun. Well, at least how I play. I have a theory if we are nice to the dealer and tip him/her, they will hit our numbers, eventually," he explained throwing two thousand dollars in cash on the table.

"How do you want your chips?" the dealer asked him with a smile. She was attracted to him, which was good for us. Maybe she would hit our numbers. Whatever that meant.

"Please split it. One thousand in blue chips for me and one thousand in chips for the lovely lady."

"What color do you want, sweetheart?"

"I would like pink tonight," a funny choice for me since I didn't like pink but owned one pink bikini. There were a lot of firsts already. Sushi, roulette and pink chips. I loved doing new things.

The dealer handed us piles of chips in a variety of values perfectly measured out. I loved how she lined up the stacks when she counted.

"Thank you, Lawrence. Are you sure?" I don't think I had ever had this much money in my hand at once in my lifetime.

"Yes, as long as you keep playing they are yours. Just cover the board with your favorite numbers. Think of birthdates or whatever numbers stand out to you. Have fun with it. If you lose it's my money so no worries."

This was so much money, I wanted to walk away and go shopping, but not at the expense of losing out on this time with Lawrence. It wasn't about the money; it was about the ride. His generosity was so attractive. I started putting chips all over the board. I always put chips on number nine(my favorite number), twenty-one (my age) and thirty-three(Lawrence's age). I placed a stack on odd or even depending on what I felt and then loved putting chips on four corners of a group of numbers. Your odds were higher, but the payout was less. Roulette became my favorite game.

Two hours later we were still there while our friends were off conquering the casino together.

Four hours later we were still there when security walked over with Makayla. Where were the others? It wasn't like them to abandon each other.

"Excuse me sir, that's my sister. Is everything okay?"

"This girl needs to go to bed. She tried to fight me," he said annoyed and shoving her toward me.

"We will take her with us," Lawrence said all chivalrous.

"I just want to sit here for a minute, don't take me back to my room," she slurred as she lay down under the roulette table.

By this point the dealer had switched out and the new dealer, a male told me, "It's okay, let her chill for a moment while you guys play. You are on a roll."

"Okay, this is definitely a first for me, but Reese, don't forget to split the zeros too. I have a feeling they will hit."

Time was special again when he was by my side and we

had a blast. I connected my sis with our other friends and they cabbed it back to the Flamingo.

The sparks were back. We kept getting free drinks. We played until I couldn't see over my chips. We hugged and kissed constantly over the ten hours together. I didn't want to stay the night with him so ten hours was perfect.

We embraced final goodbyes back at the Flamingo where I went to sleep dreaming about what we could be. I glanced at my sequined genie costume laid out for the Halloween festivities tomorrow. It would be fun. But not as fun as having Lawrence with me.

## Mid-November 2003

We kept in contact and I saw him again when I went home to San Diego for Thanksgiving break. He met my family the day before the big feast at the Cheesecake Factory to celebrate my dad's birthday. He brought his roommate, Eric, for comfort. Makayla was excited.

My dad opened gifts after dinner while we were waiting for dessert.

"Lawrence, don't worry. Makayla picked up a gift for you to give to my dad," I said reassuringly. That was so sweet of her. Lawrence looked relieved.

My dad read out loud, "TO Freddy FROM Lawrence."

He unwrapped the small box and there was a coupon book with a bow around it. My dad flipped to the first page.

"A free hug from your wife."

"What?" Lawrence said looking at me and Makayla.

"Next coupon," My dad read on, "A kiss from your wife."

Lawrence was speechless.

Next page, "A blooooo, you guys, come on!" my dad yelled and laughed. We were all dying.

"It wasn't from me. I swear. Makayla insisted I give this to you," Lawrence pleaded.

"Lawrence, I don't know what you are talking about," chuckled Makayla.

The ice was broken. Lawrence could joke with my family - he was definitely a keeper.

We kept talking over the phone until my college chapter ended. I graduated before Christmas and then moved back to San Diego for good or at least that was my plan. I rented a little house next to the railroad tracks in Encinitas with two friends. Lawrence and I began dating officially.

## December 2003

Whistler was our first destination date. We boarded our flight to Vancouver in San Diego. Lawrence and my parents surprised me with a roundtrip Whistler flight for Christmas. I like that they collaborated together on my gift. It was a sign they were building a relationship.

Lawrence was extremely stressed at the airport and it made me feel a bit stressed too. At the same time, I really enjoyed him taking care of everything. I didn't have to think about which gate we had to go to or even what airline to check in at. He organized everything and I enjoyed being in cruise control. I didn't have to worry about missing my flight or arriving on time because he was on top of it. I wondered if this was how our future would look? I pictured Lawrence always being the responsible one and carrying the stress. Was that fair? I envisioned me gliding through life with no worries. We played travel scrabble the entire flight. It relaxed Lawrence and made the time pass by quickly. Was my 'no worries' attitude just what he needed?

While I put down "OX" for a triple word score Lawrence asked, "You snowboard, right?"

I said, "Yes, I have been. I just bought my own suit and boots. I borrowed my sister's board." Looking out the plane window I was a little nervous because I had only been to Mammoth twice with friends. I remembered when we slid down half the mountain on our bums but still found a way to laugh through the pain. That trip, Laurel had brought a flask so every time we fell we made a pact we had to drink a sip of tequila. I fell frequently and boarded off the trail into a ditch. Laurel called Leigh and Makayla to have them help pull me out.

"When did you start skiing?" I asked Lawrence as he dropped a "J" on the triple letter score. I was still picturing moments from my last boarding trip. Justin, one of my best high school friends, met us there. He was with his dad and brother and they took pictures of us face-planting all the way down the mountain. I had such a great trip. I couldn't wait to make more snow memories, especially with Lawrence.

"I started skiing Mammoth at six and snowboarding as a teen. My family had a Mammoth condo, so we went all the time," Lawrence boasted proudly that Mammoth was his happy place.

After a competitive and unfinished scrabble match, we arrived in Vancouver. Lawrence got our luggage and took us to the bus headed to Whistler Village. After the two-hour bus ride, we checked into our room quickly and decided to go for a run before the lifts closed.

It was my first time in Whistler and as the chair climbed the mountain I pointed out how cute the village looked. I was planning where I wanted to go for dinner as we passed over the sheets of snow.

We got off the chairlift as I continued to take in the

beauty of the mountain when Lawrence yelled, "Alright girl, let's see what you got." He strapped on his snowboard and jetted down the mountain leaving me in his powder.

I tried to yell but he couldn't hear me, "Excuse me, how do I strap on my snowboard?" I yelled to the crisp mountain air.

"I will help you," responded a young man as he strapped my snowboard for me and gave me a little push. Now that is more what I expected from Lawrence.

Fifteen minutes had passed as I saw Lawrence jogging up the mountain. He did care about me, but I was annoyed he just took off.

"Are you okay? I was getting worried about you. You said you could snowboard. What's going on?" he asked, not the least bit out of breath from his climb. He was so fit.

"I said I *have been* snowboarding. I didn't say I could snowboard very well." This somehow transferred over to Lawrence as 'yes I have been, and I am very good and ready to ski any slope that you take me to.' I have been so few times that I didn't even realize there was easy, intermediate, and difficult runs and I clearly was not on the beginner run. Maybe next time I need to elaborate more.

"Do you think you could teach me?"

This could be some sort of bonding and he could put his hands on my hips and show me how to turn I thought.

"Sure," mumbled Lawrence.

"Two things to remember. One, follow your front arm."

This made no sense to me and I was starting to get frustrated.

"Two. Press and release."

Once again what the heck did that mean? No matter how hard I tried, I kept eating it. I was embarrassed and of course more frustrated with myself and a bit at Lawrence for having these expectations of my ability. I considered my-self an athlete but not today.

I kept trying to stay positive as the snow glistened around me, but I couldn't, there was no ounce of positiv-ity as I consistently fell on my booty. Instead of having fun coaching me he was frustrated and said, "You said you could snowboard."

"No, you idiot, I said I had been snowboarding." I re-sponded rather rudely.

"Don't call me an idiot," he defended himself. "I can't believe you're name calling while I'm trying to teach you."

"You're not trying to teach me. You're being conde-scending and making me feel like I'm not good enough for you. Sorry, I'm not the ultimate athlete like you, asshole."

"Oh, and there it is, thank you very much."

In that moment I decided I hated snowboarding; I was sore, discouraged and truly humbled. I couldn't wait to get back to the lodge and have a drink to take my soreness away.

I was also irritated at Lawrence for not being support-ive and sweet, but he felt offended. This was our first big fight and we didn't really make up. We were in Whistler. A few drinks with our new friends and we were out dancing on the dance floor like nothing had happened. Oh, when in Whistler, I appreciated the fact that we could move past our argument so quickly. On the other hand, did we really resolve it? Was this healthy? Well, it worked for us at the time.

The highs kept coming. My parents gave me the money I saved them by graduating early. Makayla had left to study in Australia. I paid her a visit. I bought a flight and pretty much the rest was covered. She rented a beach house with her college roomie and six boys.

## February 2004

"Lawrence, you'll never believe it; we went hitchhiking for the first time," I shared in excitement. Another first. He called me every day for hours and I was loving his attention.

"You girls are idiots," he said, so annoyed.

"What's the big deal? Everyone in Australia is so nice. Even our neighbor invited us over to have pancakes with him and he took us hiking in the middle of a deserted forest when the sun came up. We went looking for kangaroos," I continued.

"Okay, I don't even know if I can talk to you right now. Why are you guys being so naive?" Lawrence reacted.

"Seriously, I'm trying to tell you about all the good times on my trip and you're going to critique how we travel and have fun?" I liked how protective he was, but I can do what I want. I am a grown woman.

"Baby, I'm sending you a picture of my new haircut. I shaved my head just for you," he interjected and thankfully changed the subject.

"Oh, Lawrence it looks so hot. I'm sorry, I'll be smarter when I'm traveling, I don't want to worry you, I guess we should be a little careful."

I talked to Lawrence four hours a day and I wasn't sure if it was because he didn't want me to make any more stupid decisions or he wanted me to come back home. It was obvious he was definitely falling in love with this girl, me. Absence was making our hearts grow fonder. I felt the same way.

Every day we called each other to talk about our word of the day from his desk calendar and would say "murmur" before we got off the phone.

Well, I have to say there were more firsts for me that Australian trip besides being in Australia.

At twenty-one I didn't even know where I stood on a lot of political issues. I wasn't into politics at all. I just believed in being kind and having fun. I marched in a gay pride parade and got hit on by tons of girls with my sister. We had some good laughs. We were just walking down the street in Sydney and saw a parade so thought why not? Let's join the parade.

When I got back is when he knew he loved me. Lawrence picked me up from the airport in a green Billabong plaid shirt. I wore a short cut off denim skirt and a white Billabong shirt with little ruffles on the sleeves. It was tight, and my tan abs peeked through and said hello too.

Lawrence walked right up to me at the airport and gave me a kiss and a hug. The security guard looked at him and said, "Lucky guy."

Lawrence said jokingly, "I know she's so lucky to have me."

He said, "No, I'm talking about your girl, bro."

Lawrence said, "No, I know I'm lucky to have her. I'm just giving you a hard time."

We drove back to Carlsbad together and he flattered me the whole drive. When we arrived in Carlsbad we left my luggage in the car and ran straight for the couch. He followed me with the same thoughts on his mind. I flipped up my denim skirt, put his hand up my skirt, bent over and accepted the kisses between my thighs. He spun me around and situated my hips on the edge of the couch. I spread my legs and invited him in.

"I am ready," I said as my body relaxed. He ignored me and just kept kissing.

"Are you sure?" I knew he was the one, so waiting until marriage was already out the door.

"Yes. I love you. I am in love with you. It's been long enough."

After an hour of making out, I allowed him slowly inside of me. My Lawrence virginity door closed as another door opened full of curiosity, exploration and desire. Our bodies connected on an intimate level that I didn't know existed. We communicated better with our bodies than we did with our actual conversations. It worked for us. We were in love and for my first time I made love with my soul mate. This new first was my new addiction. If we were fighting it was always cured with sex. The firm cushion couch was turned into a soft one with all our rolling around day and night.

If we were celebrating, it was with sex. Sex was sort of my way of dealing with everything, but it was great, so it worked. When we were sad, sex could even make me happier. He was definitely my soul mate. Our bodies made a pact, but was this really love? Did I know what true love was? I would sacrifice everything for our love. I was his. He was mine.

Sex was definitely our glue and no matter what we went through sex could reconnect us. I am not sure why I even wore pants when it was just the two of us. I was always down for my new hobby or was it a passion, our passion. I couldn't get enough. I was craving it day and night.

**November 2005**

Life was fun and unpredictable during the next two years of dating and living in Encinitas. Although he had initially claimed that he was fired from McDonalds and Sears, he had actually been working in the TV industry for years. He never worked at either of these places. When we met at the races, he was on a hiatus from work and "fun-employed," which basically meant surfing and doing odd jobs to get by. His love language was acts of service. He cleaned my car, did my laundry and fixed anything that needed to be fixed. My love language was definitely words of affirmation. I complimented him daily and truly meant what I said. Meanwhile, I was pursuing my teaching credential because I didn't know what else to do with my Communications degree. I had my whole life ahead of me. Would I be a teacher? Would I be a writer? So much potential.

Then one day Lawrence was offered an amazing opportunity to work on the third season of one of the most successful shows on television. The only problem was he would have to move to Los Angeles. After living in beautiful Arizona for college, so far from the ocean, I vowed I would never leave San Diego County after graduation. I loved the beach and my family. Clearly my vow was fragile because the next thing I knew, I was packing a suitcase and my car for Los Angeles. Picturing a day without Lawrence made me sick. I needed him. He fulfilled me and my fantasies. The thought of being without him made me physically sick. I shifted my rules and boundaries for the one I loved. Hollywood, here I come. Will you be good to me?

# Episode 2

## THE WESTERN PRODUCTION ASSISTANT SD TO LA

**Soundtrack:**
**Young Dumb and Innocent**
**(Morgan Leigh Band)**

I n my early twenties, I *was* the perfect partner for any-one--in this case, Lawrence. *Was* being the operative word. Whoever he was, whoever he wanted to be, I was right there by his side supporting him and cheering him on. I would give up all my hopes and dreams to support the man I loved. My happiness relied on his happiness. I wasn't in touch with how I felt, as long as he was happy. That's love, right? And I was perfectly fine with that. To be honest, I didn't even know what my dreams were since they had morphed so many times. Some of them included being the next Mia Hamm, a lawyer, a doctor, a singer, an ac-tor, writer, teacher, a mom, a wife and even becoming an entrepreneur. The dreams I thought I had, were they even my dreams at all? Were they my mom's dreams? Were they my dad's dreams? Were they the dreams from fairy tales and Disney princess indoctrination? I thought it was honor-able to be selfless in a relationship or a marriage - my mom was the best example of that. She put her dreams aside to support my dad's potential pro baseball career. She put her dreams aside to help him through college and later found a job that supported the family when back surgery stood in the way of him playing in the big leagues. She did what she had to do, but somewhere in there she had crossroads and hard choices. Could she have had it all? Her dreams too? What were her dreams?

We use the word selfish with a negative connotation, but I have learned it's more about self-love. I used to think relationships were all about sacrifice, but are they? Well, at twenty-three years old you can't really sacrifice your hopes and dreams if you don't have them or clear goals to achieving them. You can't sacrifice them if you forget what they are or don't really know who you are. On the other hand, without firm dreams or goals you also have the opportunity to enjoy the present and see what life brings. Was there a bigger plan for me?

And so, I left my friends and family and moved with Lawrence to Los Angeles, where I knew not a soul. I didn't have a real plan but figured I could get a teaching job just about anywhere. The *Western Show* was filming at a western ranch just north of Los Angeles. They did quite a bit of filming at The Ranch which included *The Lone Ranger* and *Magnificent Seven*. Lawrence had been hired as a production coordinator and filled a position of a lady who left to pursue bigger things. The movie he was supposed to work on got cancelled and he started to realize that in this industry you have to seize opportunities as if they're your last. When we first met, he wasn't working because he had turned down an opportunity, thinking another one would be right around the corner, but then was without work for a year. That left so much time for us to bond. From then on, he cherished every show and opportunity.

Within one week of living in our studio apartment five minutes from The Ranch, a production assistant(PA) didn't show up for work and Lawrence asked if I would fill in. I had no idea what PA even meant, but I said yes, why not? I was up for a new adventure. I could work on my dreams later. Was this part of my dream? He prepped me not to mention I was his girlfriend. It was easy to keep a secret because he had his own office. I had to go in there from time to time, but he would just shut his door if we needed to talk about personal things. One day an exec told him he thought he saw a PA (me) checking him out. We would die laughing. Sometimes people vented to me about him, and I would try to keep a straight face. Of course, I would tell him later. I felt uneasy about that, a bit two-faced.

We were extremely professional at work. Lawrence was very serious when it came to his job especially after that year break and would never risk anything to jeopardize it, so he made sure to keep us a secret. One day turned into weeks and just like that I was in the Industry. People slowly found out as we hung after work at the Greens—a minia-ture golf course with a bar and live music—and attended co-worker's birthday parties together. Most people as-sumed we met at work. It made sense - we did spend a lot of time there.

This was the first time I had been to any studio and a western studio for that matter. I loved riding the golf cart down the western street to pass out new script pages. Wind and dust would be in my hair, but I didn't care. It kind of reminded me of the Del Mar Racetrack when we first met. I was in awe of the set. I just couldn't believe how real it looked. So, this was where the movies and shows were made. As glamorous as it sounds to be working at a famous studio, my job was not as glamorous. But it wasn't about the glamor for me, it was about the people and the teamwork to make something great. I had a lot to learn, but seemed to be sponging it up quickly.

As a PA, I did all the little things that most people don't know exist like restocking toilet paper in the bathroom, answering the phones, and keeping people fed. I kept the fridge stocked and drinks lined up perfectly. I made many Smart and Final runs. Ordering office lunches was a challenge during pre-production because the show didn't have catering on set yet. Hungry people were hangry people so getting orders correct was a must. I was relieved when we started shooting and catering took over. They were the best. The chef could whip up anything I was craving. Then there were the copy machines. The copy machines were friends when the script pages didn't pull and definitely enemies when they jammed. It was a game to find the jam. PA 101 should involve one hundred things to know about a copy machine. Oh, and definitely how to clean out a coffee pot well.

I was considered a day player, which meant I would work as needed on a day to day basis just filling in. I wanted a little more stability and when accounting got wind of this, Megan, the payroll accountant called me into her office.

"Reese, do you have any interest in working in accounting as an accounting clerk?" she asked while punching numbers on the calculator.

"Sure, I'll do anything, is there an opening?" I asked in an excited tone, pulling up my tube top and black jeans. The Ranch was warm so beach attire on top with tennis shoes worked in the hot months.

"Okay, I just told my friend at Smiley Studios I have someone interested. Can you go interview during lunch today?"

"Yes, let me just check with my boss. Thank you so

much," I said, but since it was Lawrence I knew the answer. Of course, he would let me go.

## Two hours later-Studio City

"Hi, I am here for an interview with Mark Davis," I said to the gate guard on the Smiley Studios lot.

"Here is your pass. Park anywhere in that parking garage to your left, then follow the sidewalk around to the right until you run into a blue house. The accounting office is in there," he kindly directed me with a smile and many hand gestures.

"Thank you," I said, grabbing the pass and smiling back.

The sun was beating on my back as I walked half a mile to the blue house. I was completely unprepared and threw a sweater I found on the back seat of my car over my tube top for the interview. Sweat dripped down my face and even my armpits. In my hurry to get to work that morning, I forgot to put on socks with my shoes, so my feet were drenched in sweaty puddles. Nervousness and heat were a bad interview combo. I walked up the stairs to the office and said "hi" to the clerk.

"May I use your restroom really quick? I am here for an interview," I asked as I felt sweat beading under my bra. I needed to touch up.

"Right there," she pointed to a door two feet from her. Great, everyone could hear me. There were five other desks where accountants sat, two men and three women.

I walked in and turned on the fan to help with what seemed like very thin walls right next to the people I could potentially be interviewing with. As I pulled down my pants, shoot! I'd started my period. The timing could not be worse. I had no tampon. I bundled up a wad of toilet paper to do the trick. I had been in the bathroom five minutes and when I walked out there was a man waiting. I was directed to an office by the clerk as cramps started brewing in my abdomen.

"Hi, I am Mark, and this is Todd," he said, shaking my hand with a very firm grip followed by a loose grip from Todd.

"Nice to meet you." I could have won an Oscar for my impressive acting. I just wanted out of there and a good quick interview was the key. I was so uncomfortable, desperately hoping toilet paper would not fall out my pants.

"Take a seat right here on the couch," Todd said as I sat on a low couch one foot off the ground. Both dudes sat on high stools. I could see their nose hairs since they towered above me. Seriously. Power play?

"I am the head accountant here and this is my first assistant, Todd. What type of management style do you prefer?"

What the heck did that mean? It sounded like they were reading out of a book. I had no idea what to say and was intimidated. The high stools were working. I could smell my sweaty feet. Could they smell them too?

"I am not sure. I just don't like a yelling environment. I don't like to be yelled at," I answered. That was the worst answer ever. The two guys just looked at each other.

"I see you work at The Ranch on *The Western.* I know the producer on that show. Why leave? That's a great show," he asked, pushing out his chest.

"Well, I work with my boyfriend and day play so it would be nice to have a steady job of my own. I wouldn't mind a break from the dust," again giving a really bad answer. As long as the toilet paper didn't fall out of my pants and I could get out of there soon, I didn't care what I said. I was not getting the job, that was a given.

"Nice to meet you. We will be in contact soon if we decide to hire you," said Todd, giving a weird look to Mark.

I definitely wasn't getting a call. I walked legs close together for a half sweaty mile, got in my car and just breathed. It would be back to day playing for me. Worst interview ever. Did I even belong in this world? Film? TV? Sure, why not?

Weeks later I got a permanent accounting position on the second half of *The Western* Season Three. The clerk was going to a new show where she was getting more pay and higher position, which made room for me. I had already showed my hard work ethic around the office as a PA, so I felt like I had the job before the interview. This time I got to sit across the desk from the head accountant and look right into his eyes with a normal conversation and no leaking fluids. This played out the way it was supposed to.

Accounting felt like an upgrade because the hours were shorter, and I was getting $20 more per day. It was very exciting passing out people's paychecks and answering the phone when agents and actors called. I loved seeing the petty cash envelopes and what people spent money on. It was fun to see the purchases in different departments every day.

Dino was my boss—I thought he was the best. He took me in like a little sister and taught me everything he knew. He unfortunately lost his sister-in-law to cancer while we worked together so I blasted Madonna to try and cheer him up. We loved colored sharpies and pickle wraps. We were always trying to eat healthy together. He was the reason I wanted to come to work every morning. My family was south in the San Diego area, but I found a sense of belonging in the production family. I was loving my "work family."

One of the highlights of working on *The Western* was Friday night lottery. At the end of each week, the creator of the show gave away two thousand dollars in hundred-dollar bills. The names of every crew member were written on tickets and they each had a chance to win a hundred dollars. Nobody seemed to call in sick on Fridays. Everyone gathered around set to see if they would go home with a lucky hundred-dollar bill for the weekend. That was almost a day's worth of pay for me, so I crossed my fingers and rubbed my ticket all over my body for good luck before it went in the bowl. I won four times.

Another person that always made my day was Raymond, the gate guard at The Ranch. Shows would come and go, but he was always there to greet you when you entered the ranch and when you left. I could tell how much he loved his job because the smile he gave me in the morning was the same smile he gifted me when I left. The Ray of light was in his name.

## April 2006

The season ended with a huge wrap party with all the cast and crew. I indulged in a few too many cocktails and apparently gave teamster, Lenny, a retired porn star, the dance of his life on the dance floor. I'll never know the actual truth since I was blacked out. Thank God it happened before cell phone videos were ubiquitous. According to rumor, I then spent the rest of the night in the ladies' room being cared for by another crew member.

Lawrence at the time was enjoying a casual drink with his bosses who some referred to as the three-headed monster. They consisted of Wyatt, Peters and Goodberg. Little did I know they would later teach Lawrence everything they knew. This was the first time Lawrence got to hang out with the big boys, the people he wanted to be someday in the industry. Was he willing to sacrifice what it took to get to the top? Did he know what sacrifices would need to be made? While Lawrence was enjoying his time bonding, a teamster, his friend and one of the few that knew we were dating came and whispered in Lawrence's ear. "Bro, I heard your date is face down in the bathroom."

"Seriously?" he said, pissed at missing out on this time to build a relationship. Lawrence got up, annoyed, while his bosses looked at him confused. He found Tom, who worked closely under him and was known for being the most attractive PA.

"Tom, can you help me? Reese is in the bathroom. I am so pissed. I can't take her anywhere," he said fuming.

Together they dragged my lifeless body through the party to the car in front of the entire cast and crew.

The next morning Lawrence was done with whatever we had.

"I am sorry, I just can't date a girl in her twenties. It's just too much work."

"Seriously?" I questioned, lying in bed.

"I spent the wrap party envisioning my future and it didn't include a wasted party girl by my side," he explained seriously.

"But come on, I'm only twenty-three. I got a little carried away, but I was just having fun." He was totally forcing unrealistic expectations on me after everything we'd been through together.

Had he forgotten I'd moved cities for him? Left my family? Given up my dreams?

I couldn't show up for work I was so hungover. I thought for sure I was fired. I spent the day sleeping, hobbling around, packing my bags and accepting the fact that I couldn't change my age. There was nothing I could do about that and I needed to accept the fact that I probably didn't have a job anymore either.

Dino called and said to just take a sick day and he would see me tomorrow. I still had a job, but now I was nervous. It's pretty awkward having to work with your ex. Well, at least we were in different departments. I figured I'd just stay on the show until I found another job back in San Diego. Even after a show wraps from filming there is still work at the office for weeks and sometimes months: "Wrap Hours." Along with packing, I spent the day jotting down things I liked about Lawrence on a piece of scratch paper. I focused on all the good things. I made peace with the fact that everything happens for a reason. I embraced the years of fun memories we'd had together. What else could I do? I was young, he was mad and it was over. How did I feel about this?

I had truly given all I could to our relationship. I had left my friends and family in San Diego for LA where I knew not a soul. I had done everything to make him happy and if he couldn't appreciate that, then there was nothing more I could do. We'd had some amazing ups and disastrous downs while dating, there was no doubt. I had a lot of poor moments but so had he. It was never perfect, but there were these magical moments that made all the bad ones disappear. Or so I thought. And if he was going to break up with me over one little thing then he didn't deserve me anyway.

But I wrote only positive things about him because I wanted him to know how much I cared, whether he read it before or after I walked out the door. Once I walked, I was not coming back. A few things I wrote were...most amazing man I had ever met, most honest man in the world, smoking hot, hardest worker ever, would do anything for me...the list went on. Despite our differences I saw so much greatness and potential in him. Despite differences like age, he was the one I wanted to have a family and forever with. Suddenly I realized what I had done... How could I live without him?

# Episode 3

## THE WESTERN, OUR RELATIONSHIP? MIRACLE?

**Soundtrack:**
**The Price of Loving You**
**(Juni Ata)**

Lawrence came home from work early and I was there still slowly packing my things. There wasn't much left, but I slept a lot that day with a headache from dehydration as a result of the reckless drinking. The only thing left to pack was a little stuffed lion, Spike. My dad had given him to me after my college break up with my first love, Chad. We had met in our college dorms and first became friends when he was attracted to the big TV I lugged to college. He was so impressed with my big TV and that conversation later led to a friendship. While polishing a case of natural ice in his Coronado dorm room at U of A we decided to rate each other's kissing skills. Smooth move on both ends because that contest led to so much more than a kiss. The kind, smart musician had melted me when he sang and played the guitar. His raspy voice soothed my soul. His dream was to be a musician, but he decided to be a lawyer and go the pre-law route. That was all too safe and predictable for me. It seemed boring to have your life planned out at nineteen.

I broke up with him and quickly moved on to a cute frat boy from Beverly Hills. Afterward, I wanted predictable Chad back; and it was too late, he had moved on to another girl. This being my first break up, my dad said I was strong like a lion and could get through anything, so Spike came along with me as a constant reminder. Spike had become a buddy to Lawrence too and our running joke was 'what is Spike doing now?' I made photo books of Spike doing activities such as sunbathing, surfing and all the mischievous things he did when Lawrence and I were apart. We brought him everywhere with us.

As I put Spike in my bag Lawrence said, "You are taking Spike?"

"Yeah, he's mine."

Lawrence started reading all the things I had written on the table. "Do you mean all this?"

"Yes." I definitely had a lot of things I didn't like too, but I was trying to be positive. "And I have a plan for my impetuous twenty-three-year-old partying problem. In the future, I'll give bartenders a twenty-dollar tip and ask that they make me virgin drinks when I begin to slur. I call it sober insurance. What do you think?"

It was totally dumb. As if that would change his mind. But I was desperate. I didn't want us to break up. Lawrence was still reading all the things I'd written down. Suddenly he grabbed my hand, pulling me to him.

"Marry me," he begged on his knees as tears ran down his face.

"What?" I just stood there in shock. "You were breaking up with me and now you want to marry me?"

"I know I am an asshole sometimes, but I can't live without you. You're not saying anything…"

"Okay, yes!" I always loved unpredictable and that is exactly what I got.

"Makayla, I can't believe we are getting married," I exclaimed, all giddy into the phone as sexy Lawrence and I drove to San Diego.

"Yay," she screamed for a good twenty seconds, "I am so happy for you, Reese. Brian's sister, Sharon, is working at McKee's tonight. Do you want to come celebrate?"

"Yes, see you there at seven. I have to call Mom and share the good news," I answered, all smiles.

In San Diego, my parents, brother and two sisters all lived within one mile of each other and were excited for the news. Seven rolled around and family and friends gathered to cheer our engagement. News traveled quickly. Brian's sister, Sharon, the coolest girl ever, was bartending and the shots flowed freely. I was careful not to imbibe too much. The music was silenced.

"To the raddest couple ever," blue-eyed Sharon toasted to the entire bar, flipping her blond hair around.

"To the raddest bartender," I yelled, thrusting my glass in the air. At the end of the night she placed a pair of our shot glasses up on the shelf for good luck. I hoped they'd stay there forever.

The next morning, we were on a plane to Hawaii to celebrate my parent's thirtieth wedding anniversary. Our group of twenty boarded together with excitement. Where was Makayla and Brian? This was my first trip to Hawaii. Lawrence offered to grab rental cars upon arrival and even planned on buying dinners since we were set with work on the upcoming Season Four at The Ranch. Hiatus with job security was the best feeling. My sister had a phone interview with Bob in Locations before the flight and I would find out if she would be joining our production family as well. Would she be a Locations PA? I couldn't think of anything better than having her by my side in LA.

Everyone was on the flight except my sister and her boy-friend, Brian. Just as the doors were closing, tan Makayla and tall professional soccer stud Brian pushed through.

"Hey," she yelled in excitement.

"You made it!" I waved. "Did you get the job?"

"Nailed it! Bob loved me," she answered as she shoved her purse under her seat. She was receiving a few stares from the passengers across the aisle.

"Don't let me down," Lawrence said, half-jokingly. Lawrence remembered Makayla asleep under our roulette table after picking a fight with the security guard. Lawrence was hesitant about how this would transfer over into her work ethic. I assured him she was smart and hard working. I really hoped I was right.

On day four of our trip exploring the Road to Hana, Lawrence got a call from Wyatt, his boss. We parked along the road to hike up to the falls. Suddenly Lawrence said, "Reese, I just got a message from Wyatt regarding Season Four. He said to call him back right away."

"I hope everything is okay," I responded, puzzled.

"Wyatt, it's Lawrence. How are you?" he asked knowing it couldn't be good.

"Did you hear the news?" asked Wyatt Somberly.

"No, we have not been paying attention to anything," he said, wanting Wyatt to get to the point.

"Sorry to ruin your trip. It's cancelled," Wyatt spit it out.

"Seriously?" Lawrence asked, punching a nearby palm tree.

"I will fill you in more later. I can't believe it either. There is talk of another show, but nothing certain." Wyatt was clearly not enjoying sharing the bad news.

Lawrence hung up the phone and just looked at me. "Turn in the rental cars. It's DEAD. Season Four is dead and we, the three of us, and hundreds of others are without jobs."

"Seriously?" I questioned Lawrence, totally annoyed and sad for my sister.

"Yes, we have to stop spending. I have no clue where our next paycheck is coming from. There is talk of a new show, but I have no details." Lawrence walked away, taking his now intense stressed energy with him.

The hiatus we planned on enjoying was now indefinite. My sister was celebrating a new job and just like that, gone. It simply didn't make much sense. The showrunner loved his show and so did the audience. It was one of the most popular shows on television. Why would they cancel it? I heard many rumors and none of them added up. This was definitely a moment in which things just didn't seem to make sense. Welcome to Hollywood.

We returned home broke and realized we had to move out of our apartment. Moving wasn't hard since our coffee table consisted of two plastic tubs turned upside down covered by a blanket. We had the orange couch, a bed, a few dishes, toiletries and clothes. We threw a few tubs in the car and then into storage.

The easiest way to cut costs was to have no home or rent. It was summer time, so we decided to visit Lawrence's sister for a week in Oregon and visit his parents at their lake house on Lake Almanor, two hours north of Chico for two weeks. We didn't mention we had no home or job. Lawrence said he always knew another job would come, but I wasn't so sure. I did love the unpredictability of it all though. The bonus was Makayla and Brian joined us on the road trip. Brian was interviewing for jobs before the trip after graduating from Notre Dame and Makayla was obviously now unemployed and figuring out her next move.

The entire road trip I had terrible motion sickness. When we pulled up to the lake house, his parents came out to greet us with big hugs. This was our fourth visit and each time the beauty remained the same. The four-story lake house had a view of the lake from every level and not just a view, but a picturesque view. The garage was full of toys consisting of a jeep, boat, golf cart and tubes for the boat to pull. I just wanted to lay down and sleep, but it was hard to say no to gorgeous walks that lined the lake for miles and tubing with Lawrence's family. Lawrence launched me as I held on for dear life.

The predominantly retired community of Chester was very quiet on the west side. The town didn't even have a movie theater. The bowling alley was my favorite place to hang at and it was family owned. Competitive Makayla and Brian challenged us to a bowling match. We won, and my sister choked on her last bowl.

Down the street was a grocery store and a revolving restaurant set-up. Each time we visited it took on a new name and cuisine. It had been everything from Italian, to American, Mexican and Chinese. Each owner hoping they would be the one to make it. I always enjoyed whatever it was, but the foot traffic was lagging. Many folks up there were snowbirds and only visited in the winter. The locals were such a small percentage of the population.

The home cooked meals were the best. His mother even taught me how to make my first bagged omelet. Days on the golf course were gorgeous with peaceful birds chirping and deer eating along the fairway. We concluded our nights with scrabble matches. One night we got his parents so tipsy his mom was giving his dad new spikey hair styles. It put his dad in a good mood after losing to me. I have a love for scrabble. I used to study the two letter words so there was no beating me on a crowded board. That's where my scrabble skills flourished.

I loved my family so much and felt so relieved that his parents were lovely people and embraced both me and my family, especially Makayla and Brian. Brian was a Catholic boy and Lawrence too was Catholic, but had doubts about the church. I now had Lawrence, my family, his family and the production family. I loved that we could talk for hours on their balcony with a bottle of Chardonnay. The bugs eventually got to us so we moved inside. Each night was so heartwarming; I was sad to leave.

After a few weeks of road tripping and living out of our car we each got calls to help wrap up the season three of the western series. Both accounting and production needed help tying up loose ends. It was really cancelled. I still couldn't believe it. It was what it was and I did need money even if it came from wrapping one of the best shows ever.

The bullets of questions came. Where would we stay? How many weeks of work would we have? There were still rumors of another show, but the question still remained, when would the next show be? Should I pursue teaching? I didn't even have an address unless I used my parent's. "Hi, it appears I live in San Diego and would love to teach at your Los Angeles school" wasn't going to work. I guess I would see how the cards played out. I so wished we knew someone with whom to crash. I was feeling so lethargic and didn't know if it was subconscious stress. I was always car sick no matter where I was. I just wanted it to stop.

Lawrence secured a few weeks of work and I secured a few days. The closest, least expensive non-motel was the Castaic Inn just north of Santa Clarita off the five freeway. It was near a truck stop and a grocery store. It was so dirty, but better than the car. I just wanted to sleep. I couldn't remember the last time I got my period, but our schedule had been so erratic that it made sense I'd missed a cycle. Just in case, I took a pregnancy test.

It was Positive.

There at the Castaic Inn, with no true job, I found out I would be a mother. I was excited and scared.

"Lawrence, I took a test and it's positive!" I screamed, not sure of his reaction.

"No way. Let's get some more tests. Maybe that one was left on the truck too long?" he said, grabbing keys for his prego test mission. I rolled my eyes. Everyone knew that if a test was positive, you were definitely pregnant. There were never false positives.

He was back in ten minutes and emptied out a bag of ten tests in ten different brands.

"Positive," I yelled from the small inn bathroom as the stick read positive. I opened another. Was he really going to make me go through all ten? I didn't have enough pee for ten tests.

"Pregnant," I yelled as I read the more expensive test that had letters instead of symbols.

"Positive." I opened another. 'Positive.'

"I get the point, you really are pregnant," he finally conceded. Duh, I thought. There at the Castaic Inn Lawrence found out he would be a father. "My boys can swim," he yelled in excitement.

I was excited too, but the questions were swirling in my head. How would I tell people? Was I going to have a boy or a girl? I should have been thinking 'where will the baby sleep?'

Lawrence turned into business mode and wanted to make sure he could provide a good life for our miracle and me. We were going to have a baby! I was twenty-four and he was thirty-five. Were we ready to be parents? We had three hundred dollars in our bank account, plus debt. We had nothing on paper, but at the same time had everything... a family. That news solidified our family and definitely our engagement.

We were engaged with plans of a November 2006 wedding. I moved my wedding up to July. I didn't want to be huge in my wedding dress. My mom and sister planned the whole wedding in five weeks because I was still car sick. While searching for a wedding event venue I laid across the back seat of the car while they met with event coordinators. They would report back to me. I didn't care about colors, location, or even what my center pieces were. I did want to get married in a church. Palm Church agreed to marry us. They were my parents' church and were the least judgmental Christians I had ever met. I also wanted Jack Johnson playing when the wedding party walked down the aisle, but that was pretty much my only demand.

## July 2006

My family paid for an amazing wedding and new dress. I had to return my original flute-shaped dress to account for the growing belly. I looked bloated not prego. Not a good look at your wedding. The second dress was billowy and flattering. It was perfect.

For everything else, we had to foot the bill. We put any other expenses on our credit cards. Yes, we were those people spending money we didn't have. I did return the engagement ring I had originally picked out and settled for the matching band. I promised myself I'd buy the ring later when I had enough money saved up. The $8000 gorgeous engagement ring had been picked out by Lawrence and me just days before we flew to Hawaii. But once we knew our jobs were lost, it was up to me to embrace a simple band. Our wedding day was perfect, I didn't need a fancy ring to bring me happiness. We had everything that was truly valuable: friends and family by our side. Many crew members were there and those that couldn't make the trip to San Diego last-minute gave us cards full of money.

We really appreciated and needed it for the baby. We had the record temperature of 116 degrees on our wedding day and the church air conditioner broke. Sweat was dripping down our bodies as we said our vows and I even tripped walking off the stage for our grand exit.

We had our reception at the Crosby. My brother worked there so we got hooked up. My parents reached their total max bar limit before the cocktail hour was over. I did not contribute to the consumption of one alcoholic beverage and unlike the wrap party night, I was probably the only one that remembers my wedding besides my parents that never drank. This was a good start to my marriage. Even my bridesmaids were tanked. Both my sisters and bridesmaids danced the night away. Three bridesmaids, Meg, Britt, and Alyssa, were club soccer and high school friends taking shots together at the bar every time their favorite songs came on. T-bone was my college friend and semi-pro soccer teammate.(I warmed the bench but enjoyed traveling with the team)The final bridesmaid was my sister's best friend, Bella. She was my blond sister and drew a crowd to the dance floor with her energy. I think she mooned my aunts while on the floor. Laurel, while not a bridesmaid, was there in cute polka dots leading the electric slide with Brooklyn, another soccer teammate.

Every important person in my life was there except one, Leigh. She passed in a car accident a few years before my wedding. This was devastating to all who knew her. She left holes in our hearts, but good memories in our minds. I invited her parents to anything I would have invited her to. Their presence lit up the room and was a reminder of strength and perseverance. During our wedding vows I thanked her in my mind for losing that bet. I knew she was at my wedding watching over us to witness her parents rocking out.

The speeches will go down in history as my sister announced I was pregnant. "I want to thank Lawrence for getting my sister knocked up."

She warned me so I thought it was hilarious. Tequila shots replaced champagne and the DJ, my dad and his friend, Ef, created the perfect atmosphere for guests to get lost in the music. My wedding was perfect, as the dance floor overflowed with great energy and the honeymoon would be perfect too.

Being broke and prego, we newlyweds decided to drive to San Francisco. The weather was a cool break from the LA heat. We spent as little cash as possible and spent our days walking miles across the bridge and town. We even ended up at Hooters with my bestie and bridesmaid, Meg, and her boyfriend because of its proximity to our hotel. Meg drove us all over to do the tourist attractions. The remaining honeymoon money from Lawrence's parents was used to pay bills. We started our marriage with a nice 30K plus in debt. Not to mention some student loans on my end that Lawrence wanted to payoff from my parents now that we were married. We started to get texts and rumors on the trip that a new show was brewing and it would be shot at The Ranch. We were about to find out if these rumors were facts.

# Episode 4

## THE SALT WATER SHOW AND CYSTIC FIBROSIS

**Soundtrack:**
**Let Me**
**(Juni Ata)**

Rumors were true, and the creator of *The Western* had a new show, *The Salt Water Show*. This was more than a treat because it was about surfing with some other creative twists. I would be surrounded by hot surfers and get to taste the salty air daily. Beach towns and beach people always seem happy to me. Have you seen an unhappy person at the beach?

I interviewed with the new head accountant and had a job again and so did Lawrence and Makayla. Dino and Megan would be working in accounting as well. With perceived job security, we used wedding money to put down a security deposit on a two-bedroom apartment. My sister was going to rent a room to make it affordable. This would be the home that welcomed our baby to the world, well, so we thought. After signing a lease, we learned the show would film two weeks in Imperial Beach, San Diego and two weeks at The Ranch, thirty minutes north of Los Angeles. I was thrilled to spend every two weeks in my hometown of San Diego. We could hang with family and friends while shooting down there. The best part is that the offices would be the penthouse of an old inn on the beach. Every window came with a view, even the bathroom. Both accounting and production set up camp in the penthouse. Crew would come in to pick up things and just plop down on the cozy sofas and throw their feet up on the coffee table to admire the view while waiting. The penthouse had three balconies and two bathrooms. It was hard to get work done at times. I just wanted to throw my swimsuit on and lay outside, belly and all.

We were so grateful to have work again especially with my growing belly. Everything was working out for us. A perfect wedding, baby on the way and jobs.

It was a whirlwind, but a fun spinning one like the high you get spinning on the beach as a child.

The producers definitely went green when it came to crew. They reused and continued to reuse many of the same crew members over and over. I looked forward to seeing many crew faces from *The Western* again every day. Like I've said before, we were like family. Working twelve to fourteen hour days with people made it inevitable to form bonds. Propinquity at its best. I now understood Lawrence's bond with Hannah in Havasu.

And there were some memorable moments from working on that show. Like, one afternoon in Imperial Beach, a star I salivated over in high school from the hit TV show *90210* threw out his back on set. I had to beg a local chiropractor to see him since he got hurt after hours. He was one of the main characters and the show needed him to film that day. The chiropractor was closing, but like many in the Imperial Beach community, was so sweet and supportive of the filming. She helped him out and he gave her the biggest hug. Gone too soon. R.I.P Luke Perry.

I got to work with other celebrities too, Ed O'neill. That was pretty cool because I watched him on TV as a kid, *Married with Children*. Some of the content was over my head.

The other highlights were working on the beach and the pranking.

Hair Bear the 27th, was Peter's assistant and you can't forget him when you meet him. He is the funniest person I have ever met, and paired that with smooth communication skills. He started a lunchtime quick surf routine. In an epic prank, Lawrence oiled up Bear's surfboard covering it with baby oil and we all watched from the production office as he slipped all over his board. He couldn't get close to standing. The laughter was contagious and all penthouse spectators tried to keep a straight face when he returned to the office.

Hair Bear did his fair share of punking so my sister came up with a plan to get him back. One day in Imperial Beach he rolled in on a brand-new skateboard. He was really adapting to the beach life with his surfing and now skateboard hobby. He had a sweet arrogance about him. When he was working away with his back to the penthouse entrance, Makayla took his skateboard from the penthouse porch and brought it down to the basketball court where local skaters were skating.

"Hey, do you mind skating with this board instead?" she asked the tan, shirtless tatted skater. His eight pack was glistening as he cruised around the basketball court.

"Sure, what for?" he answered, looking around.

"Well, we are pranking our friend and I want to see how he reacts when he thinks you stole his board."

"Okay, but I don't want a fight or anything."

"No, don't worry. He is no match for you," Makayla assured him.

It was lunchtime and Hair Bear walked out the penthouse to grab his skateboard. It wasn't there. When he looked around he could see a tough dude riding it on the basketball court down below. His face sunk. He was upset, but helpless. He was in disbelief. He paced back and forth and in and out of the penthouse.

"Makayla, some dude stole my board and has the indecency to ride it right in front of me," Hair Bear complained.

"Go get it, you pussy," she encouraged, trying not to bust up laughing.

Hair Bear walked down the steps and onto the court. Four of the local's fit friends joined the conversation.

"I think you have my board," Hair Bear said hesitantly.

"No bro, I don't know what you're talking about." The dude flexed his abs.

We all watched from the penthouse once again and were dying laughing. There was a ten second pause and then the guy handed Hair Bear his board back. It was one of the funniest things I had ever seen and have to give my sister credit for executing it.

Although each day was filled with fun and lots of hard work, in the back of my mind I was always thinking about the baby growing inside me and how I would soon be leaving my production family to focus on my own. I was excited to become a mom, but it was bittersweet. I would miss the pranking and being surrounded by people all the time but being a mom would be fun and rewarding in different ways. I was so thankful for this gift. Motherhood would also be challenging – just how challenging we were about to find out.

One day while working on *The Salt Water Show* we received news that would change our lives forever. My OB, Dr. Sal, told us I was a carrier of the cystic fibrosis(CF) mutation.

Dr. Sal explained it's not a big deal because the baby is only at risk of developing CF if both parents are carriers, and about only one in twenty-five Caucasians are carriers. So, the odds that Lawrence would be a carrier too were pretty low. I appreciated hearing this but I will always be grateful that Dr. Sal was extra cautious and had Lawrence do a CF carrier test because it turned out he was a carrier too. This meant there was a twenty-five percent chance that our sweet baby could enter this world with a genetic disease, not just any disease, but sadly I would learn, a disease with no cure and a shortened life expectancy.

At the time we got this news, the only thing I knew about CF was that a girl I went to high school with had it. I heard of someone else having it but had no clue about the details. When we found out our baby had a 1 in 4 chance of being born with CF, we tried to learn as much as we could about the disease.

The first thing I did was Google cystic fibrosis and I was led to the Cystic Fibrosis Foundation homepage. I learned CF is a progressive, genetic disease that causes persistent lung infections and limits the ability to breathe over time. In people with CF, a defective gene causes a thick, sticky buildup of mucus in the lungs, pancreas, and other organs. In the lungs, the mucus clogs the airways and traps bacteria, leading to infections, extensive lung damage, and eventually, respiratory failure.

I started to feel worried and sad and read on about what happens in the pancreas. The mucus prevents the release of digestive enzymes that allow the body to break down food and absorb vital nutrients.

Cystic fibrosis is a genetic disease. People with CF have inherited two copies of the defective CF gene - one copy from each parent. Both parents must have at least one copy of the defective gene. Lawrence had a copy and I had a copy. People with only one copy of the defective CF gene are called carriers so both Lawrence and I were carriers. We didn't have the disease, but each time two CF carriers have a child, the three chances are: twenty-five percent of babies will have CF, fifty percent of babies will be a carrier but will not have CF or twenty-five percent of babies will not be a carrier and will not have CF.

I read that CF is a complex disease and the types and severity of symptoms can differ widely from person to person. Many different factors, such as age of diagnosis, can affect an individual's health and the course of the disease. There were some things we would just have to figure out as life handed them to us. I would have to have faith we'd get through it.

"What do you want to do next? We are both carriers and have two options," I said, sharing the summary from Dr. Sal.

"What are our options?" Lawrence said pacing, arms crossed, still trying to process it all.

"We can find out if our baby has CF after he is born by the newborn screening test for CF and wait over a week for test results," I explained, referring to my notes.

"Or?" Lawrence interrupted while opening a Heineken. He was shutting down without the unknown diagnosis. The possibility was killing him, both of us.

"Or I can do an amniocentesis and have CF test results before birth. The genetic counselor will give us the results as soon as they have them. Two weeks max, but we would know way before my delivery date," I explained trying to keep it together.

"What is an amniocentesis?" Lawrence asked, defeated and still pacing shirtless across our apartment.

"The amniocentesis involves obtaining a sample of

fluid surrounding the baby, which is then used to study fetal chromosomes," I read from notes.

"I think finding out before birth is more beneficial, so our baby can have the diagnosis if needed and therefore we could have medicine prescribed pre-birth and give him a head start."

"I agree. Dr. Sal can refer us for an amnio," I said with a sense of relief that we saw this the same way. I continued to spew more info, "Research shows that children who receive CF care early in life have better nutrition and are healthier than those who are diagnosed later. With a CF diagnosis for our baby in utero we would be able to spend the last months of my pregnancy vigorously researching the disease and educating ourselves. We could spend the time processing and accepting that our baby had a disease so that we could one-hundred percent celebrate his birth and focus on the miracle and not worry about the possibility of him having CF."

I sounded positive, informed and calm. But inside I was dying. Was this really happening? I had always assumed I'd have a healthy baby. The thought never crossed my mind about anything different.

We arrived at the SD Medical Center on an overcast La Jolla morning together for my amnio. We didn't talk much that morning. Lawrence was very quiet, and I was trying to think about the positive. We would find out the sex of the baby. We walked up the stairs to patient check-in on the second floor. I barely made church, but you bet I prayed over and over.

"Hi, we are here for an amnio," I said, feeling detached from my words. I placed my hand on my growing, but not yet protruding belly and whispered to my baby, "it will be okay."

"You will meet with the genetic counselor first, so he can explain everything and your options and then we will do the amnio." The late fifties receptionist had a soothing voice. It was like she felt our uneasiness and was trying to calm us down. I was grateful for her.

"What other options?" Lawrence questioned, overhearing the receptionist. Sitting on the leather waiting room chair, he was tapping his foot rapidly and absentmindedly flipping through the pages of a magazine. I could hear his loud sighs and deep breaths across the room. We were the only ones.

"Oh, he will explain in a minute. I see he is ready for you now. Come on back." She opened the door and we walked through.

Davis, the genetic counselor, was about twenty-five, enthusiastic and bright. He spoke very clearly about the genetics of CF using visuals as well. It was a bit of a blur as all I could think about was if my baby had it or not. That was all I wanted to know.

"If your baby does have CF, you have the option to terminate your pregnancy. Some choose to terminate."

"Oh, we would never. These kids can have long amazing lives. Everything we have read says how far research has come. Our child will have a long life," I firmly said holding my stomach. I was furious inside. I didn't think I should have been given that choice to terminate for CF. This had nothing to do with my body.

"I just have to tell you your options regardless of your views and I tell everyone this," he said. This was a lot of explaining for the twenty-five-year-old and he handled it well.

"Those were the other options. Okay. That thought never crossed my mind with CF," Lawrence chimed in. I was relieved. We were definitely on the same page.

"Can we tell right away if he has CF?" I asked, hesitantly swiping my bangs to the side and slowly crossing my hard to cross legs.

"Sometimes there is a white light seen in the bowel, but still it's not one hundred percent," he answered honestly. "You will hear from me in less than two weeks with the results."

"Wait. What is the white light and why does it appear in the bowel signifying CF?" I questioned.

"The white light is echogenic bowel when it looks as bright as the baby's bones. It means the bowel, intestines or gut appears brighter than usual. The association of echogenic bowel with fetuses affected with CF is thought to be caused by the changes in the consistency of meconium in the small intestine as a result of abnormalities in pancreatic enzyme secretion. Hope that helps."

The next thirty minutes seemed like an eternity. Even though I hadn't been to church since my wedding day, I spent the amnio praying in my head that he would not have CF. "Please God, make him not have CF and I will go to church every Sunday," I murmured in desperation.

The best part of the amniocentesis was we found out our baby's sex. We were having a boy. The worst part was leaving SD Medical knowing he had CF. That possible white light sometimes seen during the ultrasound in the baby's bowel was there. We did not need to wait for our genetic counselor to call because we saw the light. It was the one time in my life when I didn't want to see the light in the given circumstance. I wanted so badly to see the darkness. It's the only time in my life in which seeing the light could bring darkness. We hoped the child would be the light of our lives despite having to go through the world with CF. Would he be our night light--bringing joy and inspiration to those around us?

Even though I was trying to mentally prepare myself for the genetic counselor's call with the test results, no parent can ever prepare for that type of news.

"Hello," I said, sitting at the top of my stairs as I answered the much-anticipated phone call.

"Mrs. Richman, I am sorry, but the results came back positive for cystic fibrosis." He continued but I felt sick to my stomach. The rest was foggy. I rolled into a ball on the stair landing. I was by myself that morning and Lawrence was already at work. I just laid there holding myself and saying sorry to my baby boy growing inside me. I just cried and cried and cried in that ball. Tears soaked my pants as my knees were pulled in so tight to my head in the fetal position. I couldn't control what was going on with my baby inside me. An hour later I called Lawrence.

"Lawrence, he has..." I couldn't get the words out. My voice was shaking as tears flowed down my cheeks again.

"I already knew...," he said and hung up the phone. He couldn't get words out either. My sister saw him shut his office door and it stayed shut eight more hours until the show wrapped for the day. I needed him to comfort me, but he didn't have it; he was crumbling inside in his own way. I couldn't give him the comfort he needed either.

I didn't feel like the same person after that phone call and wondered how long it would take for the dark cloud to leave me, maybe years? How long for the tear sessions to stop? I was helpless to fix our baby, whom we agreed to name Sterling. I wanted him out, so I could help him. I couldn't fix this, would I try to fix other things around me? Digging deep for a positive attitude was a daily struggle. Lawrence remained angry. Why our guy? Why him? Should I have prayed harder? Was this karma for mistakes we had made? The thoughts that swirled my mind were similar, thoughts that flooded both our heads. It wasn't fair to him, our sweet boy, our sweet Sterling. I got little from Lawrence, but the one thing I understood was he felt it was his fault and was beating himself up. How long would he carry the burden? How long would he blame himself? Did he blame me too, because after that day I lost the man I married. He acted as if he didn't even know me. That was the last day I felt his touch. The last day I felt I truly knew him for a very long time. I guess I can say our marriage partially died that day. Was there a disease for our pain?

We did the best we could but at moments it ate us up with suffering. I thought I loved unpredictability, but not this kind, not when it affected our precious baby. Sterling did nothing to deserve this disease. I hoped it was a bad dream. Why couldn't they give the CF to me instead? I wish this was a film and not our reality. I wanted to change the script.

After his diagnosis, we shoved the hurt aside and stuffed it away down deep. I cried in private as I tried to be positive to the world around me. Lawrence could barely talk about it. Our emotions were not in sync and we did a terrible job at leaning on each other. Finally, we decided to make a pact to live life to the fullest no matter what. This pact bonded us and was the one thing we had in common when dealing with the disease. Every dollar made would be allocated to memory-making. Money was not important to us so whenever we got some, we'd dedicate it to memory-making. I learned of another CF family's motto, "Have fun!" and shared it with Lawrence. We were going to give our baby boy the best quality of life we could. We would have fun, no matter how much pain was stuffed away. Our boy would not know how scared and worried we both were. Could he feel it? I reached out to friends and family for the support I could not get from Lawrence. Wounds were festering in him, but he didn't know how to heal them. People he worked with for years didn't know how sad this made him. The wounds were wide open. How would he handle the pain if he didn't reach out for support?

The producers and crew from *The Salt Water Show* were so supportive. They threw me a baby shower in the accounting office at The Ranch.

"Reese, we have something for you." My work buddy, Megan, guided me to the accounting office. I had just returned from passing out paychecks. There in the dim production and accounting trailer was the biggest basket I had ever seen. A child could sleep in it. I sat on the accounting office carpet with tears in my eyes. With the craziness of the show filming between Imperial Beach and The Ranch, these people took the time for me, for us.

"Thank you, I am speechless," I couldn't believe how many gifts there were from different departments. Suddenly the heavy sadness lifted. We were having a beautiful boy! The joy that new parents experienced before a child was born surfaced and I tingled all over.

"This is just a little something from all of us. We love you guys," Megan said, as many PAs and accountants gathered around.

I sat there looking at each gift: clothes, carriers, diapers, and first aid kits.

"I have been so busy with the CF research that I didn't even think about the essentials for our baby. You guys are amazing," I said sincerely and from the bottom of my heart.

Lawrence was there too and grateful. I loved my production family. Next, I opened cards and the producers had put in gift cards. It was Lawrence's dream to be a producer, but he was not there yet. He dreamed of someday making the big bucks, giving Sterling all the dreams he could dream of and continue to give him the best insurance in the world. No matter how stressful work was or became, Lawrence committed to the TV industry to provide the best insurance for our baby. Lawrence put on his blinders and focused his now tunnel vision to providing and operation memory-making. Would this take a toll on him? Was working 80 hours a week healthy?

I worked until I had huge kankles and waddled with my added seventy-five pounds. Dino, my accounting boss would keep reminding me to put my feet up while working. By my third trimester food was tasting better and I stuffed myself in the food truck with sandwiches and helped myself to extra servings in the catering line. I was like a kid in a candy store at work. There was food everywhere. My last day of work was in the penthouse of The Imperial Beach Inn.

That was the last day I worked on a TV show and the last time I worked for a paycheck. Not a bad last day typing in numbers and staring at the ocean.

Caring for a child would be challenging, but managing his health was going to be my hardest obstacle. I made the choice to stop working and it made more sense because Lawrence said he would work enough for both of us. Was he avoiding the CF?

### January 2007

We welcomed our baby boy, Sterling, to the world in La Jolla, California while Lawrence was shooting in IB. He was the most beautiful baby I had ever seen. After an emergency C-section, he opened his eyes to the world. My body was numb, but my heart was full. Lawrence had a smile ear to ear. I had never seen him so proud after cutting the cord. I witnessed my first miracle.

Family and friends visited us at what I called the hospital hotel, Scripps La Jolla. I was so spoiled there and anything I wanted I got. The service was five stars. Some of my high school guy friends and Lawrence's surfer buds came and took Lawrence out for a beer or two. Several of my bridesmaids came to take turns holding the newest member of the Richman family.

Having the first baby on my side of the family was an extra bonus because I had so much help from my brother and two sisters. My mom had four kids in four and a half years with thirty-minute deliveries. Mine was nothing like that. I pushed for three hours and had an emergency C-section. I loved my family and my new family.

I had a few challenges that most new moms don't have to experience. The first was feeding enzymes to a newborn. I broke open capsules and washed the tiny beads into Sterling's mouth with formula through a tube while trying to breast feed. Somehow, I managed but with a lot of teamwork from Lawrence and my family. I was so happy, but nervous Sterling wasn't getting all the enzymes he needed. In CF, the ducts in the pancreas become blocked with sticky mucous. The mucous blocks the enzymes from reaching food in the small intestines. The pancreatic enzymes help to digest and absorb food. Because there appeared to be a connection between better lung function and higher body weight, it was important to take enzymes with all meals and snacks. I got this all from the CF Foundation which was my biggest go-to when I had CF questions. We made many calls to Sterling's CF specialist, Dr. P from the hospital to make sure we were doing things correct.

I brought Sterling to the set in Imperial Beach eight days later to show him off. One of the nicest stars from the show held him and that was the first celebrity he met—Luis Guzman.

The picture made the credits on one of the episodes, but it was a short-lived high. The news had broken, and everyone was devastated. There would be no second season. The show had been cancelled. A writers' strike was looming, and Lawrence needed to figure out what his next job would be. Money, insurance and most importantly, our memory-making ability was suddenly at risk. I looked at Sterling and knew that no matter what, we would figure it out.

# Episode 5

## The Blues Movie and My Little Buddy

**Thanksgiving Eve 2007**

**Soundtrack:**
**Carry You Away**
**(Juni Ata)**

Lawrence got a call to work on *The Blues Movie* in LA. Not Los Angeles, but LA meaning Louisiana. We never planned to leave the state, but it was the first opportunity since the writers' strike started.

Our LA apartment lease was not fully up, but we could not risk missing out on work when the writers' strike was the famine of the feast. There was no time to eat turkey, but we had a lot to be thankful for once again: work and insurance for our sweet Sterling. We spent Thanksgiving packing up the apartment. Well, Lawrence did most of the packing and I chased Sterling around. He was walking at eight months, keeping me very busy. We loaded up our two SUVs to prepare for a long drive across the country. I was proud Lawrence was offered a movie but had no idea what to expect in Louisiana. The questions of the unknown swarmed my head once again. Where would we live? What would I do with a baby in an unknown place? What would the parks be like? What happened if he got sick? We were so far from his care center in San Diego. I felt alone with Lawrence, but Sterling would be my buddy.

My mom joined on the drive that braked in Tucson, AZ and then Midland, Texas, the second night. We took turns entertaining our bundle of joy and dispensing him his pills. We broke up his enzymes in applesauce before each meal. It was easy to give him his pills because he liked applesauce. Each time I gave him pills I was reminded he had a disease with no cure. My mom thought the world of Lawrence and how lucky I was to be married to him.

We were soon driving from Texas to Shreveport. We arrived at a Courtyard Marriott and enjoyed Frito pie for the first time. In the morning, Lawrence went to his first day of work while my mom and I searched for an apartment. Each stop was an experience.

Mom and I perused a cute baby store on Main St. I handed Sterling to her and dashed off to use the bathroom in the back. The walls were thin and I could hear some people talking to my mom. "Excuse me, ma-am, are you holding a mixed baby?" I froze. Was this really happening? What would my mom say?

"This is my daughter's sweet boy," she answered, easily avoiding the question.

People seemed extremely nice to my fair skinned, blue-eyed mom, but not so much to my half Indonesian self. I got a very different energy. I wasn't black and I wasn't white, so I had some weird encounters. When I returned from the bathroom, the couple whispered to each other and scuttled away. My mom and I just rolled our eyes and thought it was kind of funny, but definitely uncomfortable. I wondered if this was going to happen a lot in Louisiana? I hoped not.

I didn't know a soul, so I began to ask locals for recommendations of good family-friendly apartments in our budget. Lawrence would have his housing limit paid by the show. If I could find a place less than his housing allowance, we could pay off debt and even start to save a little.

I made sure I 'show dropped' while touring apartments. Everyone loved Hollywood. I was so proud of Lawrence working on a movie, but I also thought they might cut me a deal because he was working with stars. It didn't work. Southerners were hard bargainers, but I eventually found an apartment. I moved all the stuff we'd packed into our cars into the second-floor apartment and before long, it was beginning to look like home. I bought placemats and kitchen towels from the Dollar Store.

My mom had to get back to work in California, so we said goodbye at the Shreveport Airport curb. Lawrence was working 24/7, so I accepted it would be just me and Sterling, my little man. We would cruise by Lawrence's office a few times a day and he would come out and play with Sterling in the back parking lot. What to do and where to go with a ten-month-old?

I found comfort in familiar places like Starbucks, Target and Ross. I went through the Starbucks drive through every day. It got me up and going. The caffeine helped me keep up with Sterling. I ordered the same thing every time. Grande vanilla breve latte. I loved shopping with my little man with latte in hand. Sipping calmed me down and always provided the comfort of enjoying my favorite drink from home. He would hang in his stroller and eat or we would play mommy pick up around the store. Sterling would throw his toy on the ground over and over again and laugh. Hey, I got a lot of shopping done with a ten-month-old so I didn't mind this repetitive mommy pick-up game. The exercise and exposure was definitely building his immune system.

I enrolled Sterling in Gymboree hoping to meet another mom, but we were the only ones in the class. I wanted a friend so badly to hang out with. I wanted Sterling to have a buddy too. I gave him every ounce of energy I had to help him adjust to the new place. When I grew exhausted I would put *Backyardigans* on and Sterling would dance to the opening song over and over. I would lie on the couch. There had been so many highs back in San Diego and LA with the constant family and support all around us. Lawrence was working so it was just me and Sterling. I felt a sense of loss. I loved my Sterling to pieces, but I went from being surrounded by supportive people to just me and a baby. Being one of four kids, I was wired to enjoy peoples' company. I had once heard that moving is the equivalent of experiencing a death. That seemed extreme, but I definitely felt a sense of loss. Was I grieving the lack of connection from Lawrence?

Sterling and I spent hours at the Riverwalk as well, a collection of shops and restaurants. The Riverwalk trolley was free, so we rode it over and over and over, back and forth, through the middle of the stores. The Bass Pro shop was basically a free aquarium where we spent many hours staring at the fish. We only had four more months in Shreveport, how hard could it be?

The day finally came when I made a friend and so did Sterling. I was vacuuming while Sterling was rocking out to *Backyardigans* at maxed volume. There was a loud knock on the door, which may have been the result after many lighter knocks. Who knows, but we were having a good ol' time. I would chase him with the vacuum occasionally. My dad drew eyes on my childhood machine so I did the same thing. Sterling thought it was hilarious, the vacuum monster.

I opened the door to a plump security guard.

"How can I help you?" I said loudly with *Backyardigans* blasting.

"Ma-am, you are being way too loud," he said politely, but loudly.

"Sir, it's eight pm. I am just vacuuming for the first time in weeks. Did someone complain?" I asked, shocked in my U of A booty shorts.

"Yes, your neighbor under you," he explained. "She said there were very large booms coming from your apartment and she was very concerned."

"Like I said, I am just vacuuming and my baby is dancing. I will be done in a minute." Who was this neighbor? Seriously? A complaint? I said goodnight to the security guard and shut the door. I didn't want to cause problems, but it was only eight.

Then there was another knock at the door.

"What now?" I thought out loud. I opened the door annoyed and there stood a petite blond-haired woman holding a cute little baby.

"Hi, I'm Leslie." She held her hand out for a shake, with the other one holding a blue-eyed baby girl on her hip.

"Hi, I'm Reese," I said in surprise, tightening my high pony.

"I am really sorry; I am the annoying lady that called and complained. I was trying to put my baby to sleep and I just kept hearing loud noises. I haven't slept in days and was so excited that she actually seemed to be falling asleep. This is Bay. The security guard said you looked my age with a baby too, so I had to run up and meet you. I don't work and I don't know anyone in the complex."

A friendship was born. We were completely different people, but we were moms and had babies around the same age. That was good enough for me.

It was a dream come true to go to parks with a friend and let the babies hang together. They were a month apart. I still was missing California, but Leslie helped bring sunshine to my days.

One day while we were at the park a lady came up to me and said," Excuse me, where are you from?"

"California," I replied.

"Oh, are you a Mexican? You look just like one."

"I am half Indonesian and my mom is German-Lithuanian if that is what a Mexican looks like to you."

"Are you sure you're not a Mexican?"

"I am pretty sure, but California is very diverse. There are many different ethnicities there. My dad was born in Holland and his parents are from Indonesia. My mom was born in Chicago and her dad is Lithuanian and her mom is German."

"Wow," she said, trying to process all the info I was feeding her.

I said to Leslie, "Are you hearing this?"

But all blonde, thin, local Leslie replied, "You're not a Mexican?"

I was dying at the ignorance and getting a little annoyed. All I could really do was laugh. I have dark hair and olive skin. They had never seen anyone like me before.

But time with my new friend was flying. Racial ignorance and all. Our favorite drive thru was the drive thru for margaritas.

"How is this legal?" I asked her.

Leslie replied, "Oh, I just take a sip and tape the straw down in case the police come. If the straw is taped down, you are in the clear."

Drive thru margaritas were the best solution for moms whose husbands were working with no babysitter option.

We would pull up with our two babies, order two margaritas and then go sit and hang out together at one of our apartments until the husbands got home.

Something about having a wife and baby motivated Lawrence to work harder and harder. I will take credit too as I was always telling Lawrence how hardworking and brilliant he was. He soon was asked to do a pilot that took place in Louisiana, Los Angeles and Scottsdale, Arizona. It was a motorcycle drama. The producer of *The Blues Movie* let him leave a few weeks early to start his new pilot and back to California we drove. He flew because he had to start the next day, so my parents and I drove. We took the two cars with Sterling from Louisiana to Tucson in one day. We treated ourselves at the JW Marriott in Tucson and completed our journey to California the next day. I really appreciated being home, well, being back in California at least. We still needed to find a place to live. What would it be like? Would I find a place to call home? Would we make enough money to survive? Would I go back to work? What would I do with Sterling? Would I need to look for a daycare too? Is the California dream possible? How long would we be in Los Angeles? Would Lawrence come back to me? Multiplied questions with no answers.

# Episode 6

## Motorcyle Drama and Rolling Our Dice

**Soundtrack:**
**Fight Hard, Run Fast**
**(Juni Ata)**

We signed a lease on an 1800 square foot town-house. We had saved quite a bit in Louisiana and I invested the rest into Apple. I was calling it my dream house. It had an HOA so the common areas were well manicured. We even had a neighborhood pool. We had a shared driveway with four other town houses. We couldn't have asked for better neighbors. One family, the Morgans, cooked extra food all the time. They would bring over plates for me and Sterling when Lawrence was working. The Morgans also asked if they could hold Sterling or take him on walks along the dried riverbed. The fourth family, from Russia, had two girls and their mother was studying to be a doctor. We called it the Grove Cove.

When Lawrence shot in Scottsdale for a few weeks we only packed a suitcase, not the whole house. Sterling and I explored the Hotel Valley Ho and enjoyed many hours in the hotel pool while Lawrence was working. I learned from

Sterling's CF specialist that it was extremely important to keep Sterling active. This would help shake up any mucous in his chest. He also had a tiny vest that he wore to shake his lungs two times day. I jumped for joy; our insurance covered the $17,000 medical device. It wasn't too hard to keep him active because he had tons of energy. The pool was a great way to get it out. He was crab crawling around the edge of the pool and then I would drag him through the water saying "kick, kick, kick."

There were plenty of great shops at the nearby Fashion Square mall where Sterling and I met up with one of my old high school friends and her toddler.

Sterling was a year old now and still my little buddy. I bought my first item from Anthropology on the sale rack. The last time I was in the store was in Beverly Hills with my ex-boyfriend's mom in college. She was offering to buy me anything I wanted so I got a colorful knit beanie. She had insisted on getting me something. I didn't want to strip her joy of giving and really loved the beanie.

Arizona was also the first time I gave a twenty-dollar tip to a bell man for his help. He carried everything from our hotel room to our car. I really appreciated his help and the only bill I had on me was a twenty. He lit up and I felt instant joy. This would be a new habit for me even if I couldn't afford it. Giving made me feel good. This was another one of my love languages.

We got back from Arizona, and sadly the pilot didn't get picked up, but another fun experience and memory-making would go down in the books. I say fun, but it was also exhausting traveling with a one-year-old. We always made it work.

Back in LA I was enjoying our clean, safe neighborhood and three-bedroom town house. It was the perfect place to grow our family. I didn't know Lawrence's next job, but we finally had a little cushion money from Shreveport set aside in the stock market.

Pulling into a garage with groceries was the best reward. I didn't have to lug them upstairs with a baby. I didn't have to search for a parking spot at night. We bought our first treadmill and I could work out while Sterling was napping.

We decided it was time to grow our family. The chances of having another child with cystic fibrosis were twenty-five percent since both Lawrence and I were carriers. We had heard rumors about other families doing in vitro with pre-genetic diagnosis. We decided to roll our dice and whatever God's plan was going to be was great enough for us. Sterling was such a free spirit and joy to us all. We were just hoping for a baby. We wanted Sterling to have a sister or brother. He would either have a best friend with CF or a best friend without CF. They would have each other to do treatments together and understand each other. But there was also the potential to get each other sick. I hoped being exposed to most of the same germs that would be a rarity. The suspense was killing me. Either way having a child is a miracle. We believed whatever the plan was it was. Most people were anxious to find out the sex of the baby, but we were anxious to find out the health. Would we have a healthy baby? Could we handle another unhealthy baby?

# Episode 7

## Vampire Show Season 2 And Expecting a Miracle #2

**Soundtrack:**
**God, Your Mama, and Me**
**(Florida, Georgia, Line Feat. Backstreet Boys)**

Vampires were never my thing, so I thought. Until Lawrence began working on a vampire show. When Lawrence worked on a movie or show, I wanted to make sure I watched it no matter my interest in the content. I wanted to be part of his TV world, so I watched the shows to gain knowledge of what he would be talking about after work. I learned the characters, studied their IMDBs and put names with faces. The show was a masterpiece. The characters were amazing. The storylines were intriguing and detailed. I loved it. I also knew first hand that the brilliant product was the result of many hours of hard work. Some worked hard because it was what they loved and some did it to put meals on the table and provide insurance for their family. For some it was both. For Lawrence I think it was both. The long hours away from Sterling weren't easy for Lawrence and having him away so much wasn't easy on us. The credits at the end of the show were backwards to me.

If I had my own show the crew would be first in the credits and the talent would be last. Most of the time the talent could afford to fly their families in and out of locations or have it built into their contracts. They got to see their families no matter what. But the production crew didn't. I didn't. Lawrence was almost like a dream I once had. Was he even real? Was what we had real? I never saw him anymore to really know. Could he be brought back to life?

The talent sometimes worked every other day or even one day a week. Oh, believe me, I respected the talent and we needed the talent, but if credits were truly giving credit, I would love for just one show to put the credits in order of hours worked, despite the department and see what order it fell into. I guarantee you the transportation and assistant director names would be before the talent. Could just one show put the position and hours worked next to their name? It would be fun to see.

My point was, *The Vampire Show* crew was awesome. Thanks to the creator for wanting authentic night scenes, the crew literally turned into vampires working all night and sleeping during the day. Those who had families barely slept at all so they could see them. All issues aside, people were grateful for work, including me.

The man that couldn't honor Lawrence's plea for more responsibility, more pay and a better title on *The Salt Water Show*, surprisingly offered Lawrence this life-changing blood-sucking opportunity. Mr. Goodberg was a successful Hollywood exec. Lawrence never thought he would give him his next opportunity in the TV industry. We were pleasantly honored and humbled. This huge exec saw potential and appreciated Lawrence's work ethic. Lawrence needed this positive and honest role model. Knowing Lawrence worked under Goodberg put me at ease. When I worked with Goodberg on

*The Western* I got a great vibe from him. He respected me, the girl that stocked the fridge and answered the phones. He was the real deal. He paid attention to detail. I was having a rough day, a day I felt invisible, and I will never forget him stopping mid-conversation with a group of execs to ask me how I was, and if I had changed my hair color. I had. His compliment was all I needed that day to perk up. I didn't need a man to feel good, but I needed to be seen that day.

As Lawrence planned logistics for Season Two of the best *Vampire Show* in history, we were expecting miracle number two. Watching Season One, even with all the long hours, ignited our sexual chemistry and I will thank the creator for that—all the writers including my favorite known as the male deer.

I was overjoyed at the eight-week ultrasound when I heard our baby's heartbeat.

"Sounds like a healthy heart," Dr. Sal, the best OB in the world and my dad's male bonding trip companion, announced with a caring expression. I wondered about healthy lungs. Would our new baby have CF too?

Lawrence had that same proud look that blanketed his face the day Sterling was born as he heard the heartbeat.

"It's a boy. I already know. Let's name him Trent," he said so certainly with his fists clenched. He began calling him Trent. Thankfully my mom offered to watch Sterling while we had the ultrasound.

"Now you both understand there is a twenty-five percent chance Trent can have CF as well?" Sal asked, using the name Trent.

We both nodded our heads and in unison said, "Yes."

"I have the amnio referral set up at SD Medical if you want to go that route again?"

We did the amniocentesis at SD Medical. We walked

into the same office like that day with Sterling two years before. Would results prove Trent did not have CF? Would we see the white light?

We met with the genetic counselor, Davis again.

"Good to see you again, well, not under these circumstances."

We knew what he meant. His words did not blur this time.

"How is Sterling?" he asked as he glanced at his family photo on his desk.

"Sterling is doing well. He has not been hospitalized. He has a lot of energy and runs around all the time," Lawrence answered smiling. This time was much easier. We didn't have as much uncertainty as last time.

"Good to hear. I will make this quick since it's your second time," he said. Thank God, I thought, I was ready to get it over with as soon as possible.

The amnio was a quick twenty minutes this time and we were out of there. I hate needles and let's just say I forgot how big the amnio needle was. I felt a little nauseous after, but then again, I was prego.

Lawrence was right. We were having a boy! There was no white light. But that was no definite confirmation of anything.

Two weeks later...

"Good news. Trent does not have CF. He is not even a carrier," said Davis. I hung up. I was overjoyed that Trent was going to enter this world without a disease.

"Lawrence, good news, no CF and not even a carrier," I yelled in excitement as I entered the bathroom of our townhouse. Lawrence was giving Sterling a little bubble bath and held him in the tub while pouring water over his head to wash his hair.

He looked at me and put his head down on the side of the tub.

He continued to hold Sterling and lifted his head to look at his son.

"What's wrong?" I asked, so confused.

"I feel so sad for Sterling right now. I just feel bad he has CF." Sharing such raw truth was rare for him. I was slightly awestruck as tears ran down his cheeks. He was having a father son moment when I barged in. I left them alone.

I could hear him crying again. We had different emotions flowing through us in that moment. Neither of us were right or wrong. But I returned, "Sterling is a rock star, determined, audacious, brilliant and hilarious. Without the CF, we wouldn't have Sterling. He is an extraordinary boy and doesn't know life any differently. Pills and treatments will become normal to him. He has been taking them since birth. In life, tell me one person that's successful that hasn't had to overcome something hard? Sterling is going to change the world and so will Trent," I said, trying to see it from Lawrence's perspective. I wasn't Sterling and I didn't actually know what he felt or how he would feel someday. I wanted to see this as an up but understood how it could be seen as sad too. I was refusing to see it that way, but Lawrence was right. We were both right, because they were our feelings. My up was not lifting Lawrence. He needed to be sad. It was not the time for my speech. I left the bathroom to let him just be. I wanted to hug Lawrence in celebration, but our feelings did not align, and I felt alone. This was becoming the norm.

Lawrence was now shooting vampires with Mr. Goodberg, his boss. He offered us a train table for Sterling. It was like Christmas as those things were extremely expensive. Lawrence picked up the train table, not realizing it would be the beginning of a friendship. Lawrence and Goodberg discovered they shared a passion for golf. Lawrence told me no one worked harder than Goodberg. One producer had showed Lawrence the ropes on *The Western* and *Motorcycle Drama* and now Goodberg would teach him everything else he didn't know. He would be Lawrence's mentor. Goodberg, a handsome gentleman, had four boys himself so there was so much Lawrence could sponge up from this father, husband and producer.

I was catching up to Season Two while binge watching episodes I'd missed from season one and I was addicted. The love story between the lead characters was so passionate. I fantasized that was me and Lawrence. We even had the same age gap. That fantasy rolled into our bedroom. At the premiere of Season Two, the creator spoke about the numerous letters he received from women all over the world thanking him for helping their sex lives. This certainly was true for us. This was the only time we were connecting, but I would take anything I could get.

But I also couldn't help but fall in love with Mr. Muscles, a character with chiseled abs that made me laugh. Maybe a little too much. I sometimes had to check myself and keep my eye-gazing to a minimum when I visited set. Was I imagining we had a connection? Or did I feel it? I was in such a drought from connecting with my husband was it wrong to fantasize I had one with someone? I hoped Lawrence hadn't noticed. I didn't want to hurt him ever. I also didn't know how to handle the hurt I was experiencing at times.

Lawrence continued to work crazy hours and my belly was growing quickly. I started to feel like I was human and he was the vampire. I was so proud of the show he was on and his hard work, but I couldn't help resenting him for the time away and the loneliness I felt.

"We're becoming the show. We're distant. You are vampire

and I'm human. We're in different worlds," I said at five a.m. as the sun was coming up. He had just walked through the doorway. My love for life was being sucked out of me.

"Seriously, I just worked all night and you are going to give me shit?" he said, eyes half open and stumbling to our room. "I am working so hard to become a producer so we can make more memories for the family. Remember our pact? The make-memories pact?"

"Can't you work less?" I asked annoyed and pulling up my comfy socks that his mom gave me. Anything seemed to give me more support and comfort than Lawrence did. Even a pair of socks.

"It's all or none. There is so much work to be done. Please just stick with me. I am so happy to have work right now before Trent is born," he explained throwing his body on the pillow. Suddenly he was out, loud snores and all.

"Great conversation, nice talking to you," I said under my breath as he continued to snore, his body horizontal on the bed clothes, shoes still on.

The more he worked hard for the family and his career goals, the more I felt like he wasn't part of the family. He was part of a whole different family. Many people love the industry because it becomes their family, but he had a family and it was waiting for him every night. I pictured them having fun all the time at work and me home alone, pregnant and exhausted chasing a toddler. I felt left out, but I was needing friends of my own, a life of my own. I was trying to wait up late for times he finished at two or three to spend time together, but that left my prego body exhausted for Sterling the next day. Would I have his support with our new baby? Would binge watching *The Vampire Show* and fantasizing about Mr. Muscles help me feel better? Was it wrong to do things that made me feel good?

# Episode 8

## Vampire Show Season 3 and Blue Eyed Boy

**March 2009**

**Soundtrack:**
**Hallelujah**
**(Noly Mon)**

S terling was born at Scripps La Jolla and we loved Dr. Sal so decided to have Trent there too.

I stayed at my parent's long one-story house the week before my due date in case I went into labor. Lawrence would drive down from Hollywood if I started having contractions.

"Lawrence, I am having contractions," I said, excited to get Trent out and see his cute face.

"On my way." He hung up, filled Mr. Goodberg in and got in his car. He had prepped his boss that he might have to go to San Diego for a few days. Luckily, I went into labor on a Friday, so the weekend was ahead. Lawrence would not miss much work and could work from his phone if he had to.

Lawrence drove to San Diego. My contractions were getting closer together. Makayla and Brian were staying at my parent's while putting in offers on houses. Brian and Lawrence popped open a beer as Makayla timed my contractions. *East Bound and Down* kept their attention. I heard chuckles from the living room. Makayla joined them to watch this stupid, yet somewhat hilarious half hour HBO show.

"Lawrence, can you come here please. I heard that sperm can move my contractions along," I said dragging him into the guest room. His pants were at his ankles before I could shut the door.

"Thank you," I said. I appreciated him just listening to my prego requests.

Thirty minutes passed. The men were back watching TV. I interrupted Lawrence and Brian who had Bud Light and Heineken in hand.

My cervix started pulsating. "Let's go, let's go, let's go. My contractions are close!"

Trent opened his big blue eyes to the world. A gorgeous, healthy and calm baby lay bundled up in Lawrence's arms. I was so drugged up from my C-section, this allowed Lawrence to step up to the plate. He worked so hard to keep the poop chart up to date, the feeding schedule and did all the diaper changes while I was recovering from my surgery and dehydration shaking. Lawrence was so helpful, which was no different from Sterling's birth.

"Thank you so much," I said as I attempted to prop up my beached whale numb body. I wished he was always around like that. I loved his support. He was so helpful. He didn't stop. He got that from his parents.

"I want to help as much as I can before I go back to work," he said as he rocked Trent. He was definitely not lazy.

We were discharged three days later and drove to Los Angeles. I sat on a pillow because the slightest pothole hurt my incision. Trent was the easiest baby, sleeping through the night at three months. Sterling loved Trent and would always be his protector. Their chemistry was undeniable.

"Football?" two-year-old Sterling asked, ready to play tackle football with the baby.

I tried to explain, "Trent isn't quite ready for tackle."

But Trent had an amazing grip and held his bottle at three months. It wasn't even propped up. After his bottle, we laughed as he chucked it across the room.

"Did you see that?" Lawrence would say in awe. Maybe he was ready to play football with Sterling. His strength led to climbing doors and ninja courses with record times. Trent spent many hours a day sleeping. He was chilling, taking in the scenery. He had a good view of me helping Sterling with his meds and treatments in the stroller, jungle jumperoo and on the floor. I managed to do a lot while holding the little snug bug too. Sterling, my toddler, was acting out for my attention. I would occasionally have to put him in time-out and leave for a minute.

"Ah choo, ah choo," were the sounds that came from him in time-out, attempting to fake snore. I laughed from behind the corner. Soon I realized they weren't fake snores. He was coughing. And it was getting worse. I took him to the doctor and was prescribed antibiotics.

"Cough, cough, cough," Sterling was coughing so badly a few weeks later. Trent was teething and fussy and the now several rounds of antibiotics had not stopped Sterling—his coughing so violent it knocked him to the floor. His little voice begged me, "Mommy, am I dying? Please take my cough away."

Tears poured down my freckled cheeks and Lawrence guided me into a nearby room. "Don't let him see you," he reminded me as he headed back in to our son, placing a mask shooting out nebulized albuterol, hypersaline and then pulmozyme into his mouth and nose. During this half hour treatment, a vest shook Sterling's cough. The goal was to relax the lungs, shake the mucous, liquefy it and cough it out of the lungs. This took between thirty and forty minutes, depending on the nebulizer and medicines. This was Sterling's routine two times a day when he was healthy, and we increased the vest and albuterol up to five times when he had a cough.

I cried to Lawrence, "I want control. I am doing all of his treatments and giving him all of his pills. Why won't it stop? We are doing all the right things." But control was one thing I was never going to get.

Trent even seemed to develop a fake little cough. Probably saying *look at me too.*

The drive from Los Angeles to Rady Children's San Diego was luckily traffic free. Since Sterling was born in La Jolla, we kept Children's San Diego as his CF care center. Sterling and I went to his sick visit not knowing what the doctor would decide.

Lawrence was working on the third season of *The Vampire Show* in Hollywood when Sterling was admitted into the hospital. This was our first hospital experience, so we were not prepared. My sister and Lawrence's parents offered to watch nine-month-old Trent because I couldn't have a baby in the hospital with me. My parents helped relieve me from the hospital a few times to shower. My mother-in-law even snuck me in some wine. Lawrence drove from Hollywood each night to put Sterling to bed. Sterling only wanted me to sleep over. Lawrence would offer. Luckily, Lawrence was prepping the season and not shooting yet so he wasn't working nights. The first nine nights I didn't sleep and turned into a person I didn't recognize. Was I turning into a vampire? Cold, lifeless? The CF for the first time felt real and although this was not about me, I felt sad and sorry for Sterling. I projected my stress onto him and truly believed it was the reason he couldn't sleep or relax either. I didn't have the right words to explain to Sterling. Talking to him like an adult wasn't the best parenting, but it's all I had and is probably why he was wise beyond his years. I was feeling extreme guilt for not being around Trent, but knew he was in good hands. I was reminded how truly amazing family is. Friends and my Moms' Club sent cards and gifts as well. One day my sister visited and Sterling turned to say bye, slamming his head into a wall on his scooter. It was the first time a patient was stitched while being an inpatient. There was a courtyard outside his room and he still had so much energy even with a cough. I let him ride his scooter with his little mask on to avoid picking up more germs, though I forgot to put his little helmet on.

After a week in the hospital with Sterling, the doctors agreed we would do the rest of his care at home, where he could roam freely and sleep better. I could give him drugs through the PICC line myself, instead of completing two full weeks of hospital care at the hospital. My wish was granted and they sent a nurse to my sister's house to teach me at-home care. My best friend got married the day he was discharged. Lawrence told me to go to the wedding. He could handle it and his parents could help too, especially being the weekend. I was mentally and emotionally drained but threw on my bridesmaid dress, took a shot of tequila and showed up for my friend. It was a nice break from the hospital.

After the wedding, I had days where I literally had to look in the mirror and say, "Stop feeling sorry for yourself. Stop feeling sorry for him." The self-pity wasn't going to help anyone. If you are a parent of a child with a disease or challenge you know what I mean. We have those moments where we have to pick ourselves up off the floor and keep going. It wasn't just the disease bringing me down, it was the lack of emotional support from Lawrence and lack of connection. I was lacking a purpose. I had lost faith. I was carrying a burden that I wasn't equipped to carry. I was doing the best I could.

Before Sterling went into the hospital, Lawrence and I agreed to move to Carlsbad. He was working so many hours in LA this would put me closer to family for help with the kids and we would be by the ocean to help Sterling's lungs, not to mention Lawrence and I loved the beach.

The move to Carlsbad was supposed to happen after Sterling got out of the hospital, but the house we signed a lease on had a kitchen that was being remodeled and it wasn't finished. Don't ever sign a lease unless the place has a finished kitchen. Sterling got out of the hospital and we had a moving truck full of stuff from the LA house and nowhere to put it. A big thank-you went to Lawrence for doing the packing and moving while Sterling was in the hospital. We parked the truck outside my sister's house in Rancho Bernardo.

Lawrence rented the same studio we originally had when we got engaged in LA and now we would also have an adorable shared driveway house a mile from Ponto Beach in Carlsbad. We would have the best of both worlds wouldn't we?

**My Mucous Production Wife Diary-Our First Hospital Stay**

Our first hospital stay went like this:

**Friday, August 1, 2010 Pulmonology Clinic**

Sterling was coughing very badly. I called the doctor and we went to see him.

"Dr.P, he is coughing so badly I'm worried about him.

"Can you drive him down to San Diego so I can take a listen to his lungs?"

"Sure, I'll be down in two hours."

Wishful thinking—with LA traffic I would be down in 3-4 hours.

"Hi, I'm here to see Dr. P. Sterling isn't feeling well. He's coughing a lot."

"Right this way, we've been waiting for you."

First a calm nurse with a high ponytail and long hair met us at the door to the patient offices. She held the door open for Sterling and me. She pointed to the scale.

"Let me just get his height and weight really quick and then I'll take you into your room."

"Sterling, step on the scale."

"Why do we have to step on the scale?" he asked expectantly.

Toddlers always had questions and it was a good thing, but sometimes I just want to speed things up and brush over all the questions. Sometimes I don't have all the answers. With Sterling, he wasn't the kid where I could just make something up. I didn't want to answer him ever and unless I knew the facts regarding what I was saying, because he would remember what I said and he would hold me to it.

"They just want to get your weight and see how you've been growing since your last appointment."

Sterling stood on the scale and pretended to wobble on it.

"Whooooooooooo," he said, leaning both ways pretending he was on a rocking ship or was it a surfboard?

"Sterling, don't mess around. The faster we do this faster we can see the doctor," I said intense and stressed out, wondering if we were going to the hospital or not. I didn't think so. I left so quickly, trying to avoid LA to San Diego traffic, I didn't even pack a bag for him. I'd dropped Trent at my family's house on the way.

The nurse led us to our patient room and the nurse practitioner came in.

"Hi Sterling. You're not sounding so good, buddy. Can the nurse get your vital signs?" she said, sweetly increasing her volume to talk over his cough. Like he knew what vital signs were.

"Am I going into the house-p-tall?" his voice questioned.

"I am not sure about hospital. Let's see what the doctor says when he listens to your lungs?"

"So I am. I am? I really am going to the house-p-tall?" he asked again and again.

I'm talking over him. "Sweetheart, we're not sure; let's wait to see what the doctor says."

He couldn't stop coughing, but he also couldn't stop running around the small room. He was worried. So was I.

On the way down I told them there was a chance that he may have to go into the hospital. The night before, he asked me to take his cough away. The night before, he asked me if he was dying. When he asked me if he might have to go to the hospital I told him it was a possibility. Should I have lied and said no? Then we could just deal with it when it happens. I felt a little guilty for worrying him. If he didn't have to go to the hospital, then he was worrying for no reason. But if he did have to go to the hospital then I would be a big fat liar for saying no. Talking to a three-year-old about these things was very difficult. Do I worry him and tell him the truth or do I lie and deal with it when it comes?

I always told him the truth. If I didn't know, then I would say I don't know but if he asked me if it was a chance, I would tell him it was a possibility.

The nurse took his vitals and then Dr. P came through the doorway.

He was so calm and so relaxed his energy calmed me and Sterling down.

"Has your husband been surfing lately?"

"He's been to Ventura a few times but it's been a little harder for him to get out there lately with work."

"The waves have been awesome. Tell him to get out there and take this little guy too."

"Okay, I'll tell him those are the doctor orders." I chuckled a little.

Dr. P put a stethoscope to Sterling's chest as I held him in my lap. He was wiggly always. His wiggles were different. His wiggles were shaky. He was a boy that was afraid. He was a boy that was scared. Even in the most calming presence of Dr. P he was worried. I was worried again.

"Mom, you're doing a great job. He has been on two rounds of oral antibiotics now and I'm sorry but his lungs just aren't sounding any better."

"But we upped his treatments to five times a day. I just don't get it."

"Am I going into the house-p-tal?" Sterling asked again. He was so smart. But I didn't even pack a bag. I was in denial.

I knew Sterling had CF. I thought he was invincible. I thought he would have the diagnosis but the symptoms of the disease were just going to skip him.

"Sometimes you can do everything, but you just need a little bit more. Let's admit him to the hospital right now and we can have the respiratory therapists do more treatments. We can put together a meal plan for him. We will give him antibiotics through a PICC line and we will get him better. Let me have the nurses schedule that surgery," Dr. P explained.

I pretended to be so calm and so confident, but I was

freaking out inside. This disease is real. I can't control it. Sterling just kept asking about the hospital over and over and over. In every cartoon movie you see sick people in hospitals. People look sad in hospitals. So, it would make sense that my three-year-old would be confused, anxious and a little out of control while coughing nonstop. Was he feeling what I felt? I'm here. I was his mom trying to be strong and supportive for him. But I guess I just realized his disease was real. It was like I found out for the first time my kid had cystic fibrosis all over again. It was the day I got the call from the genetic counselor. I just wanted to roll up in a ball and I wanted somebody to hold me. Well, I needed to snap out of it because I had a three-year-old that needed me.

So I put on my happy face and I pretended like the hospital was going to be the most fun place in the world. He's so smart he probably read right through it but it was worth a shot.

When the room cleared from the doctor and nurses I called Lawrence. My voice was so shaky.

"Lawrence, Sterling is getting admitted but they're confident they can get him better. They're going to give him a PICC line to pump antibiotics to his heart and therefore they will be dispersed all over his body to kill whatever's bringing him down."

"OK, I'm going to shoot down to the hospital after work. Where is Trent?" He spoke in business mode, but hospital business mode.

"I dropped him off at my sister's house on the way down, so he is in good hands." I gave Sterling a hug.

"We have to be out of our house in two days in LA. This is the craziest timing. Let me see if I can get a couple guys from work to help me move out of the house tomorrow. I was reminded we were moving which hadn't crossed my mind. "Is the Carlsbad house ready?"

When it rains it pours. We were in the middle of moving all our earthly belongings.

"After we get admitted into the hospital and get to our inpatient room I will call the management company and figure out exactly when she's giving us the keys."

"OK ,sounds good. We'll talk tonight when I get down there. Hang in there. Can your sister keep Trent for the night?"

"I haven't told her what's going on yet but I will ask her. Drive safe." I hung up and took a deep breath.

Lawrence was shooting on *The Vampire Show*. Like I said before, the hours were crazy. This move couldn't be worse timing. When I called the landlord for the Carlsbad house I learned that the kitchen was flooded and they were finishing up the remodel. This was not disclosed when we signed the lease. So, I guess we just needed to pack up the moving truck from LA and park it somewhere until we got the keys to the Carlsbad house. Good thing we had plenty of family in San Diego. Lawrence also needed to sign a lease on a small studio apartment so he would have somewhere to stay when he was in LA.

These living uncertainties were adding stress to me. I tried to use that happy upbeat voice with Sterling, but I could still hear the stress in my voice no matter how chipper I tried to sound.

"Makayla, it's me. Sterling just got admitted to the hospital for a few weeks. Lawrence is shooting and, on his way down, but he can't be down here for two weeks straight; he's going to go back-and-forth every night. He's crazy. Is there any way you can help me with Trent?"

"Of course. For how long?" She answered so sweetly,

reminding me of how great it is to have family around. "Mom and dad are working but they both said they can help me with Trent as soon as I get off work."

"Hold on a sec. I'm getting a call from Lawrence, actually let me call you back." I switched over to Lawrence on my BlackBerry as Sterling was running around the room. I felt bad ignoring him for a few minutes but I just needed to get all the logistics sorted out for Trent who was only nine months old.

"Hey, so my parents are driving down right now from Northern California. They said they can help with Trent if they stay at your sister's house so they can just relieve her whenever she needs it?"

"Oh, that's awesome. I will let her know that because her workplace is letting her work from home to help out with Trent but I don't think they realize it's going to be possibly a couple weeks. Her husband can help too.

I felt so guilty. It was like I was over the limit: 'yeah, can you help with rent for a couple weeks possibly?' But is that partly what families are for?"

"Yeah, it will be great between your parents and my parents and your sister; and her husband, Trent will be in such good hands."

"Makayla, thank you so much for helping us. Lawrence is going to be coming down every single day when he gets off work whenever they wrap, so he'll come relieve you two and help out with Trent and then relieve me at the hospital so I can go and shower. I know they have the Ronald McDonald house but there's just something about going home. Wait, I just realized we don't even have a home. Do you care if I come in and shower at your house or at Mom and Dad's? Maybe I'll ask them."

"Yeah, no problem; of course you can shower at my

house. Whatever you guys need. That's so crazy–your house isn't ready yet?"

"No, it's supposed to be according to our lease but the landlord said there was some sort of flooding thing and they're redoing part of the kitchen and they're sorry but they don't know when it will be finished."

"OK, no worries. You've got my house and Mom and Dad's house. Don't worry about Trent; he'll be good."

I just couldn't fully forget about Trent so I could focus on Sterling. Thank God, Trent was on bottles. Thank God he was such an easy baby.

The nurse came into a clinic room and handed us paperwork. We walked over to the main building and checked in.

## Friday August 1, 2010 -Hospital Stay Day 1

Sterling's bed was ready. It was a crib with metal bars on the sides so he couldn't roll out in the middle of the night. The metal bars pulled up and it look like a miniature jail. The top of his bed was a plastic canopy covered in stickers. Other sick kids who used the bed before him had decorated it. Some were more worn than others.

Some stickers were Mickey Mouse and some were dinosaurs, some were large and some small and some had been pulled off completely with just a trace of their stickiness left.

I looked around and a bed for me was nowhere to be found. I asked the nurse politely, "This is our first time being admitted. Where do I sleep?"

"Oh honey. Do you see that armchair? Well, the bottom of it pulls out. You can get real cozy on it if you snuggle up with the pillows," She gestured toward the arm chair, bright pink scrubs flashing before my eyes.

"Okay. Now what can we bring to the hospital as far as toys for Sterling?" I really was a hospital rookie.

"You can bring anything you want—whatever he needs to keep himself busy for the next couple weeks," she nicely explained. "We have a toy room here too and he can schedule a time to go play in it. I will be right back." She rushed out to tend to another matter.

Three years old is a really hard age for the hospital.

I picked up my pink BlackBerry and dialed Lawrence.

"Lawrence, when you come down here can you please bring all of his Thomas the Train tracks. And a rug. Bring as much stuff as you can find for him to do. They have a play room here but I have to schedule it and make sure there is not another CF child in the playroom at the same time or another child in the playroom that could get him sick. I'm not sure what we're going to do in here for two weeks. He's coughing and he is sick but he still has so much energy."

"Yeah, I'll even buy him a scooter," he suggested. "Is there anywhere for him to ride it?"

"Thankfully this room opens up to a courtyard, I don't see why not. He's going to go crazy if he has to stay in here. Lawrence, I didn't even pack a suitcase for myself or for Sterling. I just figured he was going to be fine."

"It's going to be fine. I'm headed down. I'll be down there around 6:00 p.m. My boss said do whatever I need to do."

The nurse returned.

"I'm going to write a schedule up on the board so that we get all of his treatments in and you will know what's going on. Does this schedule work for you?" she asked, writing numbers and times on the board.

"Sure?" I responded uncertainly as everything was becoming a blur.

The respiratory therapist came in, "Time for your first treatment, little guy."

"I am not little!" he yells at her. Oh, Sterling.

"Oh, wow, he's got a lot of energy. Come on, it'll be really fun."

Yeah, he's three years old. Great observation. I was tired and emotionally drained so positivity wasn't on the forefront of my thoughts. Mama bear definitely was. I took comments the wrong way when I was tired and drained.

I grabbed the remote control for the TV and found a cartoon. Then Sterling sat down and started watching the TV as the respiratory therapist put his vest on, click click, and held his nebulizer to his mouth.

"No, thank you. No, thank you!"

He yelled as he pushed the nebulizer away from his mouth.

"No, we have to do this. It gets you better," the nurse playfully tried to steer him back on track with his treatment.

"No, thank you. No, thank you!" he yelled again, pushing the neb away from his mouth.

I was too tired to say anything. I was on the room phone and trying to order food to the hospital room. I was on hold.

"Hi, can I help you?"

"Yes, I'm trying to get some food for my son for his dinner."

"Yes, what would you like?" she asked with a little sniffle.

"Can I order him the chicken fingers and two pizzas and then the pudding for dessert later?" I rambled off quite a bit of food.

"I'm sorry, ma'am, you're only allowed to order one meal for the patient. You have to go down to the first floor and buy your own food or come here and buy it."

"Well, he hasn't eaten since breakfast and this is all for

him. I am not eating any of it." Does she think I am trying to steal food? Even if I was, how am I supposed to go get food if he needs to stay in the room?

"I don't think so. Families often try to order more meals than they are supposed to. We're only supposed to feed the patient."

"You've got to be kidding me. Our child has cystic fibrosis and he is on a high calorie diet. He hasn't eaten since breakfast," I responded with a cold tone.

"OK, well then, we will deliver one pizza and apple juice. Is that all?"

"Unbelievable, are you kidding me?" I snapped and hung up. I don't think they want to see me hangry.

I'm not going to lie. I definitely would've had a bite of his pizza. I had not eaten since breakfast either. What was I supposed to do—leave him in the room and go down to McDonald's? He's supposed to stay away from all kids so we can get better. Well, at least you'll have food, baby, and I'll see if Lawrence can grab me something.

The nurse walked into the room as a respiratory therapist had left.

"Hi, you mentioned earlier I could order something for myself from the cafeteria but they were not very friendly. Also Sterling is on a high calorie diet—hasn't eaten since breakfast, but they wanted to give me a hard time about ordering him a couple meals."

"Oh, let me call them; it doesn't say high calorie on his meal plan so we will add that and you shouldn't have any more problems," she reached up and changed his chart.

I tried to crack a joke. "OK, thank you. I felt like I was breaking the law for ordering him a bunch of food."

I myself was starving and I was getting moody. I definitely didn't plan this too well.

I hit the call button for the nurse. "Excuse me, Sterling's food is going to be here in a few minutes and I really need his enzymes. He can't eat until after he takes his enzymes."

"Sure, let me get those. Do you have enzymes on you? If you do that's fine but try not to use the pills you have because we really try to monitor how many pills he's taking here so we would prefer if you use the hospital's. I try to tell that to all the parents."

"Sure I'll wait for you to bring his." I was happy to use the hospital's meds.

The food came five minutes later. The nurse never came back. So, I politely beeped and asked for enzymes. Twenty minutes passed and still no enzymes. I gave up and decided to break the rule and give him enzymes from my purse. I tried to do it their way, but Sterling was hungry.

Sterling was eating when the nurse came in and said, "Oh, I need to get his enzymes he can't eat that yet."

"Don't worry about it; I just gave him some from my purse. I didn't want his food to be so cold," I said holding up my big pill bottle.

"I asked you to use the hospital pills," she said firmly, staring at Sterling jumping on his bed

"Yes, but I asked for them 45 minutes ago. What do you expect me to do? I'm sorry—if I don't have enzymes before his meals come, I'm going to use mine. I'm not going to make the kid wait when he has not eaten all day. And I have not eaten either so I really don't want to talk with you anymore because I'm starting to get frustrated."

Sterling just stared at me. Was I stressing him out? He scarfed down his food. I thought I would fill up the bathtub and give him a bath to relax him from this crazy day. I went to fill the bath and the drain stop didn't work. The tub would not hold water.

I buzzed the nurse again.

"Excuse me, I'm trying to give Sterling a bath after he eats and the tub isn't holding any water."

"I will call the plumber but I don't think he'll be able to come help you until tomorrow sometime. And not sure when that will be but I'll make a note of it."

"OK, I guess that's no bath for tonight," I said kind of disgusted.

I was annoyed.

"Hi, sorry, traffic was horrible," Lawrence said as he walked into the room with the scooter and a helmet along with suitcases full of train tracks and toys. There was no daylight left so tomorrow would be the day.

"Sorry, I'm so annoyed right now."

"Why?"

"It's all these little things and I'm just so not prepared."

"You knew it was a possibility, that's no one's fault but your own," Lawrence responded. What did he just say to me? "Sorry, I didn't mean that. Listen, I am exhausted too. I haven't slept in two days."

It was 9:00 p.m. Lawrence hung out for a couple hours and played with Sterling while I watched on the pullout armchair, my bed.

Lawrence set up train tracks all over the room for Sterling. I felt like the floor was dirty because there were people coming and going all the time but I didn't know where else to set it up. Lawrence even brought disinfectant wipes so I could wipe the floor over and over.

At 1:00 a.m. Sterling was still awake.

"Hey, buddy, it's time to lie down now," Lawrence said as he laid him in his mini jail cell and pulled the bars up to make it a crib.

"I don't want to go to sleep. I don't want to go to sleep."

Lawrence lowered the bar so it was less jail-like, less cage-like.

I was understanding why the bars were that way. Just in case the parents fell asleep while the kids were still awake, they needed the bar so the kid would not fall out or try to get out and fall. My eyes were fading.

"Do you want me to crash here tonight with him?" Lawrence asked.

"No, I want Mommy to stay. I really want Mommy to stay. I want Mommy to stay with me every night."

"It's fine; I'll stay," It was nice to feel needed by Sterling but I was really craving a bed.

How was I going to get Sterling to fall sleep; he was wired with anxiety and adrenaline I didn't even know how much.

There definitely wasn't room for me and Lawrence on the pullout armchair.

I still hadn't had any food since breakfast and was too tired to even try to get any at this point.

Lawrence kissed Sterling goodnight. I wanted a kiss. I needed a hug. Where was my kiss? Was Lawrence thinking the same thing? And I fell asleep. I have no idea when Sterling fell asleep. Bad mom.

## Saturday August 2, 2010 -Hospital Stay Day 2

Good thing it was Saturday. Lawrence was at the hospital with me all day to help entertain Sterling between treatments. His PICC line surgery was not able to happen until Monday so the doctors decided to start him on an IV for the time being until he could get his PICC line antibiotics.

The IV team came into the room—a group of three of them. They all had blue suits on and were on a mission to find a vein.

I sat on my armchair and watched as Lawrence helped hold Sterling down. I didn't want to be in the way and I didn't want to see him in pain. I felt the intensity of the entire scene and could tell it scared Sterling.

They missed the vein the first time.

"We are really sorry; we're going to have to try again," the man in the blue suit stated very business-like.

They missed the second time.

Sterling was crying. I think it was fear from being held down even more so than the needle missing.

When they missed a third time Lawrence yelled,

"Get the fuck out!" I was calm, but he was pissed. Is that typically how you talk to people? No, but they technically just missed a toddler's vein three times. I couldn't get mad at him for telling them to get the fuck out. His word choice wasn't the best but this was the one job that they were paid to do and Lawrence couldn't stand watching Sterling cry anymore. And I couldn't either.

I guess we would just have to wait for the PICC line surgery.

One thing we learned is that a lot of people wear blue scrubs, so every time somebody came into Sterling's hospital room that had blue scrubs on, Sterling would be traumatized.

The respiratory therapist came in wearing blue scrubs and tried to put Sterling's vest on him to do his treatment. He kicked her. He didn't know if she was trying to stab him, hold him down or what she was going to do to him because the last people that came in wearing all blue terrified him.

That afternoon we got a call to Sterling's hospital room from the nurse supervisor.

"Hi, is this Sterling's mom?" she questioned with a very soothing voice.

"Yes, it is," I answered. Dear God, what now?

"Hi this is Darla, the nurse supervisor, and I'm getting some complaints from a respiratory therapist and from my nurses that Sterling isn't behaving and we're a little concerned about his behavior. Let us give you some more support. Let us help you."

"My son kicked a nurse. He's three years old, he's barely slept and he doesn't trust anyone because of the guys that missed his veins. Are you really going to judge my parenting and my child's behavior in the hospital environment when he has nothing that's normal to him and he's being poked and probed by all these people that he doesn't know?

Go fuck yourselves." I was pissed. I was cursing sober!

I was a real peach that day. I like to make friends and I accepted that I was going to have no friends by the time we left the hospital. The one thing that was certain was that they would probably do anything they could to help us get discharged early because they wouldn't want to deal with us anymore. I had heard about at-home care and I was going to do everything I could to get us out of here as soon as possible.

Lawrence's parents brought Trent today and I was so excited to see him. I didn't have the energy to hold him the whole time or chase after him. He was barely standing, so luckily he wasn't too active. I have to say he was a pretty fast crawler. Lawrence's parents dressed him in cute little overalls that had fake tools sewn all over them.

"Thank you for all your help," I told Lawrence's mom.

"Oh thank your sister. She's doing most of the work; we're just enjoying staring at the cutie."

"Seriously, I don't know what we would do without all this help."

"Well, your sister and her husband—after just two days

with Trent—have decided they are ready to start a family so everything has a purpose. Trent is just the sweetest little thing. We watch him crawl around drinking his bottle and he sleeps through the night."

I am so tired but I keep waking up a couple times a night because people come in to check on Sterling or the doctors come in at 5:00 a.m. sometimes," I vented. I was not taking care of myself emotionally or physically.

"Honey, I brought you a little gift. There's a water bottle in the bag and it's not water."

"Oh my God; you are the best!"

That's a true mother-in-law when she sneaks a little bit of wine into the hospital. She won me over with that.

"Hey, if you don't mind I brought a bottle for myself as well. Is it four o'clock yet?" She was too funny. We didn't see Lawrence's parents much and I didn't feel like I truly knew them, but the small doses of them were for the most part pleasant. Five days a year so this was beyond their normal five day visit rule, but they were staying with my sister so still I only saw them a few times.

"It's four o'clock somewhere."

We found two plastic cups in the room.

"Cheers!"

I said goodbye to Trent and was thankful he was in their care because I was too tired to take care of both kids. I slept so well that night. Sterling only wanted me to stay the night at the hospital.

### Sunday August 3, 2010 -Hospital Stay Day 3

Lawrence ran to my sister's house to shower.

Makayla came by today with Trent. As usual, he was just so calm and happy and peaceful. There's so much change and he was still sleeping through the night and going with the flow.

Sterling was starting to adjust to the hospital a little bit but he really needed the fresh air every day in the courtyard to make it through. He took his scooter in the courtyard while no other children were around. He was so happy to show his auntie how well he was riding at three years old. I was impressed too

"Auntie, look!" he said happily as he whizzed around the courtyard. If Sterling was moving, he was happy.

"Good job, Sterling. I am so proud of you. Look how well you ride that thing."

I was so proud of him too. Good thing he didn't have his IV yet or he wouldn't be able to do what he was doing. Tomorrow would be his PICC line surgery, another first.

Makayla hung out for hours in the courtyard and later said goodbyes when Sterling's dinner showed up.

"Sterling, Auntie is leaving now. I love you!"

"Bye Auntie!! he yelled," as he crashed right into the corner of the wall. His scooter flew out from under him and he lay on the ground. He wasn't crying but when he sat up blood was pouring down his face.

I ran to him. I was hugging and holding Trent so I set Trent down for a minute as I looked at the blood oozing from Sterling's head. Makayla ran and got a nurse while I guided Sterling into the room to grab a towel from the bathroom to stop the bleeding while holding Trent .

Makayla grabbed Trent from me as I held a towel on Sterling's head. "I just called the doctor to come down and take a look at his head," said the nurse, wearing Mickey Mouse pattern scrubs. Thank God, not blue.

"Thanks, you are awesome!"

"Well, I have to say this is a first," the doctor said as he walked into the room straight over to Sterling and lifted my hand off his head.

"The good news is I think I can glue this one as long as you don't mind a tiny scar?"

"No, I don't mind at all. I think glue would be the most efficient and least invasive and least painful at this point. He's been through enough," I said, trying to put Sterling's best interest in the forefront. I noticed Sterling's helmet sitting on the table with the tags still on it. This so could've been prevented; why didn't I have his helmet on him?

The doctor cleaned up his head and glued it within twenty minutes. It was awesome.

"Mom, this was a first for me—gluing a head while a patient is already an inpatient. I don't mind him riding the scooter around; just make sure he's got the helmet on next time."

"Yes," I said, wrinkling my forehead, acknowledging my mistake.

### Monday August 4, 2010 -Hospital Stay Day 4

We walked him down to surgery. They were going to insert a PICC line that went up his arm and it would administer drugs all over his body by pumping them through the line to his heart. Because Sterling was three, it was best for them to put him under for this.

I hugged him and kissed him goodbye and Lawrence held him as they counted together until he fell into a drug assisted sleep. They wheeled him away.

My eyes teared as I walked away. I knew this was a standard procedure, but I also knew that everything has a risk. I needed to distract myself for the next four hours.

I needed to close my baggy eyes, but I couldn't. I went and sat in the waiting garden for four hours.

Probably should've tried to go for a jog, but I just sat there and sat there. It felt like the longest four hours of my life. The doctor came out and told me he woke up and my heart felt full knowing he was okay.

He was a little out of it, but when I heard that cute raspy voice I knew he was more than okay.

## Tuesday August 5, 2010 -Hospital Stay Day 5

It was just me and Sterling today. I looked at the schedule on the board and planned trips in between each treatment.

First, we went to visit the little boat.

Then we went to visit a garden that had a T-Rex. Next, we walked to the floor that had the train, known as the radiology floor.

I lost track of time and when we got back to the room the nurse said, "Where have you been? The respiratory therapist came in and you missed him."

"The board said twelve o'clock," I responded.

"Yeah, he came early today," she replied. "Sometimes things change on the board and we need to know where you are."

"Okay, we just went for a stroll. The weather is just so beautiful."

"Mom, are we in trouble?" Sterling asked innocently.

"No, even though it feels like it," I responded.

There was something liberating about walking around the hospital with Sterling. We both had little masks on together. We enjoyed exploring and pretending we were on a journey to discover all the fun things at the hospital. The train on the radiology floor was definitely a highlight. We made certain to steer away from any other children just in case they had something contagious.

Sterling also got to play in the play room today. He got to play all by himself just in case there were other kids that were contagious. They wanted him to be in solitude. It was special because he could play with any toy that he wanted to. My dad came by at this time and I thought this would be a good time to follow up on the Carlsbad house and figure out when we would be able to get the keys. Lawrence had parked our moving truck in front of my sister's house for the time being.

"Glenda, is there any news on when we'll get the keys to the house we were supposed to have a week ago?

We were hoping to overlap the two to give us a little bit of time to move, but now our moving truck is just sitting."

"I'm sorry. I can't legally give you the keys to the house," she explained with a thick accent. "and it has a non-functioning kitchen."

"I understand that but can't we at least start putting things in the house. Since we can't live in it yet, it would be nice if we could start moving some of our things into it."

"No, I am sorry. Let me talk to the owners and see when they think the kitchen will be done."

### Wednesday August 6, 2010 -Hospital Stay Day 6

I woke up at 5:00 a.m. to a doctor doing early rounds. I actually didn't know if I was dreaming because I was so wiped out.

I dreamt that I told him to get the fuck out. This seemed to be the motto of our hospital stay. When I sat up and saw the doctor listening to Sterling's lungs I asked, "Excuse me, I'm really sorry; was I rude to you?"

"No, not at all. You've just been snoring away and I didn't want to wake you," he responded.

"Sorry I was dreaming that I told you to get the F out and I just want to make sure it was a dream and not reality. I feel like I haven't slept the best even though my eyes are closed every night for some period of time. It's just all blurred together. I'm really sorry."

I started to cry.

"Mom, you're doing great. He's getting better and you'll be out of here in no time," he assured me. "It's got to be hard having a little one in here so I'll try to help you push for at-home care."

"I don't even have a home," I cried.

"What do you mean?"

"Well, we were in between moves when all this happened in the house that we're supposed to move into." I continued in disbelief. I was venting to a doctor about my personal problems. The truth is I was lonely, really lonely.

"You have a place to go, right?" he asked.

"Yes, I have my sister's house and my parent's house."

"Everything's going to be okay. Your little guy is out right now. Why don't you get back to sleep?" he whispered and quietly shut the door as he left the room. He was sweet. He genuinely cared about my feelings and I felt like I was lacking a connection with Lawrence.

Sterling and I built tracks all day and made a train track that went around the perimeter of the room even winding under his bed. It still bugged me that the floor was dirty but he was having fun. I don't know what I would've done without trains or the scooter.

The dietitian came in that day. She poured yogurt all over a napkin and started running his cars through it. She's trying to make it fun. Just trying to make food fun for him.

"What are you doing? My cars—they're getting all sticky!" he yelled in his cute raspy voice.

"It's okay for things to get sticky because look how much fun this is." Her tone was excited and high pitched.

Sterling was not having it.

"Goodbye, nice to meet you."

He was hilarious. He had this ability to be real regardless of what anyone thought. He wasn't a people pleaser and that would suit him later in life.

I was trying to be supportive of the dietitian but I just couldn't figure out her angle. I was trying to hold back my laugh because he was so funny.

He was being so polite but basically saying get the fuck out.

Oh no, what did Sterling pick up from us? Oh dear.

After the dietitian left unsuccessful, a huge basket arrived from my Moms' Club. There were notes and cards and tons and tons of toys.

I reached her voicemail, "Halle, that was so incredibly sweet of you guys you didn't need to do that. Thank you!!"

There were so many ups and downs in the hospital, Sterling and I were so ready to go home.

### Thursday August 7, 2010 -Hospital Stay Day 7

I realized Sterling's cough was becoming less frequent when my phone rang.

"Hi Meg, what's up?"

"I was just calling to check on you guys and see how Sterling is doing?"

"He's doing really well. He's able to talk without coughing, yay! I'm sorry—can't wait to get him out of here."

"Oh, I bet. I can't imagine sleeping in a hospital for one night let alone seven. I don't know if this is on your mind right now and I'm so sorry but are you coming to my rehearsal dinner? I figured you weren't going to make it but I just wanted to doublecheck."

Oh shoot, I totally forgot my best friend--her wedding is Saturday. Thank God I'm not the maid of honor. Thankfully, it was her sister.

"Okay, I am the worst friend ever, he's supposed to be in here for fourteen days, but he can't sleep in here so I'm going to try to convince them to let me bring him home tomorrow or Saturday morning and Lawrence and I can continue the PICC line antibiotics and treatments from home--well, my sister's house. Carlsbad house isn't ready yet. Long story."

"Lawrence, I'm the worst friend ever. I totally forgot about Meg's wedding. I am so thankful she has all the dresses with her. I would've been screwed."

"Honey, you have to be in her wedding; she's your best friend. You'll be OK. Even if Sterling is still in the hospital it'll be OK. We'll make it work; you have to go. I won't be shooting."

"Honey, we're both invited to the wedding. I can ask my sister to help with the kids. My parents are going to be at the wedding and my sister is going to be there."

"It's fine," Lawrence assured me. "Let me talk to my parents."

"OK, if Sterling is in the hospital still, I'm not going. If they discharge him from the hospital then I'll go if we can find someone to help with the kids. Who is going to do the PICC line then if we are at the wedding? We have to stay on schedule," I reminded Lawrence.

Lawrence hung up the phone and five minutes later called me back.

"I talked to my parents and they said if Sterling is discharged they will watch him and my mom has no problem giving him his PICC line antibiotics. I think it would be really good for you to go and have a nice break."

"OK, thank you." Whatever was meant to be was meant to be at this point.

## Friday August 8, 2010 -Hospital Stay Day 8

"I heard you might get to go home tomorrow. In that case we are going to have to change the dressings on him," said the nurse.

"Dressing? Is he a turkey?"

"Yes, that patch over his PICC line. We have to change that and it's not going to be fun. If we do this together, hopefully it will flow smoothly," responded the nurse in a hesitant tone.

She took his shirt off and slowly started peeling off the sticky rectangular patch over his PICC line. He screamed the second she pulled it off his skin. This was going to be hell for him.

"Mommy, no, no, no thank you," Sterling yelled.

"Sterling, let's think of your favorite trains and let's think of the toy shop that we're going to go to when we get out of here. What trains do you not have?" I was trying so hard to distract him. There has to be a better way.

The nurse was using some sort of alcohol swabs and was rubbing the skin while trying to pull up the dressing.

"I'm sorry but there has to be a better way of doing this. Why is this so painful for him? Isn't there something else we can put on it?" I asked. Was this what all other families went through with toddlers?

"This is all I've got, honey," she responded, certain of no other options.

"Mommy, I want another Thomas, Edward, Henry," Sterling cried.

"Any other trains you want—just keep naming those

trains and think of all the trains you know," I was still trying to distract him. It was at this moment that I didn't care if I was going to spend hundreds of dollars on trains. I just wanted it to end because when he was in pain I couldn't help but feel so bad for him and if it was going cost me a couple hundred dollars to distract him from the pain I was willing to spend it.

"Oh, I think he's playing you a little bit, Mom," the nurse said as she continued to pull up the dressing.

"Oh hell, I don't care as long as it takes his mind off you ripping off his skin," I responded rudely.

I seriously was so rude, but I was just exhausted. If she had some sort of butter cream for the stupid patch I wouldn't be trying to distract him with all the trains we can buy when we get done with this place. Obviously, not my best self again.

### Saturday August 9, 2010 -Hospital Stay Day 9

"Good news! Sterling is going home today we got you approved for the at home care as long as you guys follow all the instructions Sterling will stay on his path to getting 100%,"the nurse celebrated.

"Woohoo! That is great news." I celebrated too.

I secretly couldn't wait to sleep in a bed. Any bed, since the Carlsbad house wasn't ready. I'd be more than happy to stay at my sister's or my parents' house.

Lawrence had arrived just in time. "Go get ready for the wedding and I will wait here for all the discharge papers. Go!"

"Okay, thank you."

I hugged Sterling then ran to my car—pulling up to the attendant.

"That will be $175," he said after putting my parking ticket in the machine.

I handed him my credit card and didn't even argue with the fact that I was being charged $175 while my kid was in the hospital. It was so ridiculous but I didn't care. I just wanted to get to my friend's wedding. I was free.

I pulled up to Sara's house where all the girls were getting ready and poured myself a nice glass of champagne. I took a deep breath.

I still needed to shower, to shave, brush my teeth and dry my hair. It was so hard to even explain the whirlwind that just happened but I was so happy Sterling was getting better. It's hard to fully relax. I felt guilty being away from him but the pampering was much-needed. Mom guilt was a daily struggle for me. Was I doing a good enough job? The day still felt like a blur. The next thing I knew I was walking down the aisle with Meg's brother. A few shots later I was dancing on the dance floor. The shots helped take me away from the hospital, the sting of it all and the fact that I had a sick child, the fact that this disease was real, the fact that I couldn't know or control the future, the fact that I didn't know exactly what he was going through and the fact that I honestly didn't know exactly how to help him.

There were a few facts I did know:

Sterling is a warrior.

Trent is amazing.

My family and friends are awesome.

I was 100% terrified deep down inside.

And as much as Lawrence was there and I was giving everything I had, I was so lonely, so beyond lonely. Every night in the hospital after I fought poor Sterling to get him to lay down, rubbed his back to get him to go to sleep I wrapped my arms around myself and pretended someone was holding me. I snuggled up against the pillows and pre-tended somebody was lying next to me. How did the other parents do it, the ones that have already been through this and more? How did the parents do it that have already lost a child? I was just in the hospital for the first time with my son and he was living and he has energy and he was getting to go home. There were so many good things but I felt so alone. Did the other parents have more emotional support? I felt like I wasn't doing a good enough job. There are so many times in my life I talked myself out of things, I found loopholes to get through things, I found ways to cheat or cut corners through things that were hard, like taking the short cuts on my cross-country training runs back in high school. I even talked teachers into an A from a B+ but I couldn't find a shortcut to this one. I couldn't avoid it. This was the one time in my life I actually had to go through it, stare at it and deal with it. I was so burdened by my emotions. I questioned if I was doing enough or doing it right. The truth is, I couldn't give 100% to Sterling because I didn't have 100% to give. Sadly, my battery was running low and I didn't have much to give to anyone.

We finally got keys to the Carlsbad house. It was way too hard to live in Carlsbad while Lawrence was in LA. The double rent meant double utilities too. Every cent we had was being drained. My family was close but still forty minutes away not to mention they were all working. I also drove the kids up to LA one day a week so they could see Lawrence. We were all exhausted and instead of finding other ways to make it work, five months later we moved back to LA.

Our life felt so busy and I was not liking so much un-predictability anymore with having two little ones. I want-ed stability. I needed stability. There was so much good around me, but I couldn't see it. I won't use labels, but I was drowning. I was struggling. I drove down a street where I used to admire the flowers and I couldn't see the same beauty anymore no matter how many times I drove down it. We had a beautiful baby in one hospital and nine months later found ourselves with beautiful Sterling in another. I needed help. I needed support. We had had another fight. I looked up local marriage counselors and found one that looked like someone I would want to hang out with. Interesting way to pick a marriage counselor. I did it, I made the appointment knowing I had nothing to lose. Here goes nothing.

# Episode 9

## Marriage Counseling

**January 2011**

**Soundtrack:**
**Run Back to Me**
**(Juni Ata)**

"Hi, I thought you wanted to meet for a marriage counseling session?"

"I did. Yes, I am here." I was excited to get help.

"Well, I usually see both partners for the first session."

"Oh, well he is working and can't make it. Can we work on me? I threw a picture frame at him. I need to work on my anger."

"Okay, we can get to that, but ideally it's better to see both parties together to see the whole picture. But since you are the only one here, I guess we have no other choice," Zoey kindly agreed.

"We will discuss your desire to work on yourself, but I would like to get to know you first. What do you like to do?" I sat there a bit uncomfortable. I just wasn't happy with my life and didn't know why.

"I love playing soccer and working out. I love hanging

out with friends and family. I feel like Lawrence is never home," I said. I sounded so negative, but it was true.

"So why don't you do those things?" Zoey asked.

"I don't know why. I guess I don't have time. I feel bad getting a sitter. My son has cystic fibrosis. Who will give him his pills?"

"So why don't you make time. I am guessing you can find money for a sitter. You can teach them how to give your son his pills." That was not a question but a command. Or, at least that's what it felt like.

"I don't have a sitter, but maybe my mom's cousin's, sister's daughter can. I don't really know them since I grew up in SD, but I can ask. I heard they live in LA. Yes, I have money I can use. You're right. I can teach the sitter how to do Sterling's medications." I responded with a little light in my eyes. I missed soccer.

The next time I saw Zoey, I had joined an indoor soccer team, found a babysitter and was going to the gym. The kids could go to the kid's club two hours a day. I even started attending some mom nights out. The gym allowed me to love myself more and to make many more friends. I was working out at least two hours a day, my kids had playdates while I was working out and I finally had a really great sense of support. I started meeting friends who had husbands that were in the TV and music industries too and we could relate to each other.

I loved the new friends I was making there. We were all dedicated to being fit in mind, body and soul. Whether it was Pilates with Aly, HIT with Lyn or just running next to Mia on the treadmill, life was better. There was a great positive energy I sensed and I felt more like myself.

Not to mention Sterling was healthy and so was Trent.

Marriage counseling turned out to really be *me* counseling. I liked working on myself so much that I didn't mind that Lawrence was too busy working to make it.

I had so much I wanted to work on and so much anger and resentment I needed to work out. I didn't feel like Lawrence loved me and felt like he was hiding something. Every mile and every step on the stair climb helped me release an anger that I didn't realize was there. Even though I was the only one thrilled about going, I realized that just taking a look at myself and working on myself helped the marriage and made me happier. While I worked on myself, Lawrence would continue to put his heart and soul into *The Vampire Show* in hopes of a producer title and the opportunity for an even better life for me and the boys. I was starting to swim to the surface. I wasn't sinking. I wasn't drowning. It was getting simpler. Doing things that bring you joy make you happier and attracts happy, positive friends. I couldn't wait to discover more things that brought me joy.

# Episode 10

## The Vampire Show Season 4 and the Good Life

**Soundtrack:**
**If I Could Remember How To Love You**
**(Juni Ata)**

**2011**

There on the screen it read "Produced by Lawrence Richman" in the opening credits. Lawrence now had his first producer title. We started celebrating with trips and memory making. We upgraded to a big house, well big to me, and it even had a pool and four bedrooms. We had made it. But at what cost? The PA that cleaned crap off his director's cat over a decade ago had achieved his dream. Everything we needed was right there in front of us. Lawrence was on a show that had no end in sight and we were going to embrace the feast of the business. I increased my shopping budget from twenty dollars a week to whatever and started to enjoy fancy dinners and vacations. Most of my friends were doing the same.

Lawrence got a call from his dad right after the first episode aired, "Lawrence, hi, it's me."

"Hi, Dad," he answered, so surprised. They had a great time when they saw each other, but a phone call from his father was unheard of literally. "Is everything okay, Dad?"

"Yes, son everything is great. I saw your name on the credits last night. Congrats. Did you get a raise?" he asked bluntly.

"Ya, a good one, don't worry we are going to live off half."

"Son, I called to say the opposite," he calmly, but directly spoke.

"What?" Lawrence gasped. "Dad, I know you and Mom are savers and you have an amazing pension set for life and you always lived well within your means. That's why you retired at fifty-five."

"Son, listen, you have two incredible boys and the most supportive wife. What I am trying to say is you are young and your boys will only be young for so long. I regret not enjoying my money when I was younger. We had the money and we waited until you were in high school to take our first family trip."

"Dad, I had a blast in Hawaii. No regrets."

"Son, the point is I saved so much for rainy days and missed out on making a lot of memories with our family to save a few more dollars."

"Dad, you paid for my college; I had a great upbringing. I mean it would have been nice to eat out a little and I did think we were poor when Mom made my clothes, but it's all good. You and Mom did what you had to do."

"Son, back when my team put a man on the moon I made some investments. Your mom and I are sitting on more money than we need. I want to go out zero someday. I have never told you this, but now that you have earned every cent you have, enjoy it. I have had two strokes and a heart attack and

I can't enjoy the money the way I had planned. I didn't want you to know this until now, but we have funds set aside for your family that no one can touch but you."

"Dad, I don't know what to say. I can't accept it. I want to be self-made."

"Son, you are self-made. So, the only way this works is if you sign my pact."

"What pact, Dad? Truly, I can't take your money," Lawrence said firmly. "I don't need it."

"You might not need it now, but know it's there for Sterling or Trent should they need it."

"Dad, what is your pact?"

"Well, next week we meet with my financial advisor, Mike, at Stifel. I have known him my entire life. He took care of my parents' finances."

"Dad, get to the point. How does it work?"

"Well, I made your sisters sign it after they had kids," he paused for a minute.

"What, Karey has signed it?" Lawrence said, annoyed.

"I know I am conservative, but it's the YOLO PACT."

"Dad, did you just say YOLO?" Lawrence questioned, surprised.

"Yes. Talk to Reese and think about it. You sign the pact agreeing to turn all your finances over to Mike. He will handle everything. Here's how it works. You may never keep more than 20k in your checking account at all times. If you have 50k you will get a call from Mike. He will make you donate it to family, charity or plan a trip. Mike will transfer a large sum into an account that you can have when you turn fifty if you stick to the pact of YOLOing or living life to the fullest. Do you agree?"

"Dad, seriously I can't take your money. I can't accept it. I don't want to live by your rules. I am a grown man."

"Son, I am trying to do something nice."

"I get that. The only way I will sign it is if the money goes to the boys when they turn eighteen. I am speechless. My whole life you had this money?"

"But then you have to spend everything you make. I saved everything my whole life, but just got an inheritance from my uncle."

"Actually, I don't want it. If you want to help, donate the money to the Cystic Fibrosis Foundation."

"But, this also ensures you live life to the fullest, because you know there is a nest egg. One catch. You can't buy a house, because you will only have 20k in your account. That's just part of the deal. Your mom and I stayed in the same house our whole lives and I wish we didn't. Renting will give you flexibility to do whatever you want and applying for a mortgage would open everyone's eyes to the money you are sitting on and you don't want that. So think about it. Leasing will be general credit check and not extensive."

"Okay, bye Dad, I love you, but I don't want it. I have to call Reese."

Lawrence called me immediately. "Reese, well, you know that I say daily 'What am I working for if you and the kids are not enjoying it? I don't want to save it all if tomorrow never comes. Reese, can we make a pact? Well, I turned down a pact with my dad."

"Sure, what is it?" I asked hesitant and confused.

"We have to really live life to the fullest. My dad has some money set aside for the kids, but only if we enjoy everything I make. I was planning on doing that anyway so I told him no."

"I have no problem with that if you don't, but that sounds crazy and super generous. I know you and you don't take money from anyone. Are you okay with it?"

"My dad is getting older and has some regrets about how he lived. But it just doesn't feel right taking money with conditions."

"Agree. We don't need money from anyone."

"Promise me we will use our own money to make memories with family and friends and charities. We'll use it to make the world a better place." Lawrence made me promise.

"I promise."

So, I did, I enjoyed it, maybe even a little too much. I didn't work but hired a part- time nanny and a house cleaner to make my life as easy as possible. Is that what Lawrence meant? Make my life as easy as possible. Okay, I take it back, for every hour Lawrence worked for the studio, our family and his career, I worked too, on myself and I felt like every dollar he made, well, I would enjoy it too, especially with my amazing mommy friends and kids. If I wanted to go to Santa Barbara and Lawrence was working, I would just bring our babysitter to help me. Nothing would hold me back from doing what I wanted to do. I liked the monetary sense of freedom or at least the perspective. A shopping spree at Marshalls was so freeing and supplied temporary relief and joy.

Even though I was able to afford nice things and give my kids memories, I felt like something was missing. There was so much I wanted to talk to Lawrence about, but whenever I tried it turned into an argument. All money aside. I was still lonely most nights and when Lawrence was home on the weekends he was bombarded with emails and texts. I was trying to be understanding, but I felt like he wasn't present. He was forgetting plans we'd made and things we agreed too. This confusion led to more arguments. Although I was enjoying the good life, I was ignoring still more resentment bottling up inside of me.

I wasn't swimming to the surface anymore. I was trying, but the weight was pulling me down again. I couldn't break free from the weight that was pulling me down. But I was trying so hard. I felt like the supporting role in his drama and he was the star. He will say he was the producer and I was the director, but it didn't feel that way. I get that in marriage you support each other, but I didn't feel supported. This resulted in some horrible arguments that I still regret today. The awful things we would say to each other. Our communication was so bad and often our arguments were just lost in translation and assumption. We never solved anything and we were both never heard. That stress unintentionally projected onto the kids. Kids feel bad energy whether we want them to or not. People say parents are the biggest role models, but the truth is, we are more than role models. We are mirrors to them. I started to see them saying the same things I was saying. Things that were not nice. I vowed to cut it out. Even if it was just for the kids' sake. I continued to see my marriage counselor. I had to do better. What was I missing?

Since Lawrence was lost in his work, time would fly for him during the week, but not for me. Days would go by without us even speaking. When he came home I felt his energy and it was not warm and light-hearted. It was cold and unpredictable. At times he laughed and at times he got angry. I was on egg shells. Did he feel the same? I loved working out with my girlfriends, but the nights were lonely after the kids went to bed. I started hosting British soccer coaches just to have another body around at night. Yes, it sounds wrong and my friends would even say, your husband lets them stay with you? It wasn't like that; it was truly companionship and we even set up one of the coaches with our babysitter. After hosting guys, I started to request girl coaches hoping we could get massages and nails done together.

On the weekends we started taking family trips with the kids and enjoyed room service on whatever venture we went on. I was so relieved to be spending more time with Lawrence. We did many stay-cations and stayed in places like La Jolla Beach and Tennis Club, The Pelican, The Ritz Carlton, various lake houses and even the infamous Hotel Del Coronado Beach Village where they shot the Marilyn Monroe film, *Some Like It Hot*. We didn't stay in the hotel, but in the Beach Village Cottages with the hot tub on the roof and an ocean view. When Sterling got a cough, we would go to Hawaii for the warm salty air and ocean. The salt water had been proven to break down mucous in the lungs so it was the perfect place for him. We used up any and every travel point we could to cover part or the whole trip. CF reminded us to live a little. I was smiling, but still trying to get to the surface to breath.

Lawrence and I went on many dates dragging along a part time nanny, but even with the added time together, I still felt alone. We were making memories and having a blast, but something was still missing.

But CF always kept us present and in the moment, no matter how we were feeling. We learned to celebrate everything. After attending a CF Foundation gala, a 33-year-old speaker with CF touched my heart. She talked about celebrating every birthday like it was her last because the reality was, it could be. She was thankful to live another year and thankful she made it to age thirty-three. I had already heard and seen countless people lose their lives to CF so why not embrace birthdays even more? We rented water slides and took kids to Disneyland, just to mention a few. Then we began to celebrate half birthdays too. I wanted Trent and Sterling to have as many fun memories as possible. We call it the summer bash every year, but my kids know what it really is. A few friends have found out and bring half-birth-day gifts, but we try to keep it on the DL. Even with so much celebrating, there was still just something missing. I didn't know how or even what to fix. We were all doing the best we could. Weren't we?

The season four wrap party was so much fun. My broth-er was working the show so it was a real treat to have more people I knew at the party. My dad came along as my broth-ers plus one.

I gained so much respect for Mr. Muscles that night. My dad is the biggest sweetheart and loved the show as well. While trying to take a picture with Mr. Muscles, they got interrupted. My dad said later that night the charming actor found him and made sure they took a selfie together. I loved hearing those stories about actors. We sometimes focus on negative stories, but there are a lot of sweet actors too.

Speaking of sweet actors and parties, Lawrence was no-where to be found at the wrap party. He was busy talking to cast and crew. Did a bigger title mean less Lawrence in all aspects of life? Did bigger title mean I needed to accept this new reality?

# Episode 11

## THE VAMPIRE SHOW SEASON 5 PREMIER AND MY WILD CARD

**June 2012**

**Soundtrack:**
**Gave Up On Love**
**(Juni Ata)**

I wore a green backless dress I bought at the CF Foundation luncheon in San Diego. Twenty percent of all sales would go to CF research. Even though we didn't go down the press red carpet, but beside the red carpet, I treated all the premiers like a prom. They were different from wrap parties. Premiers were much fancier. Unfortunately the whole cast and crew wasn't invited either, but wrap parties they were. The press red carpet was mainly for the exec producers, directors and cast. Eventually we ended up on red carpet, (sometimes it was purple carpet or green carpet depending on premier themes). Getting dressed up was so much fun. It was a free adult date night celebrating the hard work of the cast and crew. It was also sometimes my celebration that wrap hours were beginning and that would mean more Lawrence time for me and the kids. Being around my darlings was rewarding and challenging, an adult getaway in Hollywood was much needed. We stayed at the Roosevelt to make an even bigger night of it. I stayed in the present and took it all in. Was this really my life? I got to sit and eat with the stars? What an opportunity that Lawrence provided. He deserved every ounce of goodness or perk that came with Hollywood.

Getting a hotel room could be dangerous with pre-partying at its best. Lawrence was always so attractive, especially when he put on a suit. He was just such a man, all of him. I wanted all of him back. I wanted to jump him, but that wouldn't be appropriate in front of my friend, Jenny, who came to help with my hair and make-up. I was terrible at curling my own hair so I often just braided it, hair sprayed it while braided, then unbraided it to create beach waves. I had met Jenny years ago when I went in to get my brows done.

It was within the weeks after Trent's birth. I was exhausted and looked it. She sensed my need for some attention. She not only threaded my brows, but did my entire face with make-up. I left feeling good about myself. She was my friend from that day forward. And now here we were in a suite at the Roosevelt getting ready for *The Vampire Show* premier. It was nice to have a glass of wine before the premier, but I didn't want to be too relaxed and fall asleep during the showing. Sometimes they showed the first episode, but that night we got a bonus. Two episodes.

"Lawrence, what's going on? I feel disconnected," I said after Jenny finished and left the hotel room. "You don't seem the same. You seem stressed. Are you excited for tonight?"

"I am not stressed," he said, pouring vodka into a glass of ice. "What is your deal? Can we just have fun tonight? Do we have to talk about this now?"

"I just want to have a conversation with you," I continued, thinking maybe I should just let it go.

"Not now. Everything is great. Come here. Cheers! Let's have fun," he said, clinking his glass with mine.

This was one of the nights I made a big mistake. At the party I walked up to Mr. Muscles in my short green dress and hair in curls. I marched right up to him and asked if we could take a picture. I already had one with him from the last five parties. There was no sober insurance needed after one glass of wine and I couldn't blame my impulsiveness on liquid pharmaceuticals.

While taking the picture, I whispered in his ear, "You are my wild card." Oops, I thought to myself. What did I just do? Lawrence was taking the picture.

He was like, "Bro, your wife just said I was her wild card."

Lawrence then joked, "Well, at least we know she has good taste. You can have her when I'm done."

That had the potential to be messier, and I felt so disrespectful to Lawrence after I said it. Good thing he was confident in our marriage because I certainly wasn't. I thought he was having an affair, but was the real affair with work? I became the crazy jealous wife wanting to know where he was at every second of the night. Things didn't add up. I became like his mother, wanting him to check in all the time. I had valid feelings for feeling alone, but I was just driving him away. I was jealous of all the time he was putting into his vampire family. I was insecure, lonely and dying for attention inside. What kind of wife does that? Me. I then tried to drown my insecurities with a second glass of wine. I had learned to stay far away from liquor at work functions or at least tried my best. I needed forgiveness. I needed to forgive myself.

The party ended, and security quickly guided the guests toward the exit.

"Will you sign this?" a man wearing a backpack asked the second Mr. Muscles stepped out the door.

"Sure." he kindly signed the one poster.

"Oh, and these too, please?" the same man pulled out a stack of at least two-hundred mini posters.

"Bro, come on?" he said, ducking past the guy and squeezing next to me as a limo pulled up to the curb.

A group of us piled in. We proceeded to the after party and arrived at the Roosevelt. There was a line, but Mr. Muscles said, "They are with me." The bouncer let us in. The room was suffocating me as I forced my way to the bar and felt a firm grip on my waist. I was hoping it was Lawrence behind me. I was hoping he had forgiven me. It wasn't him. It was a tall blond mid-thirty-year-old. He motioned for me to follow him, but I said, "No, thank you." That was the last thing I needed.

The last thing I remember before Lawrence and I headed to our room, were little people soaring over the crowds on a wire. They weren't drowning, they were flying. I wanted to fly too…

# Episode 12

## FREE FALLING AND A HIATUS FROM LA

**Soundtrack:**
**Fight Hard, Run Fast**
**(Juni Ata)**

**October 2012**

We had been going to *me* counseling for years. Was it time to throw in the towel? Perhaps change the counseling to *us?* I knew Lawrence's answer. He wouldn't have time. I didn't know. I had everything: beautiful, incredible children, a home, a successful, hot, helpful husband, and amazing girlfriends. I got to travel with them to Vegas, China - you name it. I had the perfect life on paper. But who cares about paper? What about how we actually feel together? We had highs and lows, but the lows were especially low.

This is important to share, because I believe everything happens for a reason. I had it all, but still felt like I was missing attention and support from Lawrence. When he was home, he cooked, he cleaned, he was amazing with the kids. They built obstacle courses together with zip lines, we went on walks, we all had fun together, but still I didn't feel like I was getting what I needed. I was not his priority. Lawrence was working his ass off and trying to juggle it all to give us this great life, but I couldn't feel real joy. There was always something else on his mind that he wasn't able to share with me. That's what my gut told me. I felt like there was something he was not sharing and it was eating me up. I felt like he projected his work stress on me and it wasn't fair. I was trying so hard. Life was fun and exciting on the surface, but I wasn't at peace. I could feel something was off in my gut. Friends told me they wanted my life. I had to tell my close friends they really didn't want my life. I pretended it was perfect to the outside world. Facebook and Instagram showed the best parts of our life. Did people really want to see that I was lonely? On paper, we had so much, but in between the lines is where we suffered. We were always arguing. I ended up crying in a ball some days and then shopped my pain away. Sometimes I'd get a massage, thinking that would fix it, but nothing did. We were the worst communicators and we both had communications degrees, for heaven's sakes. We threw out the word divorce every other week. I think it was mainly me. It didn't matter how amazing our trips were, I didn't enjoy them if the kids didn't come. I preferred to travel with the kids so it wasn't just me and Lawrence. I didn't want to be around him. Together we had negative, toxic energy from my bottled-up resentment. Did he resent me too? We were consistently pointing fingers, competing, comparing, and the list went on. We broke the rules of kindness, love and compassion. This wasn't love. Why couldn't we be open and honest? What were we teaching our children? Were these childhood programs of our own that we were replaying?

I was attending a wedding in San Diego where my high school friend was getting married. Lawrence and I had been fighting so badly, I told him he didn't get to come. I didn't want to be around him. He had partied in the Hollywood Hills with divorced/single friends and I had lost it. He was gone for days. I was done. His best man called to tell me it wasn't what it looked like. I was still done. There was something freeing about that thought. My reaction to his adventures in the hills were just the icing on the cake of another bad fight and I couldn't take it. The pain he caused me was immeasurable. The pain we caused each other was too much. Our inability to be decent human beings was my reason for the break. The things we did to each other, the mean texts, the white lies, the sneaking around to get away with stuff, it was childish and cruel and we were both doing it. We never resolved anything. How was this love? Was I just a trophy wife?

The best part about him working 80 hours a week was I had an easy alibi for him if we were fighting. I could tell people he couldn't make events because he was working. There was never an explanation needed. He *was* busy working. The stress from our unpredictable marriage was killing me, physically pulling my body down. My posture was terrible, shrugged shoulders and the pain in my neck, shoulders and upper back made me want to stay in bed at times. The idea of being done released a weight and all the strength I had been building working out excessively was strangely helping me move to the surface for air. The panic and tightening in my chest was releasing. Could my drowning feeling have been alleviated by separating from Lawrence? Was our energy just not good for each other? Was it as simple as just breaking up? I didn't feel this stress when I was with my friends or just the boys. Were we that bad for each other that it was the sole reason for my depression? Was I really depressed?

Brooklyn and James said their wedding vows as the sun

set over the ocean. I sat next to my brother-in-law, Brian and sister with my huge buggy glasses on. They weren't big enough to hide the tears rolling down my cheeks. And they weren't tears of joy for the married couple. Were we really done this time? Were we over? I answered yes in my head. The tears were tears of uncertainty. What next? Why couldn't I just enjoy this happy moment for someone else? Why couldn't I embrace that I was free? Everyone cheered for them as they walked down the aisle. I wiped my tears and cheered too.

The cocktail hour was a little bit of a high school reunion and I answered the same question over and over, *where was Lawrence?*

"Oh, he's working. Huge show, lots of hours. He wishes he could be here," I replied like a broken record. Then Laurel came, my friend from the races the night I met Lawrence, and greeted me with a big hug. It had been too long. I heard she was now a pharmacist. She did it! She confirmed. I hadn't seen her since my wedding day.

"Reese, meet Brandon," she said, gesturing to her plus one.

Blue eyes were all I saw as I shook his hand. Suddenly I realized I'd met him before, back in college, briefly. I took my glasses off as Laurel took off for the bar. Laurel and Brandon were buds from college.

"Hi, I think we have met," I said as we locked eyes and smiles. He was a friend of my sister's best friend, Cal, from high school and had crashed at our house in college while visiting. I remembered him more boyish, but he was now the sexiest blue-eyed man I had ever seen. A different kind of sexy, a mysterious kind, a pensive kind, a kind I wanted to get to know. I instantly felt I could trust him. What was wrong with me? I was married. *No, I justified myself, it's over*. But the voice in my head fought back, no *I am married*. Was this love at first sight? *No*, I told myself, *I am in a bad place*. Lawrence and I were fighting. But I was eating up his attention. What was wrong with me? Laurel returned and handed me a well-needed beer.

"Where are you living these days?" he asked with perfect eye contact. He was glowing.

"LA area--you?" I asked, realizing my very short Free People dress selection as his gaze wandered to my hemline way above my knees.

"New York, Upper East Side. I work in the city," he said proudly.

"I don't know what that means." I chuckled, never having been to New York. "What type of work do you do there? Are you married with kids?" What was I doing? Why was I asking him that?

"No, I just broke up with my girlfriend of five years. I work for a Bible company," he replied, fidgeting with his plaid Burberry sleeves. Suddenly he didn't seem as confident as before. I'd hit a nerve, obviously. It was the same nerve that was frayed inside me.

"Sorry to hear. My husband and I just got in a huge fight and are probably done too. Did I hear you right? Bible company? Are you religious? I should probably read one these days," I said, instantly regretting the amount of info and boundaries I was crossing. Why was I telling him this? I didn't really even know the guy, but it felt like I did. It was so weird and awkward, especially with no ring on my finger. I looked down at the tan line where the band used to sit. It was the first time I'd even taken it off. I lost my first one at an Emmy party when I fell in the bushes. It was loose. Buying a ring when you are pregnant is a bad idea. My fingers were swollen. After that I replaced it with $10 Target rings, but I always wore a ring. We'd had a million fights and I'd threatened divorce over and over, but I'd never taken the ring off. Not until now.

"Sorry," he said, understanding in a way that only the broken-hearted can. "Oh, and not that kind of Bible company..."

I must have mumbled, "Whatever, it's beside the point."

I didn't actually care what he did anyway. The sun was disappearing and my buggy glasses weren't needed to conceal tears anymore. Something about my conversation with Brandon made me feel better, even though I was still a total mess. Could he see the good in me? Could he see the love I had to give? Was it wrong to want more of something that felt good? I could tell he liked me and it was obvious Lawrence did not. We were soon seated at our tables and I grabbed a bottle of champagne from the bartenders. It was on. Operation 'let's have fun tonight.' I was going to celebrate the amazing couple because they deserved it. Love deserved it. I played duck, duck, goose with the bottle, saying 'duck' each time I poured it into a glass. But there was no goose. I ignored that part. When I completed pouring for the table I just got another bottle from the bar. I guess I was the goose, but no one was chasing me. I loved weddings, the music the positive energy. Was that the secret to my happiness? Was a positive and loving environment all I needed to flourish? I toasted my pain away with my table mates. They were all from my high school and I was so happy to be in familiar company. But when I saw Lawrence's empty chair, I grew sad again. Was this my future? The single girl at weddings? Why couldn't we make our marriage last? Why wasn't it working? I wanted that everlasting forever. Why couldn't we put our pride aside? Why couldn't I fix it? Was I too hard on myself? What was he doing to fix it?

I got up to get another bottle of champagne for the table and crossed paths with Brandon on the way back from the bathroom. Again, a sense of comfort. Goose, I joked in my head. He stopped me with a touch on the arm, "I have a lot of experience with your sort of thing, if you ever need to talk."

"Thank you, I just want to get drunk and have fun," I said freely, smiling mischievously from ear to ear. Even though I was a mess, I felt free. Did he feel free too?

He smiled and headed toward the bar. Was he for real? He was actually listening to what I'd said earlier. I smiled and walked back to my table. Why did the universe keep pulling me toward him? Why did a moment seem to pause while he was talking? I felt so present with him. The next thing I knew, while I was talking to Miguel, my friend from high school, Brandon came back over and joined us. He was persistent. The three of us were laughing nonstop for maybe an hour. It was all about how Miguel had asked me in high school if he could take my virginity. We were laughing about the fact that he had actually said those exact words. And that he'd probably asked other girls the same thing. I, of course, had said no and was giving Miguel a hard time about it, when Miguel dropped his beer and it somehow exploded all over my dress and legs. We were dying laughing as I was covered.

"Oh my God, I am so wet!" I yelled unexpectedly. That came out so wrong and all of us started laughing hysterically again.

Miguel grabbed a pile of napkins and started trying to dry my legs when I grabbed them and said, "I got it, go back to your wife." Brandon was smart enough not to help clean up my legs. But I'd be lying if I said I'd thought about what it would feel like if he had.

Brandon put his hand gently on my arm again as fiery

waves pulsed through my veins, "Listen, I am going to be upfront here and don't take this the wrong way, but that seriously was the hottest thing I have ever heard anyone say."

"Listen, you can't touch me like that. For your own good. My family is here." I totally lied. My family was there, but he needed to stop touching me because I was sorting through feelings I couldn't control. I wanted to take him in the coat closet and I could not allow that to happen. I had to shove him away.

Many gathered on the dance floor to celebrate the union of the two in-love souls. Time was passing quickly and there were probably a few minutes left when I felt like making a mad dash for the ocean. The ocean always made me feel fully free. It was a block away. Regardless of the guilt I felt, I liked Brandon's energy and asked him to accompany me. Was I playing with fire?

"Do you want to do something crazy and go to the beach for a minute?" I was crossing boundaries but wanted to do what I wanted. The beach was my happy place and I hadn't been happy in a really long time. I had met Lawrence there. Even if we were done it was still my happy place and would maybe heal my broken heart a little. It was the one place I always felt free.

"No, it's not a good idea. We can't leave the wedding," he responded firmly.

I got the message. He was right. What was I thinking?

I proceeded to listen to music and chat with old friends. Then a tap on the shoulder, "Let's do it! Nobody will miss us." It was Brandon. We were being free together. He unbuttoned a Burberry button and let me grab his hand.

I led him to the six-foot hedges outside the reception hall. We snuck through a thin gap, kicked off our shoes, released our toes and raced to the ocean. It was liberating running downhill toward the body of salt water. We had five minutes before the wedding ended. We got to the ocean and I thought I could leap down off the sand banks like in Carlsbad at certain times of the year. Without judging the situation, I leapt into the darkness. It was liberating.

I hit my head on the hard, rocky embankment and my arm was soon covered in blood. My wounds were wide open. A hand reached down and pulled me up. His healing grip cast a blanket of security immediately. As I caught my breath literally and figuratively, I could see Brandon's caring blue eyes. There was an undeniable connection. One I had been longing for. Did he need a bigger purpose like me? Did we both want to do more than we were doing? Did our souls know there was more to life?

"You okay? Seriously?" he asked, checking my arm and head. "We need to get you cleaned up."

"Brandon, look at my butt. I scraped my whole booty," I said lifting my dress for him to examine.

"Reese, seriously, put your dress down. You can't do that to me."

I laughed in embarrassment. "Sorry. I'm fine. We better get back."

We ran back and shoved on our shoes right as the wedding was letting out. I tried to sneak into the bathroom to wash blood off my arm, but couldn't get through the sea of people in secrecy.

"What happened to your arm?" Laurel asked.

"I fell. True story," I answered. But I was not in pain one little bit. I was not drowning for once. Where was Brandon? Had he had enough of me? His spell was already cast and there was no turning back at this point.

I cleaned up and followed the group to the pub. When I got there, I saw Brandon. I just wanted to be by that safe and secure energy. I needed to be by his positive energy. Is that where I thrived? But he was smart, trying to avoid me like a true gentleman. He went and sat all alone by a fire pit. Bad choice because there was a chair next to him. I, of course, sat down. I just wanted to be around him. I couldn't explain it. Why did being next to him make me feel safe, but free at the same time? I saw something in him that I saw in myself. Maybe his honesty attracted me. Did he feel free too by my side?

All of our friends were leaving and I wanted to stay. I rejected a few offers home and would just cab it to my parents' later where I was staying for the weekend. I had had no control over so many things for so long and failed to see areas I could control. Was this the night I would do what I wanted and get what I wanted?

"I really think you should go home," said Brandon, trying to put me in an Uber. This was the first I had heard of Uber.

"Please, I don't want to go to my parents' right now. I am going to the beach for a while to clear my head and then I'll catch a cab home," I said, trying to convince him I was fine.

"You shouldn't go alone," he urged, exhausted now that it was 2:00 a.m. "Please let me get you a car," he begged with his blue eyes.

"I am twenty-nine years old. I think I can manage," I said as I walked down the street to find the beach.

"I'm coming," he said reluctantly. "Follow me, this way." He motioned to avoid a group of people already setting up for a Sunday street fair. I must have been swaying a little. Several bottles of champagne will do that to you.

"My feet hurt," I complained, realizing the walk was farther than I'd imagined.

"Take your shoes off. You are in four inch heels," he suggested, pointing to my feet and laughing.

"Okay, but I'm tired. I just want to go to the beach. Can you carry me?" I asked in a sweet whiny voice.

"Get on my back," he offered like a perfect gentleman, succumbing to my request.

We approached stairs and he gently set me down. "We're here and you are a stubborn one," he smiled.

"Fuck you," I said playfully, "Just joking." Swearing was a bad habit after a few too many drinks. I wasn't a fan of cursing when I was sober.

"Oh, and a spicy one too," he joked back.

"What happened with your husband?" he said, as we descended the stairs and crossed the sand. We sat next to each other, waves crashing against the rocky cliffs to the side of us. A few seals lay on the sand in the distance.

"We have everything and all we do is fight. It's just not love. This can't be love. We have torn each other apart and are so cruel to each other. I have been in *me* counseling for years, but I just can't be happy. Money can't buy happiness. We were happier living in a studio apartment with nothing. Our son has a chronic illness and we just can't give each other the support we need. I honestly don't feel like he loves me, but likes the idea of having a wife. We have broken each other down mentally and physically. He is off working all the time and I feel alone facing the disease on my own. I think he truly is doing the best he can or thinks he is. We don't bring out the best in each other. We bring out the worst. This can't be love. We are toxic and I am part of it. Two great people alone, but together we are horrible. I fear a divorce would bring out even more bad parts of us. I fear its ugliness. I believe in marriage, but I think we have become wrong people for each other. I can't fix it on my own. I don't want a divorce, I believe in marriage. I love my boys. The commitment. Through it all I still love him as the father of my children. He created these gifts, our children and for that I will always be thankful. I am trying to forgive myself. I am trying to forgive him, but, like I said, this can't be love," I rambled on with help from the champagne. But I was being one hundred percent honest. It felt good to say it like it was.

"I really think you can work it out," Brandon responded after he had listened to me. I wasn't expecting that. Again, such the gentleman. I imagined him holding me in that moment and kissing my neck. I imagined what it would feel like to touch his face. What would it feel like if he held me for a minute. Could it heal my pain, maybe for a minute, maybe for a second? There was one thing certain. Was I willing to risk it all, what was left of my marriage for one second in his arms? He nudged me out of my hallucination. He didn't hold me, but sitting next to him would be good enough. He gazed into my eyes—a stare that made me feel light and warm. I wanted to kiss him. I needed to ask something quick.

"What happened with you and your girlfriend?" I asked, giving him a chance to talk since I dragged him to the beach and threw a curveball into his night.

"She was amazing and we had a lot of good times, but we just weren't meant to be," he explained.

"It sounds like you can still maybe work it out," I returned his positive relationship advice and put my arms inside my sweater to warm up.

"No, it is better for both of us. There's something missing. We weren't married so it's completely different scenarios." He had a good point.

"True," I said, lying back into the sand and staring at the sky.

Brandon lay back as well and created an invisible bubble of security I was longing for. I wondered if I could bottle it up and take it home with me. Was I that deprived of it that I needed to take it from someone else? How did I allow this to happen to myself?

"For what it's worth, I think you are wonderful and I love your smile. You're truly an amazing person. From the way it sounds your dedication to your family is so admirable and I think you can make it work. But it does take two willing partners."

"Yeah, well, you have gorgeous blue eyes and a perfect smile yourself. Tonight, when I first saw you I thought you were super-hot and mysterious."

"Well, I'm flattered, but I am a groomsman in a wedding tomorrow so that's why I have the mysterious air. All groomsmen do." He smiled, trying to dodge my flirtation. "I had a great night with you. Can I get you an Uber? Or you can crash in my hotel room and I'll sleep on the floor? I swear I won't touch you. I would never touch a married man's wife," This solidified every good vibe I'd gotten from him. He was a good one. It was so nice to totally trust and admire a man again.

"You are so sweet. I am in a foggy emotional state and if I'm going to be totally honest, I'm super attracted to you and haven't felt this good in a long time so I think I better take that Uber."

"It's two minutes away," he said, looking at the app on his phone,

"We better get you up these stairs." He grabbed my hand and gently led me up the stairs.

"Brandon, thank you," I said, looking into his eyes one last time.

"For what?' he asked, surprised. "I did say if you ever needed to talk, right?"

"Thank you for everything," I repeated. "Listen, I will

probably never see you again, but you will always be my wedding angel and I will never forget it." I got a little teary and tried to hide it. It was probably just all the champagne, but I liked how I felt next to him. He filled that hole in my heart longing for connection.

I was so tired, he was practically having to drag me up the last stairs.

"Listen, since you think I am an angel, if you ever want to feel my presence, just go to New York. I'll always be somewhere in the city."

My Uber, an Escalade, sat at the top of the stairs waiting.

"Joe?" Brandon asked the driver in a business-like tone I hadn't seen yet.

"Yes," he answered, getting out to open the passenger door.

"Figured you are the only Uber by the beach at 3:30 a.m. but wanted to double check. Can you take this girl wherever she wants?" he asked, reminding me of a scene in *Pretty Woman*. The last time I'd felt I was in any way like Julia Roberts was back with Lawrence at the sushi restaurant. I remembered being happy with him back then. What had truly changed? Was it me? Was it him? Was it both of us?

I wasn't going to be rescued that night by Brandon and I was grateful for it. I had to rescue myself. I had to do it to save my family and myself. But being told how amazing I was over and over had been a healing balm that I needed to lift myself up and create a game plan. I finally felt totally honest with myself and it was powerful. I could do it. I could save things.

I hugged Brandon with a good squeeze, knowing I would never see his blue eyes again. I jumped into the Escalade, shut the door and rolled down the window. I looked at him one last time.

"You have a lot of potential, Reese. Don't ever forget that," he said and walked away. I had a sinking feeling for a second that he wasn't even real. Maybe I was just passed out drunk in the toilet of the reception hall, dreaming about this cupid who was subconsciously steering me in the right direction of self-preservation?

But the bumpy ride led me to believe it was all real. I left his side, reminded of how amazing I was. I promised myself to always fall back on that moment whenever I was struggling. I would remember the sense of safety and security and that everything was going to be okay. I *was* strong enough. I *could* keep going in whatever direction our marriage took, whether or not it was the dreaded path of divorce. I was capable. I had forgotten how amazing I was – constant fights with the person who is supposed to love you the most will do that to you.

My wedding angel had been a life preserver. I vowed to stay at the surface of life's rocky ocean and breathe no matter what.

He was light in my script of darkness. He was my night light that night. I vowed that no matter what he did with his life I would find a way to support his journey. I would always root for him from afar on whatever journey he took.

He lifted me out of my depression. He gave me hope that things could get better. Was this really goodbye forever?

# Episode 13

## The Vampire Show Season 6 and Marriage Retreat In Vegas

**Soundtrack:**
**Stay Together for the Kids**
**(Blink 182)**

**Sometime In 2013**

I wanted to tell everything to Lawrence, because I felt guilty for having the feelings I was having, but what was the point? I would hurt him again. Was I prepared to be hurt by him if he had something to share? We were married, but we were so far from honoring our vows. We should not have been married.

Both of us knew something was off with our marriage, okay, way off, clearly, but didn't know how to fix it. I was motivated to make a good change. We were drifting with two separate lives. Were we still even friends? I thought I'd dive right into the deep end and try a marriage retreat. We could fix this; I could be open and honest with my feelings and so could he. We could get help.

But the truth is, a marriage retreat in Vegas is a very bad idea. We were so distracted by everything around us that we couldn't even focus on what was left of our marriage, if anything at all.

Let's start with the good things. At check-in, I had a smile on my face and persuaded the front desk to give us the presidential suite. I had no idea how it happened, but I told him I was there for a marriage retreat. Maybe he really wanted to help. Firstly, the room was overlooking the strip and came with its own pool table. The retreat soon became more of a group date as many couples came to party in our room and enjoy the space. So much for time together. Second, how can you have deep, honest conversations if you don't even remember them? We were given a workbook to do, just the two of us, but ended up doing it with another couple. The other couple was arguing so much about the answers that we didn't even have to look at ourselves.

"What is one thing you and your spouse enjoy doing together?"

"Laundry," my friend's husband, Fab, replied.

"Laundry, are you serious? Why would we ever enjoy doing that together?" she asked in a frustrated voice.

"Baby, I thought making pairs of socks together was nice because we get it done and we hang out."

"This is why we don't work. You are not even answering the question. It's not what *you* want to do together, it's what we both enjoy doing together and why would I *ever* enjoy doing that?"

This was sort of hilarious. Lawrence and I had to mediate. We couldn't judge. We were far from a perfect marriage ourselves. All the attention was on their arguing. It sounds so wrong, but one weekend was not enough time to fix our marriage. We made one out of the ten sessions and ended up at the pool. At the end of the retreat, we held a sign and took a picture that said, *we still do*. We didn't get divorced at the retreat, but made no progress. Quality time made a little progress, well, if hanging with other couples meant quality time. We didn't argue the whole trip, so that was definitely a win.

I always tried to observe other marriages in Hollywood. What was working for them and what wasn't? I needed encouragement to make mine work.

While in a box suite at a King's game – there are seriously great perks working in television - I quizzed the wife of another producer in the TV industry. They'd been married for twenty years so she was sure to have some sage advice. The men were in the bathroom and I seized my opportunity. "So tell me, what's the secret to making it work?"

"Oh, honey. It doesn't work."

"What?" I gasped.

"No, I am serious, it doesn't work," she stared me right in the eyes.

They were divorced months later.

Six months later we were at an Emmy party and some girl had her arm around Lawrence, chatting it up, probably harmless. I said to another producer's wife, "Seriously? That's so weird. I would never be caught with my arm around my old boss like that."

"Oh honey, if my hub wants to go for another woman, I say have fun! Go for it! He can't do better than me." She was so confident and matter-of-fact, it was disturbing. Was I supposed to be that way? Why couldn't I be more secure in our marriage?

# Episode 14

## THE VAMPIRE SHOW FINALE AND OUR MARRIAGE?

**Soundtrack:**
**Took So Long to Say So Long**
**(Juni Ata)**

**2014**

By the time Lawrence was working on the finale, season seven, I had many hilarious vampire stories regarding the kids. Lawrence and I talked about the show often, especially with me being a fan.

When Sterling was little, his pre-school teacher stopped me in the hallway at pick up.

"Excuse me, Reese? Can I talk to you for a minute?"

"Sure," I was nervous.

"Well, at school today Sterling was telling all the children he wanted to take their heads off. It's not like him to say those things. I asked him where he was getting those words and he said, "Daddy's show.""

"Oh, dear," I said, "I'm very sorry. Last night we were watching *The Vampire Show* and somehow fell asleep. The show sometimes repeats and he must have crept into our room. I do remember waking up and seeing him staring at the TV, but in my tiredness, I didn't know what he'd seen. Now I know. There is a scene where Vampire Goliath takes all the heads off a group of pedestrians. That must be what he saw. I will talk with him tonight."

"Thank you. I thought he must have seen something so I just wanted to make you aware," she said calmly. I loved pre-school teachers or at least ones like her. They were not quick to make judgments and were so calm.

Lawrence and I talked about the show often, but never allowed the children to see it. At open house in our son's kindergarten class, we walked around the room reading our son's work. We got to Sterling's and it said, "I love my family because... they let me watch *The Vampire Show*. It was there large and bold for all the parents to read. All we could do was laugh.

We sounded like parents of the year, but knew how innocent it really was. He had just remembered watching it from that one time in pre-school.

We did tell them a lot about the show in kid terms without the blood and guts. They loved *The Vampire Show*, just from the characters we told them about. We told them vampire hero stories they could relate to, but left all the mature details out. Well, most of the details.

The vampire talk must have confused them because when my dad took them to Sunday school, Trent came home with an inappropriate picture.

"What did you draw, Trent?" I asked, seeing the big sheet of light brown paper in his hand.

"We had to draw a picture of Jesus, so I drew a vampire. He is strong and powerful and has long hair, just like Jesus."

"Oh, that's lovely," I said, trying not to laugh. Oh dear. Well, church is the one place they shouldn't be judged so I can't worry about it.

I took the kids to Hollywood as much as I could to visit Lawrence. There they would play pretend work at the PA desks, like the one I had back at The Ranch and put post-its all over. They even went around telling people "You're fired." There were plenty of good laughs. They loved checking out sets with me when the show was not filming. The T-Rex on Highland and Hollywood was always a treat to drive by. And once we got to the set, they'd be super excited if there were any major stunts being filmed. After one explosion scene, the kids had a ball climbing all over the fake debris.

When a show goes seven seasons there are incredible bonds between cast and crew. Sometimes when I visited the office I tried to observe. I simply describe it as if there was a big secret everyone knew, but no one wanted to tell me. As much as I tried to stay involved and in tune, I felt left out of his world. I felt like the show was my husband's real family. I gradually had to rely on my own social circles to keep busy. I began to take advantage of getting babysitters even more. As wrong as it sounds, I still had a joke with one of the female producers on the show that we were sister wives. Only because she saw my husband more than me. Again, she was his work wife and I was his home wife. We were told at a party that the crew relationships were never like real family, but I felt like the fake wife – she was, after all, getting to be by his side 24/7. I was totally isolated from his world. Yes, I had the freedom to do whatever I wanted with myself and the kids, but I wanted to be with him. I wanted him back. There were people he worked with for years and I felt left out.

Were my hardest moments because of my own insecurities? At one party a coworker came up to me whom I barely knew. "Hi Reese," she said with perfect posture, blond wavy hair and a smirk stretching across her lightly blushed peach cheeks.

"Hi, Lacy. How have you been? You look so pretty," I replied being sincere. She was beautiful. Lawrence introduced her to me on set a while back. "Lawrence just loves working with you," I continued, genuinely complimenting her.

"Thank you! Yes, we really just get each other. We know what each other is thinking and truly understand each other like no one I have ever met. There is no one else I would want to spend so much time with. He is my best friend."

That was a little more than I wanted to hear. It was extremely awkward for me because I already felt left out of his world. Why was she telling me this? I sensed a connection with them. I wanted that connection. Why did she get the fun Lawrence that I fell in love with? Why didn't he treat me like his co-workers?

A few days later my neighbor, Stacey, approached me frantically, "Is your son alright?"

"Yes, I just dropped him at school. Why do you ask?" I was on my way out the door to the gym—and now so confused..

"We saw ambulances at your house this weekend. We've been praying for you all weekend," Stacey said sincerely.

"No, my son is healthy. I was in San Diego with the kids. My husband was home, but he would have said something. Are you sure it wasn't the neighbors?" I combed through every detail in my head.

"It was parked in your driveway at two a.m. A few weeks ago I saw a black Mercedes parked there too." she ranted on. "This is not the first time I've seen an ambulance."

"Excuse me, I think you're jumping ahead here. It must have been the house next door to us. My husband didn't say anything. I will ask," I responded kind of shocked. Why wouldn't Lawrence have said anything?

"Here, I want you to have this." She handed me a brick

red book titled "Jesus Calling" that had devotions for every day of the year. I hadn't been to church since our wedding day. I remembered the peace I felt sitting there with my family every Sunday. It was the one day a week we were guaranteed to all be together. I remembered putting pencils on my shoe laces and poking my brother when he sat in front of me.

"Thank you. I will check it out," I told my neighbor, getting into my car. I really was going to. Was this my sign to be present and find my connection with God? Is this what our marriage was missing? Could this save us?

"Let's get tea sometime!" Stacey said as she walked home.

I randomly flipped to page 235 and started to read... August 12th, Come to me when you are weak and weary... weakness stirs up my compassion...Accept yourself in your weariness, knowing I understand how difficult your journey has been.

I was freaking out at how relatable it was to me, okay maybe I would read it daily, but for now I still couldn't wait to get to the stair climber. I needed a Starbucks first.

There I vented to my workout pal, Everly, who was married to a successful actor. I filled her in about the annoying co-worker and sequences of events. She sported bright yellow lulu lemon pants with a crop top. She could pull it off and did with her obliques.

"Listen, I know what I married and you just have to kill them with kindness and be secure. It sounds like you were kind."

"I was, but I didn't want to be," I said, increasing my intensity to ten as the climber beeped. I took sips of my breve vanilla water. My friends wondered how I could work out and hike with a coffee in my hand.

"Listen, my husband had a scene where he had to pretend to go down on a girl. Do you think I was throwing a party? No, but it comes with the territory and you have to be secure or it will tear your marriage apart. Lawrence also needs to do things to reassure your trust. If things are not adding up with him, of course you will be insecure about aspects of your life," she said, so matter of fact, while wiping bullets of sweat from her forehead with a white hand towel.

"Well listen to this...the other night I was at one of his work parties and I thought a girl offered me a shot while I was standing next to Lawrence. And I said, 'Sure, why not, we're celebrating, right?' And then she was all like, 'oh, not you, honey, him. It's for him, Lawrence.' Everly, I was like, what a beep? Seriously?" I continued. "I lost it that night on Lawrence, not her. He took the shot and was upset I was getting mad at his co-worker. He didn't stand up for me. I broke my no hard alcohol rule at parties—I got my own shots."

"Well, you married an attractive man, so what do you expect? Take it as a compliment. As hard as it is, you not only married an attractive man, but a successful man and with that comes competition," Everly explained, trying to change my perspective.

"You're right," I agreed, struggling to keep my small five foot, four inch frame on the stair climber. I lowered the intensity.

Everly looked over as she was starting her cool down. "Want to do weights next?"

"I'm good. I'm going to try and run six miles next to Mia," I answered, scouting out an empty treadmill and wiping the sweat off my arms and neck.

Lawrence will claim he is not successful, but I beg to differ. We had ups and downs, but there was no doubt in my mind he was successful. He was the hardest working man

I knew, besides his boss. He went from cleaning shit off a director's cat that crapped all over itself on a plane, to becoming an assistant, and then arriving: running one of the biggest and most successful shows on television. This was so sexy. It wasn't sexy how hard he was on himself with work. I did realize it didn't matter whether Lawrence got an increase in pay or a higher title, he wouldn't allow himself to enjoy it. He was never satisfied. He was so critical of himself. It was getting worse and worse. He beat himself up all the time and my frustration wasn't helping his self-destruction. "You have to want success like you want air," he would say. He couldn't remember where it originated, but he borrowed it.

One thing I realized in the final season was that I needed more for myself. I needed to achieve more for my journey. I was happy and grateful for all the fun memories Lawrence and I were making with the kids, but I realized I needed a greater sense of achievement for myself. I started a few at-home businesses selling jewelry and spa products. I wasn't good at it, any of it. I gave half my profits away. I didn't want to have ulterior motives when hanging out with friends. I just wanted to hang out. I had friends that were great at it and didn't see it that way, but I did when I was selling to friends and I just couldn't handle the model.

I started throwing small charity events on top of participating in CF walks, CF Gala and CF Ladies Luncheons I attended annually. The small fundraising events created a greater sense of self achievement. I was raising money and giving some of Lawrence's profits to cystic fibrosis research and enjoyed it. It was my new passion. I was helping Sterling. It gave me a greater purpose. Giving really made me feel better.

I liked throwing events, but didn't like asking friends and

family for donations, as happy as they were to give. It was my Achilles heel. And, I just got tired of asking. How could I expect my friends to take from their savings or sacrifice for my cause when we were traveling and staying at fancy places? I was not cutting back entirely or sacrificing much. It felt hypocritical.

I wanted to generate enough of my own money to give more. One item on my bucket list was to raise $1,000,000 for CF. How could I raise more money? How could I generate my own money to give away without asking others? How great it would be to attend a CF Foundation event and donate $100,000. I had my goal and I was going for it.

There were many hard nights and moments for me on that final *Vampire Show* season. There were the usual nonstop work texts and no matter where we were, I felt like Lawrence was still always working. While he was making television history, I was drifting out to sea. While he was working hard for the family, I was longing for attention again and the need to accomplish even more with my life. I wanted it all. Was I like Lawrence that way, never satisfied? I fought the loneliness, daily dreaming of running into my wedding angel. I needed a refill of whatever he had. I went to Instagram and found him. It sounds kind of stalkerish, but it was innocent. He had quit his New York job, whatever it was, and was traveling around the world searching for a greater purpose. He was doing it and I had to too. I wanted to reach out, but that wasn't our purpose for meeting. It was to recharge one another. Give each other a little boost. Just seeing him happy in his photos was a little recharge for me and I would send him good vibes in my mind like an energy pen-pal. Was I the only one writing? Would praying for him be more beneficial?

I joined a novel writing class and drove to Griffith Park

one night a week for months with another one of my work-out buddies, Beth. Everly introduced us and she transparent-ly opened up at the gym about her marriage struggles and just like that we were friends. She had me by fifteen years on this planet and was like a big sissy poo. She had a heart of gold. She never forgot a friend's birthday. All her friends and family looked perfect, so I did wonder if she would still be my friend had I not been attractive? I was shocked I made the cut at times. Those were my own insecurities. No, there was so much more depth to her than one would know. Behind this perfect-looking model and talk show host there was a solid friend that would do anything for me. She was my Filipino angel. I finally completed my first novel and so did Beth. It felt great to complete something, well not fully, it still needed to be edited, but it was close to completion. I learned how much I loved writing and it taught me so much about myself along the way. It reminded me that happiness comes from within. It was the one job I could do when I wanted and it didn't cost any money, just pencil and paper or laptop. I was trying to balance being a wife and a mom while pursuing something for myself. It felt like I always got really close to being satisfied with myself, but it was never quite enough.

When I wrote, I felt like I went to a peaceful place be-cause I was working through emotions. Music on, volume up, Starbucks grande breve vanilla latte to my right—I played the keypad like a keyboard. Every time I typed a word I felt a sense of relief and a sense of escape from whatever anxiet-ies filled my head. I felt lighter, like I was working through pain, hurt and abandonment. Writing was my drug. I felt free, truly free–like the night I met Lawrence, like the night I met Brandon. I didn't need moments and memories to feel free...I was the co-creator of my universe with God. I was reminded of this as I continued to read my devotional.

But it was reminding me of how many years I'd spent not doing anything for my own sense of accomplishment. I had just been there for the kids and Lawrence. Why had I sacrificed myself entirely? The realization of not pursuing my own achievements for so long brought up even more resentment toward Lawrence and his long work hours. He gave us every pressured second he had, but he was exhausted. Sometimes he'd even fall asleep on double dates at restaurants. He was burnt out and I didn't feel supported. I can't imagine him feeling supported by me either.

On Monday nights I played indoor soccer with tough-as-nails, Barca, with my cuz and then the "Babes" (I loved this team name). In addition, I started playing tennis at a tennis club. Then, a few days per week, I also was hiking with girlfriends.

I was so lucky to have this time to do all these activities for myself while Sterling and Trent attended school. The tennis and hiking became another pleasure. I truly had the best life and the most amazing family. I even started playing in a league with my friend, Kaydie. Mr. B, my tennis coach, would go down in history as one of my favorites. He was like a dad, and probably the only person that was a hundred percent honest with me. The more I played the better I felt. We even started having margarita tennis nights and slipped our beverages down to the court. It became an annual ugly sweater tennis night around the holidays with a gift exchange. We laughed so hard until they shut the lights out on us.

"I wish our wives had this much fun," the dads on the other courts would say to us. We knew how to laugh. Why didn't I feel this way with Lawrence? He used to make me laugh.

Sadly, the more independent I became with all my

hobbies, the more I felt finished with Lawrence. Was it healthy to live in the constant back and forth on the court of marriage and divorce? My tennis partner, Kaydie, was married to a famous boy band singer and was the best example of a wife and mother. She was so supportive of her husband's career and so positive when she talked about him. She had had a career in the entertainment industry as well and was now an amazing photographer. I learned to try focusing on the positive. She reminded me that tennis was our time to have fun and play hard. She reminded me how lucky we were to have this time to play. She kept me in the present. We often danced on the court. She was all luv and surprised our group of tennis girls with backstage tickets at one of her husband's shows. The band took photos with us. The same love and positivity in their songs was exactly what I felt when meeting them. It was nice to meet such down-to-earth people after all their success.

God placed some amazingly strong women in my life. From hike buddies, to school moms, to my soccer teams, tennis moms and girlfriends... All my LA friends played such an important role in helping me keep my head up and family together every time I wanted to walk away. They also let me know that as friends they would always be there for me no matter what path I chose. My flight attendant friends were always reminding me about that. They had cool lives, always flying famous people around the world. They reminded me they were just people. I started going to tea with my neighbor, Stacey, once a week and continued to read the devotional she gave me. She was a saint now, but shared so much of her journey toward contentment in marriage. It wasn't easy and she seemed to figure out how to make hers last. She was also adopting her 4th child. I could not believe how selfless she was.

I needed to stop my pity party and embrace the amazing life I had. I needed to enjoy what was right in front of me. The ability to breathe. My friends kept reminding me that my husband got to come home every day after night shoots. Most women never saw their husbands during the day. Military families go without seeing each other for months and some sadly don't come home. If it weren't for the amazing, strong supportive women in my life, the show finale would have been the finale of our marriage.

I was looking at my life from the wrong perspective and so focused on what I didn't have for so long. I didn't need a refill from my wedding angel; I needed to find that peace within myself. I realized I was like a single mom with a trust fund, as bad as that sounds. I continued to enjoy front row concerts and travel with the kids. Lawrence jumped into the memory-making on the weekends when the kids needed him the most, and I finally just got over myself. I had a great life and I was going to start enjoying every part of it, including my marriage while finding inner peace and self-love. I don't need affirmation from another to have peace and love. That comes from within. I needed to take control over my life. Would our show, our marriage be cancelled? Could I continue to live in the constant unknown? Could shifting and working on myself even more fix us?

# Episode 15

## THE ROBOT SHOW AND BACK AT THE RANCH

Soundtrack:
Peace
(O.A.R)

2015

P rep at The Ranch for Lawrence's next show was possibly going to follow *The Vampire Show* finale. Thank God it didn't. Lawrence needed a break from the stress. He appeared to be losing some hair which was strange since both his grandpas had full heads of hair. Could stress really cause hair loss? I had my husband back and for six months we could finally walk two times a day. We took the kids to Mammoth every other week, snow or no snow. Lawrence seemed weaker than normal and struggled to pull the kids around the mountain. His balance seemed off. I thought trips to Mammoth doing the things he loved would bring him back. I was so attracted to his athleticism even if he wasn't 100%.

"Boys, write down on a napkin cold or tropical," Lawrence suggested to Sterling and Trent as we were eating breakfast.

"Let's see what you wrote," I said, so excited, while moving my mommy go-to-braid to the right side of my neck.

Blue-eyed Trent unfolded his napkin. T-R-O-P-A-C-L-E was spelled out. Lawrence and I gave a sweet smirk to each other. Too cute.

Next was Sterling. He unfolded his napkin and it said SUNNY.

"How does Hawaii sound?" Lawrence asked the kids as they started to jump up and down. This was the Lawrence I loved–the unpredictable, generous live-life-to-the-fullest guy.

We didn't know if Lawrence would get this time back with the kids so we booked a trip straight away. We drove to LAX that day and got on a plane. We missed a few days of school, and were burning through money recklessly but once he was back on a show, who knew when we'd see him again? It was wild, impetuous and possibly irresponsible. Just like the night I carelessly charged the set of waves on the beach with Lawrence. I smiled.

We lived it up. We didn't know if this big chunk of time would ever come again and planned as many vacations as we could. We enjoyed even more trips to beautiful Mammoth and couldn't believe how fast children progress on the slopes with no fear.

"Lawrence, we shouldn't spend everything you have worked for. Should we slow down? We can still do trips, but don't have to stay at the most expensive places."

"Can we not worry about money? What if I die tomorrow?" he'd answer. "Remember the pact with my dad that I turned down to do it ourselves?"

"Okay, as long as you're okay with it. I haven't looked at the bank account in months." Memory-making was in full force. May the force of memory-making be with us.

Our frequent trips led to friendships with Trent's snow-board instructor, a husband and father of two himself. It was great for Lawrence to have a friend that wasn't crew. Captain James was Sterling's instructor and they connected instantly. He had lost his close cousin at a young age to CF and knew all about it. In private, he recalled memories to me of slumber parties where he'd heard his cousin cough all night.

He'd been a child actor and had donated the earnings from his first film to the CF Foundation. He was an amazing guy. One day he brought Lawrence, Trent and Sterling to meet Dave McCoy, the founder of Mammoth Mountain, and hung out on his property for the day. What an honor and memory for my boys as they went to bed watching a DVD about Mammoth's history.

I knew I was lucky. How many people got six months off with their family? And there was one extra wonderful detail during that period –both boys were healthy.

When Lawrence was offered work on *The Robot Show*, a new high-quality drama written by one of the best writers in town, Lawrence couldn't be more satisfied. It was also going to be shot at The Ranch where many of our western memories were made. It was an honor for him to work with several of his favorite A-list actors, too.

I stopped by The Ranch to visit Lawrence one day and was greeted by Raymond. My old buddy. He'd saved a card I made him on *The Western Show* and showed me where it was pinned to his wall. He was still his cheerful self and remained proof that happiness comes from within.

Unfortunately, Sterling was admitted into the hospital in San Diego during the filming of the first season. I thought I had our family back, but the hospitalization threw me into a rut and Lawrence was gone again—emotionally and physically. Lawrence was more drained from *The Robot* season than he had been in six seasons of *The Vampire Show* series. Driving back and forth daily from LA to San Diego Rady Children's hospital will do that. Lawrence was gone again, emotionally. A very famous film director, screenwriter, actor and composer all signed a poster for Sterling that said, *May the force be with you.* Along with the poster, Sterling received a Star Wars hat and shirt. I never met this famous man of many talents or his staff that orchestrated the swag, but I will always have a special place in my heart for the smile they put on Sterling's face. This was where we stopped looking at CF as a disease, but a challenge Sterling had that was going to make him even stronger. His health improved quickly, and he was back out running on the soccer field and jumping around on the trampoline again with his infectious laughter and spirit. Had the hospital care changed that much since Sterling's last visit or was it our attitude as a family and our perspective? Was it knowing what to expect? Maybe it was knowledge I gained from other families at my small charity events or parents I was seated with at the foundation events. Did I feel more supported? One thing for certain: Sterling was older and we could explain procedures to him. He was inquisitive and asked lots of good questions. This time I didn't stay each night in the hospital. Grandparents offered to be with Sterling some nights and he wanted them too. Lawrence was able to sneak away from *The Robot Show* set. I was able to give Trent some much needed attention. Trent was relieved Sterling got better so fast because he did not like spending nights without his big brother. Although Sterling had CF, Trent went through it too. Siblings often experienced more than parents realized. He experienced all the ups and downs from a different perspective. "Trent, you are the best brother in the world," I'd always remind him. Their brotherly bond was strong and it was strengthened when they had to rely on each other in new places that lay ahead. Where would the next adventure be? As smooth as the hospital seemed, I took a few steps back in my inner peace search. I was fighting a current again. Why? Everything was fine. How long would it take to get Lawrence back? I didn't need him to be happy for me to be happy. I already knew this. Why couldn't I let that go?

# Episode 16

## The Demon Show and North Carolina for the Summer

**Soundtrack:**
**Richest Man**
**(Juni Ata)**

"Makayla, guess where Lawrence's next show is?" I teased in excitement with my phone on speaker.

Makayla is the one person I always confided in about industry stuff. She was a vault. She had no idea who half the celebrities were so it was fun to bring her to parties. "Where? What show is he on?" she asked, excited for me.

"North Carolina! I am so excited. Another state we haven't been to. I can't wait to explore. "

"What show?" she asked.

"*The Demon Show* second season," I answered.

"I have never heard of it. Let me look it up, googling right now... I can't find anything on it." she said, but I figured she was spelling it wrong.

"Maybe nothing is out yet," I suggested, thinking maybe I heard Lawrence wrong.

Makayla said, "No way. A big premium show. There has to be something online in the Hollywood Reporter."

She was right, whatever. I was sure it would be good. The first time I arrived in North Carolina, I felt like an outcast because of my SoCal accent. Also, no one had heard of the show. Did it really exist? Where was he going every day when we visited if there was no show? I wish I could say this was a Hollywood thing, but this was a Lawrence thing. Things never seemed to add up. Should I just accept this? I didn't want to get stressed over it. I wanted to focus on the kids and me. All I can control is myself. I learned this in counseling and it had helped a lot. I knew the kids and I were going to have a great summer regardless. The attitude I reflected always set the tone for the kids so I was very careful how I played things. I'd finally learned that lesson. I now knew that each show Lawrence filmed, whether it was at home or away, was an adventure and a learning experience. Throughout Lawrence's television journey, I worked on my journey. I'd already planned my next move after North Carolina. It would be walking five hundred miles on the Camino de Santiago through Spain to raise awareness for CF and DMD, also known as Duchenne muscular dystrophy. This walk was also to prove to myself and my children what I was physically capable of.

I was still working toward my goal of getting $1,000,000 to the CF Foundation. I wanted to teach my kids that raising money and giving back was one of the greatest gifts one could give and receive. This would be my biggest charity event and possibly my last one. I thought I was done asking for money, but partnering with DMD and this group of people made me feel like I could try one more time. It was going to be a big achievement for myself.

But first it was time to live in the present back on the balmy East Coast. Our North Carolina summer began with catching fireflies on a sweltering night. Luckily, the area we were in was not mosquito-filled like I was warned. We rented a huge house for half the price of our California house just outside Charlotte. The street had twenty boys on it and our next-door neighbors would become friends for life. Did I mention the house had a movie theater?

The kids wanted to attend Lego camps, soccer camps in the a.m. and wanted to play hoops afterward, while I worked on my charity goal. I was working with a team through email. The best part of charity is meeting selfless individuals. Four out of our seven team members would walk the five hundred miles together.

Christine, from a nude survival show, also known as *The Chef,* would be one of the pilgrims, along with her husband, Volcom, and mom, Lindsey. Davidson, from an incredible production company, did everything behind the scenes for us along with his wife, Leanna. They were extremely generous with their time and expertise. They created a website, trailer, and multiple videos for our CF/DMD project. This walk originated as The Chef's dream that she turned into a bigger cause. I started planning a charity event to take place in Los Angeles that would kick off our trek. But at the same time, North Carolina had lots of adventures in store for us.

We were weekend warriors. Sterling and Trent were the best explorers. They were up for anything. We went on an alligator tour in Hilton Head while celebrating the fourth, not my choice, but it was enlightening. The only alligators we were told to fear were the ones that were big enough to eat us and fast enough to catch us. Lawrence burned his hand that night while trying to legally light fireworks on the beach.

"Dad, are you okay?" Trent asked as Lawrence screeched in pain.

"Yes, I'm okay," he answered like it was no big deal. A

firework had just exploded in his hand. I couldn't believe what a good actor he was.

"Dad, I think it's okay if you don't want to light anymore. Look over there," Sterling said, pointing down the beach where hundreds of huge fireworks lit the sky. Hilton Head was a fun place to be and Lawrence gave up on our baby fireworks. They didn't compare to the local's versions anyway. We sat as a family enjoying the homemade shows around us, and for the first time in a long time, I felt content.

When room service arrived that night, Sterling was doing his CF treatment, the vest which entailed the shaking of mucous out of his chest with a vibrating vest while doing nebulizer meds.

"Are you okay?" the young male asked as he set down the tray on the kitchen table.

"Yeeeeeeees, IIII aaaaammmmm gooooddd," Sterling replied as his lungs shook.

"Yes, he's okay. Just doing a treatment for his lungs," I explained.

"Does that hurt him?" he asked, looking worried for Sterling.

"No not at all, it's like a massage," I tried to explain.

"Oh okay, well sign here please and the service fee is added in too," he said as Lawrence came and signed.

It was strange. I was feeling like a regular mom on a great vacation. I'd almost forgotten CF was something unusual. And I suddenly realized, this was a great thing. Lawrence noticed my inward smile and touched my hair gently.

We continued on after Hilton Head and proudly celebrated our ten year wedding anniversary with our children at the Omni in Homestead, Virginia—first time to Virginia for all of us. There were waterslides built into the hillside and a lazy river. This was my favorite Omni we had ever stayed in. Lawrence and I floated in the lazy river for hours while the kids rode the water slides. I felt chemistry again. We got more fireworks. It was their 100th anniversary so we were treated to birthday cake every night and more fireworks. Lawrence and I were laughing that we both ordered roses and champagne to the room for each other. We each took down a bottle to celebrate.

But the Biltmore, the largest privately-owned estate in the country, was our family's favorite weekend trip. There were a lot of favorites. We tubed down the rivers in Asheville, off-roaded on the Land Rover driving course and even fed chickens. There was a mini Land Rover driving course for the boys. They had to complete Land Rover driving school before they were set free on the course. The live music and wine tasting weren't bad additions either. It was a perfect summer and the boys even saw a Carolina Panther's game and NASCAR race. North Carolina Film Commission was so kind to our family.

My dad flew out to visit and we had the time of our lives in Charleston, South Carolina. We stayed in a Bed and Breakfast where George Washington ate breakfast and the kids ran through the fountains at night. My dad was the best energy ever and best travel buddy. He always helped with my boys and never resorted to anger with them. He even brought his guitar with us. He could talk to anyone which was a bonus when wanting to learn more info about places.

After summer the kids and I went back to our LA home to prepare for their school year. Lawrence flew home every weekend for the next four months. Major bonus points for family dedication.

I was relieved when this show was over because the boys had their dad back in LA full-time. The sad part about it was the fact that there was not going to be another season and many locals would be without jobs. Lawrence heard many relocated to Atlanta where there was an abundance of work.

Back in LA, I had to return my focus on the upcoming charity event. It was time I made my dream come alive. The event would be one more step toward my goal and I enjoyed learning something new every time. My book would need to make whatever money this event didn't.

I'd managed to create an event where 150 guests were all coming to support CF. The CF and DMD Barefoot Ball. I had to include something about the beach in everything I did. I'd chosen a stunning country club to host the evening and everything was humming along perfectly. This was the last event I would throw, and I teamed up with my dear friend Christine, *The Chef*, adventurer and philanthropist, and mother of two, along with Patricia who was a successful executive in the music industry. She was a mother of three and sadly her son, Price, was diagnosed with DMD at the age of six.

Christine introduced me and Patricia and, just like that, a special bond between our families and kids was instantly and effortlessly made. We each had children with a disease that had no cure. I refused to say terminal anymore, but sadly that was the harsh reality for most DMD children and some CF. My final event was hosted by a well-known heart throb actor and radio host. These nice people took the time to support CF and DMD. When other celebrity guests arrived, my heart grew fuller. My doubles partner in tennis showed up with her superstar hub and would always be much more than a doubles partner. They were the epitome of a perfect celebrity family.

The humble couple walked through the doorway barefoot and stood with both Sterling, Price and Price's service dog, Beatle, in front of the organization's step and repeat banner for photos. The kids were thrilled.

The silent auction concluded as people were seated for dinner. The energy in the room became serious as all eyes were on Price and Sterling and their speeches. They spoke openly about their diseases and I had never seen a ten and eleven-year-old capture an audience like they did.

"Do you see me walking around all depressed and mopey? No, I am living life to the fullest and skiing from the top of Mammoth with Captain James. Nothing will stop me from living my life. But, we need you and we need money so we can help other kids that don't have as much money. We need to help others with diseases like me," he triumphed, throwing his fist in the air. I was so proud to be his mom. Lawrence was at the back of the room at the bar balling his eyes out. This was rare to see Lawrence show vulnerability. I wanted to comfort him, but I could not leave the side of the stage.

Each table at the CF and DMD Barefoot Ball had two pictures. One picture was of a boy with CF between the ages of one month and eighteen. The other photo was of a DMD child, aged four to fifteen. A lot of the shots showed them in a wheel chair because that was the reality for most children with DMD, a gut-wrenching genetic disorder characterized by progressive muscle degeneration and weakness.

Price and his parents spoke next. Price talked about his dreams of being a scientist. Patricia talked about the dream of watching her child go to college and see his dreams come true. Dinner napkins were used as tissues as there wasn't a dry eye in the house.

"We need to let these kids be kids because it's just not fair to them," I announced. "Thank you for taking the time to support CF and DMD. Thank you to our sponsors, Emergency Restoration and Feather Inc., for being so generous with their time and money. Thank you to my dad, the DJ, for coming all the way from San Diego to provide great tunes and last, thanks to the hosts," I announced. Lawrence was sitting at our table and I was the one in the spotlight for once, up at the podium, addressing the packed room full of generous supporters. He grinned up at me and I grinned back.

"And now for our very special auction." This was by far my favorite part of the event and I'd been waiting eagerly for it. Price had painted a beautiful sunset picture with him and Beatle, and Sterling had drawn a Minecraft image. Both had been put onto canvases as priceless art. They were displayed on gorgeous wooden easels for everyone to appreciate.

"Do I hear two thousand for these paintings?" The host asked the audience with enthusiasm in his soothing radio voice.

"Two thousand dollars," Lawrence said, holding up his paddle.

"Do I hear twenty-two hundred dollars? We are going to help some amazing kids," Mark said looking around the room.

"Twenty-two hundred," the pop star said, standing up.

"Twenty-two, going once, twenty-two going..." The host spouted out.

"Three thousand," confidently spoke a man in the middle of the ballroom.

"Thirty-five hundred," battled Lawrence.

"Ten thousand," yelled the pop star coolly, flipping up his paddle, smiling and leaning against a pillar by his table.

"Man, you are awesome," yelled Lawrence

"Shit, it's the least we can do," he said, looking at his beautiful wife.

The host smiled, "Ten thousand going once, going twice... Sold!"

Everyone cheered.

"Thank you!" I cheered, so excited to help these very deserving children. It was an amazing way to end an amazing night. Lawrence grabbed my hand and we celebrated with all the other couples on the dance floor. It was one of my favorite songs, *Come Together* by the Beatles. We had.

# Episode 17

## THRILLER AND A 500 MILE WALK

**Soundtrack:**
**I Would Walk 500 Miles**
**(Kenny and the Scots)**

**2016**

The thriller wasn't out, but I had read the book and loved it. It was an easy, quick, dark twisted tale, that I read in an afternoon. It wasn't a surprise it was so nefarious. The author's other novels were the same and just as page turning. I read the book as soon as there was a rumor Lawrence might be working on it. I was so proud he'd be working on another amazing story that TV audiences were going to love. It was shot in LA with some parts shot in Ukiah.

The kids and I drove to Ukiah. We had a great car ride, playing music and telling stories. There was one that had me confused again.

"Mom, Dad always talks to this lady on the phone." Sterling said as we were driving.

"I am sure it's just someone from work." I replied, hoping I was wrong.

"It's not because he always says doctor when they talk." Sterling was a smart kid and knows when something is off.

"Maybe it's his set doctor he is talking to," I suggested.

"Mom, set doctors are called set medics and dad's set medic is Martin. I looked on the call sheet." He said very matter of fact.

"Okay, honey, I'll ask your dad when I see him. Don't worry about it."

They were going to hang around set with Grandma and Lawrence while I walked the five hundred miles for my charity project. I was leaving for forty days. I was overwhelmed with excitement mixed with guilt, but I was determined to enjoy the few days I had with the kids before I flew out to Europe.

In the few days we were there, the kids met an actress on the show and star in many super hero movies. She invited Sterling and Trent to have breakfast with her family each morning. My kids would set their alarms to wake up and walk out the door across the meadow to have breakfast with Superman's girlfriend--well, so they thought. She did look a lot like Lois Lane. They were convinced her actress routine was just a cover – superheroes did stuff like that so why wouldn't their girlfriends? I didn't ruin their fantasy with the truth.

"Are you sure you want them joining your family?" I asked nervously.

"Of course! I invited them," she replied.

So, morning after morning, the kids ate with her family. That meant a lot to them. They also spent time in the mineral baths with her family as well. I felt like we should be giving her space, but she insisted the boys come hang. Very sweet.

I can't say enough great things about the director, Sean, and his exec producing partner. He agreed to give the kids their own shot in a scene.

The director and Sterling had a whole conversation.

"Hey, Sean," Sterling said, chest puffed out. Something amazing about kids with chronic diseases, they don't waste time asking for what they want.

"Hey, Sterling," Sean answered matching his tone.

"Can you give me a shot in the show?" Sterling joked

"Oh, I'll give you a shot," he said, laughing, amazed that this young kid even knew what a shot was.

And no lie, the next day, Sean had a shot set up for the boys. What a trip and how lucky for the boys to be at work with their dad and get direction from an Oscar winning director. Things like that just don't happen every day. Unless you are a Production Wife. It for sure had its cons, but on that day, it had its pros. In a way, a person on TV lived forever.

The next day I said goodbye to the kids in Ukiah and I was off. Although tears filled my eyes under my sunglasses that hot day, it hadn't really hit me how long I would be away, and did I mention that we decided to permanently move to San Diego while I was gone?

Our timing was always impeccable--not. When I came back from Spain, I would be returning to our new home in San Diego. Lawrence would be moving the whole LA house on his own. He didn't want to spend money on a moving company; he wanted to save it for a trip. We would keep a small studio apartment in Studio City. Which we thought was pretty funny. The studio in Studio City. It was more like a dark hole that came with a neighbor's barking dog 24/7. Poor puppy and poor Lawrence.

Why move? Well, we liked our LA life, but I really wanted to be closer to family. The kids were involved in great sports and activities, along with having some very nice friends. Like I said before, I had amazing friends too. There was just something off and missing from my kid's childhood.

It's hard to explain, but my gut agreed with Lawrence's. I'd tried moving once before closer to family. But I'd learned the hard lesson that if you are going for that reason, you'd better move right near them. Last time, a half hour away was still too much. This time we'd be right by them, only streets away.

"They can't get this time back. They seem a little too stressed so young. These are the good ol' days. It should all be about family right now, right?" Lawrence said to me and I completely agreed.

We played a part in that stress at times, but the school vibe was what was really off. My kids had amazing teachers and we met amazing families, but there were just too many rules.

"Well, it's now or never." I added up my reasons for relocating. "I am in love with how well the school nurse helps with the CF, but come on. No playing tag, no hanging upside down, and no touching? They need to be kids."

"Sterling is going into fifth grade so it's literally now or never. I am not moving him in middle school along with Trent," Lawrence firmly spelled it out. "Will this make you truly happy? Because if it will, it's best for the whole family."

"It will make me truly happy, but you will have to make the biggest sacrifice—not seeing the kids every night," I said. "I really believe that if you love the community you move to, you are bound to love the school vibe. I truly believe there is no place better to raise our children. It takes a village, but I think this is the best village. I promise. My childhood town, a city in the country not far from the beach is all about family and truly embracing the kids. It's a 'You can have it all there.' Not that LA doesn't; it's just that there is something unexplainable about this place, most comfortable to me."

"I agree it's a better life for them down there and that's

where your family is. That's where Sterling's doctor, hospital and CF care center is too. I'll be able to take out-of-town shows more if I have to and not feel so bad leaving you in Los Angeles without family," he said, as I was reminded that this selfless man was one of the reasons I married him.

So we decided to move back to San Diego, just miles inland from Del Mar, but this time for good. No turning back. If we made this move, it was San Diego forever, because by this point, Sterling had moved eight times. Lawrence could now take any show anywhere in the world if needed to keep our insurance and I could have support from my family whether he was home or away.

Lawrence explained he would do the move while I was walking in Spain.

"Reese, you need this walk. It will be good for you. I read online that a walk through the woods can make you happy. Can you imagine what a 30 day walk in nature will do for you?" He said it so sweetly, I could tell he really wanted me to go.

"I just feel so selfish. The timing is horrible. Who leaves their kids for thirty days? Yet, somehow I am already happy. I'm doing this to raise awareness and funds for CF and DMD, but there is guilt doing this for myself too." I needed more reassurance from Lawrence.

"Listen, if you don't enjoy it and feel guilty the whole time, then you have wasted this amazing experience and all the people helping with our kids. It's all for nothing if you are going to be miserable. Go. This is a once-in-a-lifetime opportunity. Enjoy!" he said.

I was impressed. I was convinced. I could do this. I had to and I needed to. If I was happier I would be a better mom and better wife. Things can affect your marriage and I didn't realize it. I was so sad for a while. He was angry. Put that together and try to be married. When we married we were both happy and vibrant. That's why we worked. Then we both became sad and angry, not the same marriage and not the marriage I imagined. We had to figure out who we were before we could come together again. **It's kind of like getting married**, getting divorced and meeting all over again for the first time. **Let's say I was sad dating for the first time**, I would put off sad energy and we would put off angry energy. We would attract sad and angry people. **I was so down and negative about life and how I talked about people and situations**. It was never my fault. I wasn't able to step back and see the big picture at times. I was in survival mode just trying to make it. Being in survival mode is good at times, but being in survival or the pons all the time is exhausting.

"Reese, do you think you're depressed?" Zoey, my counselor asked.

"Me, no, I can't be. I have a home and beautiful kids, my husband has a good job right now--never a constant in the industry--we make lots of memories. I have tons of friends."

"But you said you feel alone often? You said you feel lonely every time I see you."

"Yes, but that is because he's working."

Zoey, chimed in, "But your husband was home for six months. You were not alone. Do you feel alone even when he is there?"

"I do feel alone sometimes even when he is there. There is no way I am depressed. I am happy," I pleaded.

"You are on the outside, but are you sad on the inside? Is your soul sad? Are you a cheery person because of your personality, but your soul is crying? Does this sound like you? Have you considered that Lawrence is not good for you? Your happiness does not rely on someone else's. It comes from within. But some people are not good for each other. You have been here for years now. Where is he?" I knew this.

"No, I am happy, I have a perfect family, I come from a perfect family. I can't be sad. It doesn't make sense."

"Go home and just think how you feel, just be in touch with your feelings, who you are and specifically how you are feeling. How do you feel around Lawrence? You have a child with CF you are caring for, so have some compassion for yourself. Look at all the work you're doing." Zoey suggested in her calm counseling voice.

"But Lawrence isn't home, he is making me mad and sad. Something is wrong and it has been off for a long time. I feel it. What's wrong with me? I feel like he is not being honest with me," I exclaimed, blaming him for my feelings.

"You only have control over yourself and your happiness. It doesn't matter what he is doing. There is nothing wrong with you. Some people are just not good for each other. You do need to trust your intuition. The feeling in your gut is there for a reason." She continued. I had heard it all before. Year after year.

"I don't know how I truly feel around him," I said sadly. I blocked out a lot and tried to accept what I could not control.

"Are you still concerned about his drinking?" asked Zoey. "You mentioned at one time you thought he might have a problem. Do you think this? Is this why? "

"No, he has been so amazing and supportive of the move to San Diego and my 500 mile walk. No, I mean we party and have fun, but probably no more than our friends, I think I was overreacting," I answered, not knowing if I was being 100% honest with that feeling in my gut.

"Reese, listen to me. San Diego is exactly what you need.

A change in environment can lift you up. You need support. You have support here, but too many mutual friends. When things get bad and **it will get bad,** know that your family is there to help you." Zoey continued. "Be very careful who you talk to."

"Zoey, you are crossing the line here. Everything is fine. My life is great. I drink too, we all drink," I pleaded. I had created a perfect image of the family I wanted and that was how it would stay.

Was I sad? Was our drinking affecting me, us? No. We have the perfect family. Everyone drinks a few drinks a night.

I cried three times yesterday over Sterling's cough. I did not want to get out of bed, but I do--good thing I had an appointment with my trainer, a tennis lesson with Bob, and Pilate's classes on my schedule. Good thing I had a tea appointment. I don't know. I hated labels. It's okay to be sad when your kid is sick. But I guess his health is a roller coaster. Was this healthy for me? Was I depressed?

I subconsciously must have scheduled activities to pull me out of bed because if I didn't I would drop the kids at school and go back to bed.

Everything seemed hard to me. **Was I being honest with myself** ?

Was I really sad? Can marriage struggles and a disease do that?

I googled **Coping while caring for someone with cystic fibrosis.** Cystic fibrosis was not the main cause. It was part of it, but so much more was our relationship, and that is the truth.

I really do hate labels but google said sometimes parents can get depressed or develop anxiety, and you can't ignore these things.

I kept reading...

I asked myself all the questions.

What were my answers to the symptoms?

Let's see:

**#1. Physical problems including Headache, stomach ache, back pain and sleeplessness?**

I've been to a doctor three times in the last three months for neck pains, headaches and nausea.

Oh my gosh, I haven't slept in two days.

At night my thoughts just race and race; they just won't stop.

**#2. Emotional issues such as**
**Frustration, sadness, loneliness**
**anxiety, guilt, anger, resentment**
**Decreased enjoyment in pleasurable activities , social isolation**
**Blaming?**

-shoot!!

Oh my God, so many of these are me.

Is caring for a child with CF really capable of making me feel this way? Is it my unhappiness in my marriage? Or is the way I feel making me unhappy in my marriage? Is it just normal stress that comes with life? I had heard at a CF national conference that sometimes caregivers can get PTSD in a less severe form. Was that me? Was I just going to have to accept the waves of depression that come with caring for a child with a chronic illness? Or did I have to deal with the waves of depression from being in an up and down disconnected relationship? Even though my son is healthy. If I was struggling to fight these small waves how would I make it over the larger ones?

Is it living away from my family? Well, then a move to San Diego will fix that.

Well, of course I'm going to feel sad if I'm not around

all these crucial people in my life; that is a normal emotion, right?

Is it okay to have feelings, to feel something? I needed to keep working on myself.

**#3 mental issues-forgetfulness, mental exhaustion, more frequent accidents, trouble deciding, poor attention and memory, confusion?**

I honestly couldn't even remember why I was wandering into each room in my house. Because the boys asked me three times to make them something and I would get distracted and forget to feed them. But isn't this normal? It happened for a while each time I had a baby. Is it normal to forget things as you get older and after you have kids? I joke that half my brain left me when I had kids.

**#4 spiritual issues including alienation and hopelessness?**

**My wedding angel had helped pull me out of that for a while.**

There were days I felt I didn't deserve to be living. There were days I felt like I didn't deserve anything I had.

Isn't this normal, though, to just have some down days?

But you can't ignore them. I needed this walk. I needed something to trigger me out of this slump. I needed a Camino angel, much like my wedding angel. Just that person that comes into your life to teach you something. A connection, but not in an intimate way, in a friendship way. I loved guy friends. I had lost many when I left San Diego. We just lost touch. I loved hanging with the guys, but it changed when I got married. I missed Justin and Kirk, my best guy friends from high school.

I was no doctor, but these were things to be aware of moving forward. Let's see if a 30-day walk could help me have clarity?

Christine gave me a journal for The Camino and the cover read...Make today great.

Inside the cover she wrote:

*"The journey of a thousand miles begins with a single step."*

*I am so thankful to walk this journey with you. Thank you for introducing me to being a warrior for CF. You inspire so many. Keep fighting, mama. Proud to call you friend and sister.*

*Now let's go kick this 500 miles in the butt!*

*Love, Christine.*

## Camino Diary:
## Monday, May 25, 2017

*We arrived in London today from Los Angeles and I am so happy to be here. The best part is they speak English so I felt right at home. We are staying in a posh neighborhood before boarding our plane to France in the morning. I lucked out with my own room, small, but nice to have my own space. Life has been so crazy with our move to San Diego and Lawrence's show shooting up north for a few weeks. I guess I wouldn't do life any other way. My hand is already hurting because I don't know the last time I have written. It's been a few years. I am beyond thankful for this adventure. I will miss my boys dearly, but this is truly a one in a million chance to do something so good and so inspiring. I promise to embrace it all and stay positive. The credit doesn't matter. It's the journey and intentions that sit within our soul. I truly want to help people and feel blessed to be a role model for the kids and other moms.*

## Monday May 29, 2017

I have skipped a few days, but at least I am writing ☺ Today we walked 10 miles, yesterday 12.5 and the day before we did 20 miles. Day 1 of the Camino was hard because it was so long, but I found today challenging because of the rain or maybe I was sore, but needless to say we made it. We won't stop. I am having a blast. I was nervous about traveling with Christine, her mom and her husband, Volcom, because before this trip I really only knew Christine and only for a year. I was nervous we would all drive each other crazy, but I have to say we all get along great and laugh a lot. It's only day 3 on the Camino, but I am confident our banter will continue. I really was tentative about this trip in all honesty. Yes, I wanted to raise money for children, how could I say no? I will do anything to raise money for children and help my kids, this being for Sterling and to raise awareness. I am certain there is another purpose for this trip for me in addition to these kids. Thankful we all had enough money to pay for our trip so all the money would go right to these kids. Every dollar. We wanted people to know that too. The money we raised was not paying for our trip. I appreciate life and I wanted this trip to REALLY REALLY appreciate life, my husband and kids more. They are amazing human beings and I miss them dearly. Sometimes distance and time can make that appreciation and gratitude grow even stronger. I don't know how I got so lucky with a perfect life, but I want to keep it going. I feel so lucky and blessed and don't know how I got this lucky. Lord, please help me to make good choices and see the good in everything. I want to be a better mom, better friend and better wife. Help me to give more grace and be more forgiving. That is hard for me. Help me to trust others more, which is too hard for me because I have been *badly hurt. I want to leave this road with a fresh start and give everyone in my life forgiveness and a fresh start as well. I am hoping to figure out how to truly forgive those who have hurt me, like really forgive and really trust again...hoping this road will help.*

### June 11, 2017

*WE ARE HALF WAY!!*

*I have not written too much, but I have a ton of photos and memories. I miss my boys so much today and every day!! Thank God for facetime!!*

*What I miss... Trent, I miss your eyes, your smile, your snuggles, your helpfulness, your voice and your hands when you put them on my face. I miss your singing, your sweet comments, your hugs when I am mad, your willingness to please and do what's right. I miss how thoughtful and selfless you are. What a great friend you are to others, what a great son you are. I miss watching you play sports. I miss when you put the car window down and enjoy the air blowing in your face. I miss you helping me cook. I miss how cute you are when you ask to slumber on the floor with rolled up comforters for your bed. I miss watching you come downstairs when you wake and miss seeing you snuggled on the couch with your blanket. I love how sweet you are and the list goes on and on. Trent, you are the sweetest soul and God blessed us so much with you.*

*Sterling, you are so compassionate and giving! I love that about you.*

*I love your channel and how you are using it to do great things. I love that you inspire so many people. Like your brother, you are a leader. You taught him how to be one. I love that you are strong and bold and stand up for yourself and what you believe in. You are so handsome and wise beyond your years. You are an extraordinary competitor. I miss your laugh. I miss you challenging me and calling me out. I miss your smile and watching you play sports. I miss your jokes. I miss how creative and funny you are. I miss how you say sorry to your brother by rubbing your hand on his lips and making him eventually laugh. You are a gift and I can't wait for you to discover more of your gifts.*

*I miss you boys so much. I miss how loud you boys chew and how loud you slurp slushies. I miss laughing and exploring with you guys.*

*I miss movie nights when Sterling talks a lot and Trent falls asleep before the movie finishes. I miss when you boys come downstairs to ask for water, food and snacks just as an excuse to hang out with me. I miss bath time when we all hang out with Sterling in the master bath (in your trunks, of course). I miss the tennis ball game you play with Dad and our Mammoth trips. I miss beach trips with boogie boarding, sand and soccer, catch. I miss so much about you boys. I miss how you boys laugh together, wrestle together, stand up for each other and love each other like brothers.*

*Your bond is UNBREAKABLE.*

*Lawrence, I miss everything about you! I miss your smile, your laugh, jokes, sex, how much you touch my feet, my face, everything. I miss our walks Thankfully we get to talk, but I miss your arms, abs, butt, hair and smell.*

*I miss when you BBQ chicken, everything!*

*I hope you all can forgive me for the times when I am not perfect. I will forgive you...I already have. I promise to work on staying calmer and embracing your own journeys even more.*

*Sterling, when you are frazzled, I promise not to get*

*frazzled. Instead ,I will give you more love, affirmation and assurance.*

*Trent, I promise to be more patient and give you even more love and affirmation.*

*I am so lucky to have you boys and can't believe I get to raise you, love you, and watch you grow. My angels* ☺

*Let's embrace everyday...the 4 of us.*

*My Goals:*

*Stay calmer*

*Breathe*

*I am doing a great job*

*Plan less, stress less*

*Appreciate more*

*Enjoy every moment*

*Breathe*

*Be more positive*

*Check emotions at the door*

Well, long story short, I did it. I walked five hundred miles along the Camino de Santiago in thirty days with nothing but three friends and a backpack. I was officially a pilgrim. People from all countries and all walks of life walked the Camino for a variety of reasons. I met many cancer survivors that shared their stories. One lady placed a rock in each city to honor those that had passed from cancer. Many people seemed to walk it after a death or divorce. My reason was neither. Each day of the thirty days we walked for a child with either CF or DMD. Like I said before, there was a huge personal achievement benefit for me. The money raised would be divided between the thirty DMD and CF kids, in addition to the funds raised at the Barefoot Ball. The kids would use it for medical expenses which could stack up quickly with such serious diseases. I was hoping to raise a million, but settled on fifty thousand. I was not done giving to these children or diseases. Family was the beans to my burrito. Could my writing generate more money to give?

I found a Camino family as I walked. I think the trek should be a college graduation requirement. I met so many different people from all over the world and literally all walks of life. I talked to random people along the long path to learn their story and their reason for walking. Our closest walking buddies were from Kansas, Italy and Canada. Our group of four grew bigger and smaller as we met people and adjusted the pace of our gait.

I walked proudly, remembering how everyone had joked that Christine, nude survivor, would probably end up carrying me. They thought I had lost myself in all my luxury travel experiences and could no longer rough it. They were wrong. I still had my will. I read my devotional daily from my neighbor, Stacey. Well, to reduce backpack weight I had ripped out 40 pages and brought them with me. I would put them back in my devotional when I got back. I realized praying and connecting with the heavenly father could not hurt ever. I did my journey my way.

Kansas, a Marine, made me feel safe at all times. He was carrying the ashes of his beloved grandmother and sprinkled them along the way. I called him my Camino angel. He reminded me I was an amazingly beautiful woman and I needed that. I was so hard on myself; that affirmation was always nice. We bonded over music—we both loved Ed Sheeran. He also played "I'm a fucking unicorn song" over and over. Some drunk Brits made it up at a hostel one night on the Camino. It made me laugh. He became besties with Christine's husband. Kansas and Volcom spent every night with us and if there was a noise they were the first ones up making sure everyone was safe. When I was being an ass Kansas would let me know. I needed that too. The last day he did say something I will never forget. "I hope this never happens, but if for some reason, you and your husband split please come watch a Chief's game with me."

Canada, a fifty-year-old software entrepreneur, kept me entertained with his stories, stiff drinks and amazing style. Italy, a businessman, showed me he was a hopeless romantic and how to use google translate. He showed me all the things he did for his fiancé including proposing to her at the Eiffel Tower. The three joined our group of four and became like brothers to me.

I returned to the United States forty days later, twelve pounds lighter and with a whole new appreciation for life. I was at peace. I flew from Spain to France to London to Vegas to Atlanta, where *The Thriller Show* was filming.

We sadly got in a fight the moment he picked me up from the airport. We had so much to be thankful for. We were a family together again, not home, but together in Atlanta. What was wrong with us? Why couldn't we see eye to eye?

Expectations were the problem. I got off the plane in Atlanta after a stop in Vegas. Lawrence bought me a first-class ticket as a treat for completing the walk. I was so thankful, but I would have been grateful with any seat on the plane. After living out of a backpack you learn to appreciate what you are handed. I didn't come from money. My two hard-working parents worked their tails off, sometimes two and three jobs to give me and my siblings everything. Lawrence and I still didn't have money, but we could have had it. Instead we chose to enjoy luxuries and make memories with our kids. The walk reminded me how little we needed to be happy. I was so happy. I had nothing to worry about. All I had to do was get up every day and walk.

As I walked down the terminal to baggage I called

Lawrence. No answer. I saw some drivers with signs and some kids with homemade signs for their parents. I didn't want a sign. I wanted to see Lawrence and my boys. I was ready to give him a huge hug. He was my best friend. I was so grateful he pushed me to go on this trip. My head and my heart needed it. I got my luggage and still Lawrence was nowhere to be found. My kids were nowhere in sight. How silly of me to expect a warm welcome. It was 10:00 p.m. They were probably sleeping. I picked up my neon green North Face backpack out of the luggage carousel and walked out to the curb. I looked for Lawrence and the kids, but still no one was there. Were my expectations too high?

"There you are," I said, kind of annoyed as Lawrence pulled to the curb in a Nissan rental car two hours later.

"Hi, sorry I'm late, the valet at the Ritz took forever," he explained sensing I was annoyed.

"It's fine," I said, "sorry, I was just so looking forward to seeing you at baggage and hugging you." I was real with my feelings.

"Well, I am here now. You can hug me now--you're welcome."

"I was just telling you how excited I am to see you."

"I am excited to see you too, but I am doing the best I can. The guys took forever to get my car." I noticed a bandage on his arm. I didn't bother asking for an explanation. He seemed off.

"It's fine," I said, sad. I was so sad. All that time reflecting on myself and our marriage–this was not what I had pictured after not seeing each other for a month. I plugged my Camino playlist into the car and put on "Life's better with you." We sat in silence.

There in Atlanta, when I finally got to the hotel, I hugged

my boys so tight we rolled to the ground. They cried to me, "Never leave us for that long ever again."

"I won't," I said, hugging them and kissing them all over their cheeks.

Unfortunately, Lawrence, the man that supported me in going on the journey and the man that was so helpful with the kids while I was away, did not react the same as the kids.

The next day we explored Atlanta, Georgia. My time zones were way off, but I rallied. I had just had a 30-day break and I was excited and motivated to be with my boys. We explored the aquarium, sports hall of fame, world of Coca Cola, botanic gardens and more. We even stopped by Dr. Martin Luther King's childhood home. We enjoyed Atlanta, but we couldn't wait to go home to San Diego—our next chapter. I hoped the fights would stop. They had to. I wasn't going to let them affect me anymore. I was in control of how much pain I let into my life. We had everything any family could ever want and more things than most people. I'd learned that from my time on the trail and I was determined to put my new knowledge into action.

# Episode 18

## Transition, LA to SD and a Leap of Faith

Soundtrack:
Beach Drive
(John Rhey)

2017

With the feast and famine of the TV industry, leasing had seemed to be the best option for us. We were also terrible savers, especially with the pact. With our lifestyle of enjoying every moment, memory-making, and you-only-live-once mentality, it was easier to move up or down in house size with a lease, rather than a purchase. We also loved to treat friends and family to unforgettable experiences. We loved to give and that was a very attractive quality about Lawrence.

You never had to worry about what the market was doing. Friends kept telling us to buy, that we were throwing money away. But we were all about minimizing stress. When leasing, you have no stress about repairs or the cost of them because the landlord does it. When you lease, if you don't love the house or like the freeway noise or have discovered you have an irritating neighbor after you move in, then you can easily just move out. So, although we saw the upside of earning equity, it didn't support the freedom we craved. You can't have it all in that aspect.

So we rented a $2.5 million dollar home and were loving it. It was a home with views of hot air balloons over Del Mar and we were in heaven. Could we have bought a $2.5 million dollar home with our lifestyle? No. But leasing one was not a problem. We were not responsible for the upkeep so this was a huge weight lifted.

We were originally just looking for a three-bedroom, two-bath home with a pool in my niece and nephew's school zone. We needed a particular school for the late start time as well; Sterling needed time in the morning for his treatments. I searched Zillow, Trulia, and Redfin daily to find something nice, but nothing fancy. There was nothing available during the small window we had to move in. But then my brother-in-law sent us the listing for a mansion right before I had left for The Camino. We'd never even considered something so fancy and pretentious, but we remembered our goal of memory-making and having the best time we could together at all times and bit the bullet. And we could see what it was like to live in such a huge house to help decide if we wanted to save to buy something similar one day. Sterling and Trent always dreamed of living in a giant house like so many of our celebrity LA friends. But after being there for a while, we concluded that unless we had sixteen kids and unlimited funds, the mansion life was not for us.

We reminded the kids, "It's just for fun. We're not living in a place like this forever. You don't need a giant house to be happy. We're not rich, just rich in spirit."

We also explained to the kids that the move to the big house in San Diego was until they finished high school. No more big moves. We would maybe move one more time in the same five-mile radius, but their schools and friends would be the same.

After the move, Sterling claimed some of the kids said they didn't like him because he was rich. I was crushed. So much for splurging to enjoy life to the fullest. We encouraged him to explain that just because you live in a big house didn't mean he was rich. But even if he was, that didn't make him a bad person. They soon became fast friends. Thankfully, it had been that easy with my social circle since I moved to my hometown. Would the new community provide the same good ole day memories I had? I had no doubt.

**But first, let me go through the pros of our new digs:**

- Made friends with the neighbors down the street that had seven boys
  - "love your neighbor" they greeted us with hugs.
- Private roads- kids could ride golf carts, motorcycles, anything they wanted for miles and *almost* nobody cared
- Empty lots for riding all the toys, when it rained, kids could ride through puddles
- Gold fire hydrants
- Getting space from each other was easy
- Beautiful Spanish architecture
- Beautiful pool
- Dog poop bags provided every mile, in any direction, when you went for walks
- Privacy
- View of sunset over the ocean
- Security-gate-feel so I felt safe when Lawrence was away
- Security guard greets you with a smile and a wave

- No surprise visitors like in-laws lol, just kidding
- Resort feel
- Fountain
- Huge yard
- 6 bathrooms
- Lawrence and I each had our own toilet in our master bathroom
- Pure air for Sterling's CF - no freeway nearby.
- 80 doors with screens for breeze, the kids enjoyed tag through all the doors(screens popped right off)
- Huge wide hallway – the kids could ride go carts in them
- HOA was dedicated - plants were always kept perfectly manicured
- Famous neighbors, ball players, YouTubers
- Gardener
- Pool guy
- Most all the neighbors were friendly
- Media room
- Rooftop garden
- Balcony
- Amazing kitchen
- 6 fire places
- Plenty of parking
- 20k garage doors (maybe that's more of a con)
- Hide and seek was amazing
- No complaints about music or parties, with empty lots surrounding the mansion

And here were the cons, hence why we would never buy the house. These problems are going to sound ridiculous, but here we go:

- Homes were so spread out you could go days without seeing a next-door neighbor. Some even had private gates on their driveways after the neighborhood gate. I took those as *don't bother me signs*, but doubt they meant that.
- Laundry room was 50 yards away
- There was a repair needed once a week, we thought the fancy bathroom sinks were all clogged at first, but the plumber came out and told us they were slow drain. I didn't even know that was a thing anyone would want.
- You can't always find your kids
- Guests get lost with 80 doors to choose from
- Delivery companies also don't know which door to deliver to
- If plumber is needed, often repairs for fancy parts are upwards of $1400
- Things take months to fix due to their fancy nature
- Electric bill was outrageous and we weren't allowed to install solar. At least 4k a month. We were not going green at all. We were embarrassed to tell people what we spent.
- Water was also expensive with such a big garden and lawn. We averaged $1k a month.
- A broken sprinkler was easy to miss, thus adding to the water bill.
- It wasn't very environmentally responsible watering all the time.
- Constantly telling kids to turn off lights, but it was hard to figure out which ones and in which room. Each room had a panel of ten buttons.
- Light timer would go on and off all the time and there were so many different buttons for all the different lights it got very confusing.

- Cleaners and gardeners all charge above average per hour when you live in a fancy place, as they assume you have lots of disposable income.

We loved the house and couldn't say enough great things. But there were definitely a lot of cons to a bigger place. Things I'd never realized. It all took more money, more organizing and sometimes, a lot of effort to keep everything going. Bigger isn't always better as they say.

And to make sure I was still keeping things real, I'd go visit a very special place, just two miles from our house. I walked there once a week with my "sisters." Only one of them was my real sister. Di and Kay were sisters and Kaleia was Di's sister-in-law. I can't forget Tiff too, AKA plus one. She was so busy professionally dancing that we made our plans and invited her after. If she could swing it she would be there last minute. We did all of our girl trips together, we just called ourselves "the sisters." I liked it. Not to mention Kaleia's family was our travel family. These girls walked with me and gave me the support I needed to handle the disease and life once a week. We started at my house and walked there and back. That sisterhood was definitely a perk of moving back. Each week we visited the memorial for a boy who lost his CF battle at nineteen back in 1998. It was a must visit for me, as emotional as it was. Kay had lost a friend to CF too, so I feel it was special to her in a different way. It talked about how he used humor to deal with his battle. It was a great reminder for me to laugh it up more with Sterling and Trent. Sterling was hard-working, tenacious and cracked me up a lot like a few of Justin's characteristics. He seemed to understand Justin's way to cope. I just needed to figure it out a little more. I always had fun with the boys and Lawrence, but I didn't feel I was laughing a lot again. Things started to feel easier when Lawrence was gone working. Why was this? I needed to change that, and fast. The years were whipping by and who knew how long we all had to be together, enjoying each other?

# Episode 19

## THE MAMA DRAMA 2 AND GEOGRAPHIC SEPARATION

**Soundrack:**
**Foolish**
**(Morgan Leigh Band)**

While adjusting to our new place and enjoying the San Diego beaches, Lawrence was asked to work on season two of my all-time favorite TV show. We were trying to get the hang of having the LA studio apartment and the San Diego house, get the kids adjusting to a new school, sports teams and friends. Well, my intuition was right and the kids adjusted and coped with the move better than I could have asked. The village had only changed a little over the last decade and the foundation was still there. Children and family were the priority in this town. At first it was a little rough being the new kids, but within a few months they had a larger circle of friends from classmates, sports teams and activities than before, not to mention they had family and other family friends in SD that we had known for years. Kids were good! I will always be thankful that Lawrence took the leap of faith with me. He took a leap to go to where it all started, where we fell in love. Symbolically that meant a lot to me. And with that leap, a wonderful opportunity fell right into his lap. There are no words to describe. A mini-series, my favorite one, that was so loved turned into a season two. Not only do I have so much admiration for the talent, but the whole creative team and crew, especially the same director, now exec producer, from the last thriller Lawrence worked on.

It was also set in beautiful Monterey. It was definitely my favorite location so far. The flight from SD to Monterey was only an hour and twenty minutes. Easy for me and the kids. Easy for Lawrence to come home. The views were breathtaking, and I was pretty sure they were going to let the kids jump into a scene. Even if it was just a shoulder caught on camera, we all felt lucky to be on the set of such an inspiring and empowering show. We needed more like it, more shows that explored the complexities of relationships and more importantly, women's inner lives. Not to mention abuse against women.

We'd been invited to the Golden Globes to celebrate their season one debut, and the irony was not lost on me that I was there representing a show about abuse toward women whilst getting a little verbal abuse by some ass in a tux. All the women were wearing black in honor of the #MeToo movement. We'd just heard an incredibly empowering and passionate speech, when some jerk decided to thumb his nose at the whole thing.

"Sir, I am so sorry," I said apologetically after spilling a little white wine on the gentlemen's shirt. I spilled some on myself as well. No big deal, it was white wine and I bought my dress for forty dollars at Ross that morning. Sometimes I gave myself goals to spend as little as I could on a fancy dress. I always tried to buy dresses that had roses on them. Kids with CF often learned it as 65roses. It was easier to say.

The guy was glaring at me, but in my defense, the party

was super crowded and it was impossible to get through sections without bumping into someone. The man continued to look at me with his annoyed expression, but had no response. I started to squeeze through the crowd some more, when he decided to respond.

"Why don't you come over here and lick it off, bitch," he said rudely, but with a laugh.

"What did you say?" I clarified.

"I said why don't you come lick it off my chest? You heard me," he repeated clearly as his friends and him now laughed.

"What a jerk," I mumbled under my breath as I tried to find my way through the sea of people to Lawrence. At this point, I had been to tons of Hollywood premiers and this was the one time I was going to be disrespected by a man? Surely everyone was being a little more careful of what they said and did at a #MeToo event? Not so much, apparently. But I didn't know why I was so shocked, it was Hollywood, after all - a place that was always full of surprises.

During the prep of *The Mama Drama* second season and thinking about our geographic separation once again, Lawrence and I had a respectful and honest discussion involving mutual feelings of divorce when he was home for the weekend. He said he needed space and couldn't give me what I needed. The tension began when I got a call from the hospital early in the morning after we had been at a 40th birthday for our SD friend.

"Hey Reese, it's me. I am in the emergency room and they won't let me drive. You need to come pick me up." I was speechless. I thought he had gone for an early morning walk with Lassie but I was wrong. When I got there the receptionist took me back to him.

He wasn't talking. It was the same feeling from set visits

when I felt like everyone in the room knew something I didn't know.

"What's going on?" I questioned looking at his frail body.

"Your husband fainted while walking the dog and a good Samaritan brought him here. He is dropping your dog off at home right now."

"Why didn't they just bring him home? I could have taken him?"

"Ma'am, your husband is sick…"

Lawrence interrupted, finally with something he had to say, "Honey, can you leave the room for a minute? I need to have a word with the doctors."

Everyone just stared at me while I walked out of the room in disbelief. All I wanted were answers.

Why was everyone acting so strange? My gut told me this does not add up.

I was sitting in the waiting room. A nurse walked out. "Excuse me, Reese. Can I talk to you?"

"Yes, please. What the hell is going on here? I would love to get more information."

"Here, this is for you," she handed me a packet.

I read the pages quickly. To sum it up, my husband had a disease and needed rehab. Why didn't they just say that? I guess he tried to quit on his own a few days ago and the withdrawals nearly killed him. The nurses gave him big hugs goodbye as they felt sorry for him. Sorry for him? What about sorry for me? Where is my apology for not being open about his disease and putting our family through this? There was no way he was an alcoholic. Alcoholics don't produce Emmy winning TV shows. We partied, we drank, but he was successful. I was mad at him. I was mad at all of it. Where was my compassion? Why wasn't he honest with me?

He walked out to the waiting room and we walked to the car.

We got in the car and he asked if we could go to church. I was an emotional wreck. Who am I supposed to call? He's so private. He doesn't want anyone to know anything. And he is asking to go to church.

He looked sick, really sick, but I was hoping for a miracle. Strange. I didn't remember him having a drink last night. It doesn't make any sense. My head was spinning. I didn't understand. Drinking is a choice. He chose to drink. He chose to stop. What's the problem? Alcoholics choose to drink. Why are they telling me he has a disease? I had asked him to stop for years, but he chose to keep going. It's his fault. I stopped drinking around him to minimize the arguments, but then gave up.

I told the kids Dad had a headache, a really bad headache called a migraine, so I had to get him at the hospital. I hated lying to the kids for him and covering up for him.

I was pissed at him. Makayla, the only one I told said, "I think he needs support."

I was a really supportive person; I was just angry. I had thought it was a problem for years and then talked myself out of it. Everyone drinks too much sometimes.

"Get your shit together; you're a dad," I said. I was more angry because he lied to me about it being a problem and got upset so many times when I'd asked him to stop. He would tell me I was a nagging bitch when I had my concerns.

It still didn't add up. Divorce had been thrown out over the years in anger a million times before, but this time was different. This time we were seriously considering it. I can't help him. I can't fix him, especially if he was not getting help.

I read all night and talked to my counselor. If he was indeed an alcoholic or struggling with addiction, then he had to help himself. I threatened, "Lawrence, it's rehab or divorce," praying he would just go to rehab.

"I am not an alcoholic. Work has been stressing me out. I just need some space. Why are you asking for a divorce when I am going through a hard time?"

"Excuse me; we were just at the hospital and they said you needed to get help," I said assertively. "If you refuse to get help then I have to force you to. You will thank me later."

"Reese, I appreciate you getting me from the hospital, but they said it was just really bad anxiety. I'm fine." He said confidently.

"I don't care what you think; I know what I saw and I am done ignoring my intuitions. I saw a packet form the ER doctor stating that you needed to go to rehab or counseling. I paid the $8000 retainer fee for the lawyer and if you don't go to rehab I will have the lawyers file and start the process." I hated being so cold and aggressive, but there was no other option. The doctors said he needed it and my counselor agreed. If I didn't give him an ultimatum, I didn't love him. I hated tough love, but it was my only option.

He needed to help himself. He needed to send himself to rehab. And it was in exploring the reality of separating that I truly found myself again. I never thought that in considering divorce genuinely, that I would be able to finally appreciate Lawrence in a way I never could before. I needed to let go of it all. In finally owning my life choices and weighing out the pros and cons of divorce, I was able to take responsibility in the failure of the marriage on my end. Accepting that our marriage was over, was when he became my best friend. I could support him and his disease without the expectations I had as a wife. We didn't hate each other; we did what we had to do for years and had some epic times. For every terrible thing he did to me, I reciprocated with something even lower. In our poorest moments, I had to tell the kids that it was not healthy. To not copy us. That we were what *not* to do in marriage. We had many rough patches, but we didn't hate each other. When we communicated about divorce or separation and what it looked like, I didn't realize this decision would allow me to respect him again and give him the space he needed, the space to get help. We had not told the kids our decision.

Lawrence came to me and said, "I don't think I can give you what you need and I never will." He refused to go to rehab. He seemed to be okay so I just moved forward with the separation, accepting that he was not going to get help and was on his own journey.

"You're right." I didn't fight him. He was right. He couldn't give me what I truly needed.

We were geographically separated and we both had a part in this arrangement. He was doing the best he could to provide insurance for the family and provide a life of comfort while making quality TV shows. On my end, I wanted to raise the kids in San Diego near family and near Sterling's CF care center. I felt extremely safe and relaxed down there. I wanted it all and so did he. So as much as we loved each other, we agreed to being best friends and giving our kids an awesome life without tension, anger and resentment.

If we were separated, I could make the space to have someone around that could give me the attention and support I needed in hard times. He could find that someone too who could satisfy his needs. He had nothing to give me or anyone until he got help. He could go to rehab if he decided to. I was done being angry at him. All this time I thought I was competing with some female doctor (Sterling had mentioned he heard Lawrence on the phone with one)and other females, but I was competing with alcohol-Vodka. I don't even know who he is right now. Our individual needs could be met if we were separated. We would both not be alone. We would both be happier. For the first time in fourteen years, I felt a calmness like we were on the same page. We had so many great memories and so much to be thankful for, but our lives just didn't align anymore. We were actually able to communicate at times because I accepted he was on his own journey. He was not my responsibility and never was.

Our choice was going up against every family and religious tradition we both had. Like that, we were just giving up. If we loved each other, then why get divorced? We loved each other, but in a different way. Family and friends looking in would never understand the hurdle we were up against. I loved Lawrence as the father of my children and he loved me as the mother of his children. We were two different people. We had been up and down for so long we just drifted. Many separations and divorces were nasty and ugly, but we both agreed that being truly happy for each other separated was healthier than being resentful and angry together.

We were doing so well as friends with no expectations of each other. We were so much better as friends than husband and wife. I started to forget about his struggle with alcohol. I never saw him drink anymore. He said he had been working on it with his counselor. Did we actually have a chance? Was I going to be vulnerable and let him in again? Was forgiving a fault of mine?

We *both* started seeing counselors to help with the potential separation. We had never done this before so we wanted guidance on how to separate with dignity and respect. We needed guidance to put the kids first through the split, if that is what we decided. We both had parents with forty plus years of marriage. We couldn't get advice from them. It was obviously going to be to *stay together and work it out*. We both never saw our parents argue or fight. Where did we get it? We both never saw our parents resolve marriage conflict. Now that part makes sense. There was no manual for raising kids, and there most certainly was no perfect manual for how to do marriage.

He finally decided to get help from a rehab center in Beverly Hills and I was getting the help from mine in San Diego. We were spending $4000+ a week ($16,000 a month) on rehab/counseling so we would call each other and compare, we wanted to get the most for our money. It was unorthodox but it worked for us. He had advice that helped me and vice versa. His was saying don't do it and mine seemed to lean in the same direction. But we were already in the divorce direction. Divorce or not, we were both working on ourselves so much and sharing advice to help each other. This was the first time we both worked on ourselves at the same time and it was relieving. He was sober. His boss was the only one that knew about rehab. Lawrence was the first producer to produce three episodes of an Emmy-winning show from rehab. We were blessed to have the funds, but we truly were blowing through every penny coming in.

I left him alone for weeks to have his space unless he called me, and when he got out he didn't touch a drink. I was so proud of him, but he looked like he got hit by a truck. I was still worried about him. Would I be able to trust him again? He was losing hair. That didn't seem genetically possible.

I felt like Lawrence was truly making an effort. There were three divorce vows I learned from my counselor, Alma. She wasn't suggesting divorce, but if that was what I decided, using her separation vows would be the only way to put the kids first in her eyes. I thought they were brilliant so I wanted to share them with Lawrence. She also asked if she could meet with us before we told the kids.

We decided to work on being our best selves for the kids and to follow her rules before having the serious talk with them.

Some say failure is not an option, but sometimes failure is the best option, at least for us. For the first time in a long time, I felt truly happy and at peace. I was pretty sure Lawrence did too. Maybe we were never right for each other, but sometimes vows, pacts, contracts and religion can trap couples into unhealthy circumstances.

# Episode 20

Soundtrack:
Hung Over and Hung Up on You
(Juni Ata)

OUR DIVORCE VOWS
(as given by my San Diego counselor-
Alma and CEO of BRAINWORX)

**1) CELEBRATE WHAT WE HAVE; OUR AMAZING BOYS, STERLING AND TRENT, AND THE AMAZING MEMORIES WE HAVE HAD TOGETHER WITH MORE TO COME.**

In order to celebrate the kids, parents must get along in order to attend all important events of the child and not bring tension into the child's important moments. The child's moments are about them, not the parents. For example - sporting events, holidays and birthday celebrations.

**2) EACH PARENT TAKES 100% RESPONSIBILITY FOR THEIR SHARE IN THE SPLIT**

- These were mine:
- I was disrespectful
- I had trust issues
- I was too motherly and nagging
- I did not trust my intuitions
- I was hurtful and mean at times
- I relied on others for self-love
- I had my own insecurities and wounds
- I didn't believe I was enough at times
- I didn't love myself enough
- I reacted instead of observing
- I took things too personally
- I didn't believe how great of a mom I was

Alma explained that if I didn't work on some of these beliefs, I would make the same mistake with someone else. The more I worked on self-love, the more positivity I would attract into my life. I was open and began re-thinking everything. It would help me become a better, more attractive person inside and out. Realizing my shortcomings would also prevent me from bad-mouthing and shaming Lawrence, which would not be good for our children.

### 3) BE 100% HAPPY FOR EACH OTHER

I would have to be ready to be happy for Lawrence in his job, life decisions and future relationships if I was truly ready for a separation. If I was not ready to be happy for him, it would cause jealousy and anger that could subconsciously be projected onto the kids and that would not be putting them first. I would have to truly be happy for Lawrence so I would not say mean things about the father of my children.

Putting the kids first meant making peace with their father and not tearing him down.

In working on self-love with Alma and changing some of my subconscious beliefs through a technique called rewiring, I was determined to make the rules work. There were so many 'programs' given to us from our parents, good and bad. The idea was that sometimes we failed to achieve our dreams because of subconscious beliefs in the programs we were given. There was a lot involved with rewiring and I discovered more about it through a system to which Alma introduced me. I believed in medicine, it kept Sterling alive; but I was also open to looking at alternative options for reducing stress and anxiety in my life. I did not want to numb it with pills. In the program, I began looking at what truly brought me joy, not happiness, but joy. Writing, music, and event planning is what I came up with. I loved putting my thoughts on paper. The program focused on shifting my perspective, so I could succeed at achieving goals or better handle anything life handed me. This program wasn't faith-based, but I combined the rewires with my morning devotional book from Stacey.

For example:

I would read my devotional...Jesus Calling by Sarah Young. (this can be a devotional for any religion, but I was given a Christian one)

*April 26:"Welcome problems as perspective-lifters. My children tend to sleepwalk through their days until they bump into an obstacle that stymies them. If you encounter a problem with no immediate solution, your response to that situation will take you up or down. You can lash out at the difficulty resenting it and feeling sorry for yourself. This will take you down into a pit of self-pity.*

*Alternatively, the problem can be a ladder, enabling you to climb up and see life from My Perspective. Viewed from above, the obstacle that frustrated you is only a* **light and momentary trouble.** *Once your perspective has been heightened, you can look away from the problem altogether. Turn toward Me, and see* **the Light of My Presence shining upon you.**

***2 CORINTHIANS 4:16-18; PSALM 89:15***

I would then follow this with a rewire:

*Rewire: "I embrace each day and celebrate my life."*

I would repeat this while doing exercises to get it to the subconscious.
I changed the rewire to:

*"Dear Lord, give me the strength to embrace each day and celebrate my life." I would do the PACE exercises and end with a prayer.*

I repeated this prayer while doing PACE.

1. Drink water, hold in your breath, swallow water
2. Massage your chest area with right hand and left hand on your stomach, switch.
3. Touch right knee to left hand and touch left knee to right hand. Repeat 20 times while repeating rewire/prayer.
4. Then cross legs right over left while crossing hands and arms, hook up. Switch. Breathe and repeat rewire/prayer.

5. Put both hands together with fingertips touching. Tap each finger together one at a time while repeating rewire/prayer.

The program also helped me become aware of my triggers and then try to subconsciously change so that the same things would not repeatedly trigger me. Habits can be hard to change at the surface if we don't break through the subconscious. With God, I felt I had nothing to lose with trying the rewires.

In months of loving myself more and putting myself first, I realized I had found my dream job. Writing was a dream come true. I was thankful to have so many experiences to write about that Lawrence and I created together. Writing released stress and took me to a place of relaxation. I could block everything else out around me when I wrote. I got an adrenaline rush. Writing was a good addiction and cost me nothing, compared to my many, crazy shopping marathons. And it was helping me understand fully who I really was. My love for writing and music worked hand in hand. I typed on my Apple like I was playing a piano. The particular song decided the speed at which I typed and it was like music to my ears.

We needed the time apart to discover what we both wanted out of life – Lawrence had to work on his show and I wanted to dedicate more time to writing. So, Monday through Friday we did not see each other at all. He stayed in Monterey and I held the fort down in San Diego. Facetime is a beautiful thing for families and parents that work hard and away. Before when we spent time apart, we saw it as a sign that we were fine by ourselves, but now that we were consciously making a choice to be apart, we started missing each other. Was it as simple as allowing space to grow?

Freddie Rae Rose

I got excited to see Lawrence when he came home and the days we went without speaking became less and less. In fact, I couldn't wait to talk to him every day. I started complimenting and encouraging him again. He then shifted and started doing the same for me. We had stopped giving each other cards years back, when all of a sudden, they were turning up on my desk, along with surprise gifts.

We were growing together again. We were speaking each other's love languages.

With the large house, we thought one room could become his and I would keep the master. Well, it didn't last. We missed each other. I sat down with him and said, "For years I have been angry at you for working all the time. But I am at peace and no longer feel that way. I am going to embrace the time away from you because I enjoy my freedom. I want to make the best out of all situations."

The happier and healthier you are, the happier your children will be too. Alma taught me that. And now I was seeing the truth of it. The kids were so happy and relaxed now that Lawrence and I were content. I continued to read the devotional text to help with self-reflection and life gratitude. I continued to do my rewires and pray. I remembered the quote "progress not perfection." It wasn't about labels or declaring religion, but seeing the world through a new lens and appreciating the small things. Could anyone find a religion, power, a higher being who works for them? This was my life. Whatever I needed to be my best self was perfect for me. If everyone is trying to be their best self, does it really matter what religion we are? Is being our best self having different perspectives and yet being non-judgmental?

I listened to morning affirmations every day as well and had a sneaking suspicion that God had a plan for us. I didn't

222

know what it was, but I knew something had shifted for the better and I was just going to go with it.

I learned a lot from Lawrence and would be forever grateful to him for making me a stronger and independent person. I learned to stop reacting and start observing. I learned that happiness is perspective. I was happy with nothing before, so why had I gone down such a dark hole? I needed to shift my perspective. I was happier and calmer in San Diego – sometimes location does change how you feel about life. Accepting that and embracing it had been the right thing to do. I had a better attitude about everything now that I felt I was choosing my life rather than it being forced upon me. The kids felt and mirrored the new me and life was opening up in amazing ways.

### A FEW OF MY TIPS TO GREATER HAPPINESS:

- **Get a dog** (adopted two from the humane society. No words can describe the joy they bring to our family. They make me feel safe and protected when Lawrence is away. They bring the boys joy.)
- **Morning affirmation** (YouTube-Many to choose from. The point is to breathe and relax)
- **Work out-SELF LOVE** (running, soccer, hiking) Mia was the girl who I looked up to at the gym—the girl that could conquer 10 miles on the treadmill. I always wanted to know where she was running to.

Perhaps San Diego was in her mind, and when I moved to San Diego I realized she moved there at about the same time. I didn't join her in the gym on the treadmills. I joined her on the road in beautiful Del Mar. She felt freer in San Diego too. When I lived north I never imagined an amazing friendship. We were just gym friends. But now I consider her a great friend.

She's a very strong Catholic that firmly sticks by her principles and beliefs without judging others. The beauty of it all is we have many different views and respect each other's opinions.

My indoor soccer team is a second family and amazing support.

- **God Time and rewires** (read daily devotions. I fail at going to church, but strive to have a relationship with God. I thank my LA neighbor Stacey for giving it to me that morning. I cherished it)
- **Support from friends (the sisters) and family**
- **music** (make a playlist for every mood)
- **build a strong bond with my children** (make little traditions with them, strive to be a better mom every day)
- **writing**
- **quality time with the kids, being fully present when your mind is in a calm place**
- **scrabble**
- **travel-** find a travel family where you all enjoy each other and book as many trips as possible. This family was so supportive and provided more happiness and memories than they realized. Find a group of girls to travel with. I did mystery trips. Venmo $25 a month to one girl in the group and let her plan a fun surprise trip. Rotate who plans each trip.
- **Morning coffee routine/Starbucks-** Thoughts on Starbucks or any coffee tradition

I refuse to make coffee at home, but I get it. If you are trying to save money, better brew your own. But if you have a neighborhood Starbucks with a great vibe, go there! I have received way more joy from my local San Diego Starbucks and each experience is priceless. I enjoyed when Ellen started calling me by my first name when I came to order. One of my bridesmaids used to be her neighbor. Then I enjoyed when Ellen, Marc, Stella and Gab had my drink memorized. Then I enjoyed when they had it on the counter before I swiped because they knew I was coming in at a certain time every day.

Every day I walked in excited to see the Starbucks crew. Same drink every day Grande vanilla latte with breve.

I love my drink and something about the routine of getting my coffee and starting my day makes me feel great. My vanilla latte tastes a little better when I go to this particular Starbucks. It's mixed with love, laughter and something new. Stella and I enjoyed chatting about kids in school and what it was like for her when she was a teen and a kid. She was young and beautiful and not far out of high school. I really valued the advice she gave me since she went through the same schools as my boys attended. Ellen, a mother of two amazing softball players, always gave me another perspective on life. She's a mom and she's raised two amazing girls so I loved hearing about their journeys and the fun stuff she does every weekend. She always found the special dessert places around SD. Ellen read me so well that when I had days when I felt a little down or something was stressing me out she seriously asked me if I was OK. "You seem a little sad today" she would nicely point out. I'm like how does she read me? I was trying so hard to be positive but she truly could sense when something was off with me. I found it very interesting how this mother of daughters had some special intuition.

And then there was... Marc. He was always hilarious. I always laughed when I ordered my drink from him. One day a lady came in and ordered a drink with 30 requests.

She said, "Add this, not that, little bit of this, a little bit of that, take this out, I don't have that, and a little bit of the other, and then throw this in and then not that, but half of that, and two times the usual, and then not that."

When she walked away Marc looked at me and said, "I hope she doesn't ever come back. Just kidding."

I knew he didn't really mean it—he was just trying to deal with four minutes to describe one coffee. And we couldn't help but chuckle. Could you imagine her ordering dinner?

He was always going out or doing a spin class if he wasn't working. He shared music lists with me too.

There was also...Gab. She was going to be a teacher so I loved hearing her stories about her future career as a teacher and her journey as a student teacher. She sometimes subbed in my son's class. There was the regular four and then there were new barista's from time to time and I couldn't wait to know a little bit about them. My point is every morning I don't know which of the four will be taking my order but I know every day that vanilla latte will taste just a little better because one of them made it.

The idea of a latte went deeper than just going to Starbucks. Wherever I traveled—wherever I was—it was the one thing I tried to find before I started my adventure for the day. While walking through Spain I sometimes walked five miles to find a latte. It was the journey and a process of finding my latte that made the latte extra special. I took pictures of lattes whenever I went to a new place or new country. I prefer Starbucks lattes—that's just the preference of my taste buds so I try to find a Starbucks vanilla latte first. If they are not available then any vanilla latte will do. If I can't find a vanilla latte then a plain latte will have to do. And if I can't find a plain latte, a cup of coffee is still always appreciated to start my day.

One thing is for certain- I enjoyed the journey of finding my vanilla latte.

When life has so much unpredictability, my vanilla latte was always the one constant thing that I knew would happen every day or at least most days.

I can't forget the hearts or other art that came with the drink as well. I took some amazing pictures of lattes along the Camino de Santiago as well as when I went to China. My all-time favorite place to drink a latte was definitely at the beach on a cool day.

Each sip of my latte allowed me to relax and take in the world around me. Each sip of my latte reminded me to be present and appreciate everything around me and where I had gone to get to here, right now in this moment. I was happy and I was at peace.

In marriage you are on a journey together, but sometimes those journeys become separate for good reasons. Lawrence was on his own journey to sober up, but so was I. Would our worlds collide again or were we too far apart? Regardless, I was finally living the dream...my dream. In finding and seeing the perfection in myself I was able to see even more perfection in my life and all around me. I was literally stopping to smell the roses.

On the *Mama Drama* show, I was envious of Lawrence having an assistant, fridge stocked with monsters, and the cooked set meals he got every day. I was jealous of his days spent working on the beach in Monterey and Malibu, but I realize maybe it was jealousy. Did I want to achieve career goals too? Well, I needed to be happy for him. He sent me many photos from Malibu, but why was he in Malibu so much. Wait, hmm? Things didn't add up, but I needed to stop, I needed to be happy for him. That was all the work I'd been doing and it was time to implement it. Was I trusting my intuitions? I had to assume these were our divorce vows we were working on.

"Do you vow to celebrate what you have with Lawrence including your boys, your memories, family and friends?" asked the officiant as I noticed Lawrence had lost twenty pounds. Did he meet someone else? If so I needed to be happy for him. That's why we're here—to be the best for our kids and be happy for each other. They deserved this. They didn't deserve divorce, but if divorce became the only option, they deserved the best case divorce and parents that got along. Parents that loved each other.

"I do," I said with confidence. I wasn't wearing white as I said these vows. My Black Orchid Denim and Free People body suit would do. Unlike the professional hair and make-up on my wedding day, I had put on my Ned lip balm and some tinted moisturizer. I liked simple. It was time to find that again, especially within myself.

"Do you vow to celebrate what you have with Reece? Do you vow to celebrate your boys, your memories, family and friends?" Bryce, the divorce officiant, said with a calm tone. He was a tall handsome brunette and friend to both of us for years. Who knew the man Lawrence met on a drunk golf day with his studio exec would be the officiant for our pre-divorce vow ceremony?

"I do," Lawrence agreed flashing his soft green eyes. A piece of paper peeked out of his pocket. Did he write down his answers to the questions? Did he have something to read? We didn't write our marriage vows, why write divorce vows?

"And back to you. Do you vow to take 100% responsibility in your part of the failure of your marriage? Do you vow to forgive Lawrence for his mistakes in the marriage?" This felt surreal. I felt a different energy from Lawrence. The stressed workaholic seemed at peace. This was good for both of us. Clearly.

"And Lawrence, same to you. Do you vow to take 100% responsibility in your part in the failure of your marriage? Do you vow to forgive Reese for her mistakes in the marriage?"

"I do," I said as I looked Lawrence in the eyes. I gave it all I had. I did my best.

"I do," Lawrence agreed. We had rows of empty seats. Not one family member or friend supported us in our divorce. Well, one did, Bryce the man reading our divorce vows to us. Our parents had 90+ years of marriage altogether. They always said to make it work. That's when you know you have clarity and peace within, when you don't care what anyone else thinks.

"We do," we said in unison.

"And this is the hardest one. Reese and Lawrence, do you vow to be 100% happy for each other in future relationships, job decisions and life decisions?"

"We do," we said in sync taking these vows as seriously as we did on our wedding day, hopefully more seriously.

"By the power invested in me I now pronounce you happily capable of divorce or legal separation. Your six-month waiting period can begin." This divorce vow ceremony was something we learned from one of our counselors. She wasn't always for divorce, but if a couple chose that route, these were her vows the couple had to work on before filing. The vows focus was to keep the children the priority during the transition.

I closed my eyes. How did we get here? This was an interesting way to celebrate my birthday. Was I 100% sure about this? Yes. Many years of traditional marriage counseling, years of non-traditional marriage counseling, individual counseling, two marriage retreats and over 200k spent in saving our marriage. Yes, I was 100% sure. How did we get to this point? We did invest almost every dollar, well after memory making, into saving our marriage. The truth is even after all the pain, I found a way to love him as the father of my children.

I walked away in my wedges. I turned around and he smiled at me. I kept walking. It just didn't add up. We could have been so good, but still the trust wasn't there. We had everything but trust. He couldn't trust me and vice versa. The vows, I agreed to the vows, but the trust–I had to remind myself this is why I am doing this, but still something just didn't add up, it never did. I had to remind myself we brought out the absolute worst in each other at times and we just couldn't take it anymore. It was time to forgive myself and forgive him for the faults of our marriage. I did my best. Could he say the same?

# Episode 21

## LAWRENCE AND REESE TOGETHER AGAIN, SEASON 2?

**Soundtrack:
Don't Go Breaking My Heart
(Backstreet Boys)**

I once read a perfect marriage is just two imperfect people who refuse to give up on each other. The crazy thing is, the more Lawrence and I worked on ourselves and stuck to our divorce vows, the more we shifted and were attracted to each other again. The things I thought I needed from him were really things I needed from myself. I was on a flight from Monterey to San Diego, tapping away on my laptop, getting some good writing time in. The kids had just been background extras on Lawrence's current show for a few days and my SD family and friends had joined us. It was the perfect trip. I can truly say that I didn't know what the future would bring, but I was at peace and was hopeful of being in love again with Lawrence. Was it realistic to give us a shot?

"Come here, Reese--come sit out here with me," Lawrence said, guiding me outside. A few weeks had passed and he was back home with us for a weekend.

"Okay, you are so sweet," I said, looking at the salmon

dinner he had cooked for both of us. He definitely showed his love through acts of service.

"Surprise," he said, smiling and pulling out the bench for us to sit, facing the hot air balloons while we ate. The whole time we'd lived in the fancy mansion, I'd never appreciated the hot air balloons. This was the first time. It was stunning and moving seeing the giant colorful orbs float right before us.

"And my favorite wine, Moscato. Thank you," I said giving him a kiss as he started to screw off the cap to the cork free bottle.

"Cheers," he said as he handed me my glass of wine. I couldn't help noticing his green eyes, and his long eyelashes surrounding them, but then something felt off again. He took a sip and smiled.

"Cheers," I said right back, "I like us right now."

I was pondering these thoughts, knowing full well that both Sterling and Trent were at friends' houses for sleepovers. No kids, just me and Lawrence. Wait, I thought he was sober. . I don't want to ruin this moment. Should I ignore it? Everything is so peaceful. This just doesn't add up. It never does. He went to rehab. **Why is he drinking?** I am going to let it go. We are perfect. Life is perfect.

It's called falling in love again. It's about being able to find a soundtrack that you both enjoy together no matter who else is around you or what's going on. Marriage is a series of scenes and I truly believe you have to keep fine tuning and changing together to find harmony and sync.

We enjoyed our first dance, but if I had to choose a last dance with Lawrence, I guarantee it would be very different and maybe even more enjoyable –If you've done the work.

From the contemplation of divorce almost a year ago to the present moment, I finally believed that miracles did happen. I was still married and couldn't wait for our next adventure together. Life was good and life was hard at times, really hard, but I had accepted the amazing hand of cards I had been dealt, and had begun making some of my own luck. I had truly accepted myself for who I was. I still wore a ten dollar wedding band from Target on my finger although we had way more money to our name than we started out with. The most important things had remained the same. We were a family and we always did things our own unique way. But what had genuinely changed was my understanding of perspective and that had been a game changer.

But having a child with an illness always tests you to see how strong you really are, no matter how good a perspective you have on things. It questions how hard you want to fight to get to the surface. Because if you give up along the way, you drown. But no matter how hard the weight pulls you down into the darkness, you have to keep fighting. You have to fight for love, you have to fight for your family, you have to fight for your children, but most of all, you have to fight for yourself to live the life you want to live.

If there's a hand trying to pull you in a different direction away from the surface, ignore the hand and keep swimming to the top. There are hands coming from the surface so look up, reach up and grab those hands or grasp the edge. Those hands are your friends. Those hands are your family and those hands are your support, the life coaches, the counselors and, at times, strangers. And if you feel that little push edging you to the surface, please believe in angels because they are all around.

And when you get there, breathe and feel the joy, the triumph and the strength you used to fight. Celebrate how far you have come. Don't take that breath for granted, because I did for way too long and it was one of the main reasons I was unhappy.

Next time you sink, remember the feeling of getting to the surface and seeing the light. Try not to go back into the depths. It's a long road out. The more you change your perspective and work on yourself, the easier it is to stay at the surface and bounce back if you fall in again. You will not have to fight as hard. You will be stronger and you will be lighter. I wanted to feel loved, but I just had to love myself. That was the real answer for all of us. That answer we were all searching for. I wanted to feel free, but I just had to free myself of sadness, painful wounds and worries and darkness. I wanted to be heard, but I just had to listen to myself. I wanted joy, but just had to open my heart. I wanted to be held, but I just had to hold myself up – I was always strong enough. I wanted someone to take the pain away, but I had to do that for myself. I was looking for someone to be my everything and that's where I had gone so wrong. What I really needed was to be all those things for myself and appreciate my life and what my husband brought to our marriage. And that was a lot.

I already had freedom. Lawrence was hardworking, not absent. I could do whatever I wanted, my only limitation was me. What had I been so sad or worried about? I was already free. New perspectives brought new meaning to everything. I could embrace and enjoy the smallest things all of a sudden. The TV industry gave my husband something I couldn't. I got what I couldn't get from my husband or my girlfriends. Escaping to work gave him what he needed. Everybody talks about downs in life. But I can look at it like a personalized diet. Not all of our bodies are the same so why would our formula to happiness be the same? Alma did that for me. It's about getting to know who you are and being present in the moment with who are you. Being present is what keeps you calm and keeps you yourself. When we are aware of ourselves we are able to truly know ourselves and when we know ourselves we are able to be in harmony.

With my boys and Lawrence by my side, working on a happy, healthy marriage and achieving something for myself, I am living the dream I wanted. That was always my real dream. Back when I was younger, I didn't think I had a goal, but I did. It was always about family and communion and that's exactly what I had. When I finally realized that what I got in life was not only what I needed, but actually what I wanted, it was a big shock. But a good one. Sometimes the best, most beloved shows do get a second season. Will ours? Happy 12 Years, Lawrence.

I gently placed our Season 1 book in the mail and addressed it to the Peachtree studios in Georgia. It had been six months since I saw him at our divorce vows. Inside the cover I wrote...

# Season 2

# Episode 1

Soundtrack:
The Secret of You
(Juni Ata)

December 29, 2017

*T*o my Lawrence:
*The day at our divorce vow ceremony there was a weight lifted off my shoulders. We were happy for each other and we had grown to love and respect each other. I was happy that we gave it our all and we chose to become better people for ourselves and for our children before the divorce. I was happy for us, but most of all I was happy for the better man you became. At the same time, I was sad. I was sad because in my gut I knew something was off and something didn't add up. How can this amazing man still have lies and secrets that he keeps from me? Was 100% a divorce right for us? It doesn't matter how much you have if you don't have trust. Then I saw a piece of paper in your pocket. Was there something to say? Was there something I was missing? You didn't say anything so*

*I walked away and started writing. Here is my gift to you. This is our amazing love story and how hard and rewarding marriage can be. I hope you can see it. But unlike that day you proposed to me, I am really leaving this time. I wanted to write a letter to explain to you how great my life is with the real you in it, but I know you are not a letter guy so I wrote you a book, and hoping you could be a book guy, I wrote this for you. Here is our love story. The good, the bad, and the ugly. Maybe you will find the answers as to why I am walking away for a while, hopefully not forever. Maybe you will find the answers as to why you should walk away from me. Look within yourself. Only you know what I am talking about. I hope you will understand why. I will always keep a space of hope for you. I will always love you. This is it, now is the time. Do you have something to say?*

*I did my best and that's all I can do. Thank you for this beautiful life. Please forgive me for the mistakes I have made. I forgive you.*

*Yours Truly,*

*Reese*

# Episode 2

## His Script Notes

**Sound Track:**
**Half Hour**
**(Juni Ata)**

An envelope arrived in the mail with a letter from Lawrence. it was folded. it read

Open me: what I had to say that day at the divorce vow ceremony.

*Dec 31, 2017*

**B**abe,
I'm sorry I've been so distant and I'm sorry I have not been there for you these past years. Perhaps my timing for honesty is too late. I just want you to be happy, though I question my role in that. I agree to be happy for each other, but today is the day I promise to be honest with you forever. I was diagnosed with a fatal disease and they gave me five years to live if things don't turn around. My disease has progressed so much it will be hard to cure

*it. I have a team that is trying to help me, but they say I am in denial of how bad my disease is. I have been battling for a while. I have ups and downs, I have good days and bad days, good weeks and bad weeks, good months and bad months, good years and bad years. I had not mustered up the courage to be 100% honest about my disease, along with the fact that it's not going so well. I feared the disease would take me before I told you. I have enjoyed working on myself and working together on being better people and parents. The studio I have been working with knows and they have let me get help while shooting on location. It's not because I don't want your support; it's just that I want you to be able to give all you have to our kids. I want you to keep Sterling healthy and I don't want to take away from the care you give him. The boys need you the most. I'm sorry I don't hold you enough or touch you enough. I know you may hate me because I kept this from you for so long. That is why I have been taking out of town shows, including the one no one has heard of. I pretended to work on a show out of town to try a new center.*

*I have received treatments from several hospitals depending on my location. Work has distracted me from the fact that I won't be here much longer, even though I tell the doctors my disease is not as bad as they think.* Every day is a battle. I don't know how else to explain it.

*I didn't want you to spend years in sadness, knowing this because I feel like you just became happy again.*

*I'm still going to fight. But the memories we make every weekend mean the world to me.*

*Just know it's not that I don't love you more than the world itself, I just could not hurt you more and the kids.*

*You have all your friends and family in San Diego and you have all your LA friends as well so I know as long as* you stay in southern California you're pretty much covered for support. The reason I agreed to move to San Diego was because I knew this was your best shot with the kids when I am gone or when I go into treatment again.

I know it appears that I've been working so much the last few years but for part of that time I appeared to be working I've been in the hospital working on myself too.

My assistant has been helping me as I have not wanted to be a burden to you.

I've also saved up enough money so that you can continue to make as many memories as you want with the kids and never have to work again.

I have also saved up enough money to pay off your parent's house so they can help you with the kids and allow you to pursue your dreams as well. Residuals are a blessing. Good thing I produced a lot of syndicated projects.

I'm sorry for the shadiness, the lies and my affair with my disease during my treatments. I don't know how much I have left or how much time I have, but every second spent making memories I am a little bit happier. I know we made a pact to make memories for our kids but I didn't realize the memories were for me too. I am glad we live the way we live. I'm glad that we live for today. I'm sorry for keeping this from you. I love you more than you know. Thank you for standing by my side all these years even when I'm an asshole.

Do me a favor and no matter how hard times get, continue to make as many memories as possible.

So before you walk away and go through with any big decision. Yes. Something has been missing from our marriage and a part of it is me. You are strong enough and you are independent enough to make it without me. You are going to have to be; you can do this. You already have.

*During our divorce vow work, I decided it may be better for us to get divorced so you could find a man that could fully support you emotionally and be an amazing stepfather to our kids.*

*I know you were thinking it was maybe what was best for us and our relationship in general but the only reason I was agreeing to do it was to give you the opportunity to meet someone else because the doctors say my disease is getting worse. I try so hard and I just can't get better. I am trapped in my body and am battling every day for you guys and it's just not enough. I never would've agreed in a healthy, free state. I realize my honesty was missing from our marriage. I can't even be honest with myself. I thought for the greater good, but I am regretting that choice, although I know it's the best choice. I know you are the most loving and caring person to a fault and after all we have been through you still wanted to work on it.*

*I just want you to be happy. I didn't think I would make it to now. But here we are. A blessing I am alive, but sadly this may be it for us. Can you forgive me? You are now happy, but I am sad and I need you to understand that. This is a battle you can't fight with me or for me.*

*There is the best marriage retreat in the country, June 5th. meet me there. Sundance, Utah.*

*Lawrence*

# Episode 3

## Hɪᴀᴛᴜꜱ

**Soundtrack:**
**I Am the One**
**(Juni Ata)**

was beyond confused again. That was so much to take in. Was it cancer or was it alcoholism? I thought he already got help. I thought he was sober. He didn't say cancer. It has to be cancer. He is not an alcoholic. He is a TV producer. He drinks too much at parties, but *I* never see him drink too much. Gosh, I drink too much at parties sometimes. He is always cooking and cleaning when he is home and always playing with the boys. You can't produce number one shows on television and be an alcoholic. Is that the disease? No, it can't be. Is that the reason for our fights? Is that why things don't add up? No, it can't be. I am not married to an alcoholic. The father of my children is not an alcoholic. I started to cry. I don't get it. It doesn't make sense. My parents never drank and I was never around it in my childhood home.

If it's alcoholism, he shouldn't be drinking at all, and if he is still suffering from it, does he or does he not have cancer? I can't do this. Nothing adds up ever. Is alcoholism a disease?

We can't be together. I don't trust him. But now I feel terrible; I want to help him. Here we go again. My fix-it tendencies of wanting to help someone even to the neglect of my own needs. I don't trust him, I have dealt with lies yet I still want to just forgive and move on. This is the struggle of my life with Lawrence. Loving him in a healthy way. It makes sense. I can't help but love a man that is sick because I want to take care of him and fix him to the point that my needs are not met. He knows that and he did it for me. He agreed to get divorced. It is the best decision for us. We can't be healthy together and if we don't have a healthy reciprocated love, then we will both never be fulfilled. We are happiest apart with space. You can't work on a marriage if you don't have a sober partner. It's pretty much impossible. There was only thing I could control and it was myself.

"You know what? Really, he wants to do a marriage retreat? Fine, I will go." Was I crazy to try?

## Marriage Retreat Diaries
## Pre-Retreat Counseling (over the phone)

Lawrence scheduled the pre-retreat phone call, but they said we had to do the interview together. Lawrence flew home form Monterey for five hours and headed back. We did our phone session, but agreed not to talk until the retreat with a third party.

During that first pre-marriage counseling phone meeting Lawrence farted while we were on speaker with that counselor, Terry. I couldn't stop laughing.

The director proceeded to tell us that it was a non-alcoholic retreat and asked if there were any drinks we wanted in the refrigerator we could request them.

I quickly responded with, "Red bull and blue Monster for Lawrence."

Terry returned with a pause and said, "We don't promote energy drinks here." Lawrence agreed to bring his own.

Then me, not being any better with caffeine intake, asked, "Where is the closest Starbucks?" He said I could walk down to Sundance Resort for a latte or make one at the house.

Our conversation was very nice as we answered simple questions as to how we met? Where we met? The things we hoped to gain from the retreat? Terry seemed very kind and Lawrence and I were throwing funny signs and faces at each other while trying to answer the questions seriously. It was fun.

Terry asked what drew us to each other and how we met. I said I was attracted to him initially and then also said I was attracted to the fact that he was hard-working like my dad.

Could anybody fulfill the things I wanted? I felt bad for thinking this. No, others were not the fathers of my children. No one gave me these gifts—my boys--except him. No one could replace the father of my babies.

Then Lawrence said...he was attracted to me because I'm spontaneous and I have good family values. I didn't know if he intentionally didn't say anything positive about the physical characteristics and being attracted to me that way. It's okay because I'm confident enough in myself but it is sad that I am questioning the fact that he didn't say anything or if he intentionally didn't say anything and that was scary to me.

Before this retreat—in the weeks leading up to our initial call--Lawrence said he would do anything to make our marriage work. He suggested the retreat and booked it. But now his attitude seemed to be negative. It was frustrating. He asked me to go meet him there and was now being resistant. This was not adding up again. I was only going because he asked me to meet him there.

I shared some personal stuff about a friend after our phone call. It was horrible stuff that she's gone through and he broke down crying, "She's been through all those things and we're worried about going to some stupid little retreat."

I said, "What our friend has gone through is sad, but I think our marriage is important and you were the one who wanted to do this with me. You don't make any sense."

Then he tried to explain himself, "I'm just saying I can't believe we have to go to this retreat to figure out our crap."

And that's when I realized the words he said to me did not appear true. He didn't truly want to go to the retreat and he didn't want to work on the marriage together and have serious conversations, while I thought the retreat would be good for that.

It really hurt my feelings. After everything we'd been through and us both having a desire to work on our marriage, he made it clear that he did not have any desire to go to this retreat and didn't want to go. I was really looking forward to it. It even happened to begin on my birthday. After the retreat we were deciding if we were going to stay together or go our own ways in peace, but either way we were going to go in peace.

I was hurt the most because he'd talked to me as if he had wanted to go to the retreat. His letter!!! What changed again? I was the one that caved in, wanting a separation because I couldn't physically and emotionally handle being in a marriage where something is missing. Aside from all the good times, there's just something really strong that was missing. And when we were talking with the counselor on the phone I realized something: *neither one of us said that we liked the way we made each other feel.*

I said I wanted to be in a marriage that had peace and joy and he said he wanted better communication and less stress and anxiety.

I'd really tried to be supportive of his job and tried to be really supportive when he asked the counselor if he would be able to use a cell phone if he needed to work while we were at the retreat. It made me sad that the thought which crossed my mind was like "is there another woman?" This is not healthy and this is part of the reason I really wanted to go but from all the books I'd read it takes two people that want to work on it. We both had tried to work on it on our own but a retreat was supposedly something that we both agreed on and he said he really wanted to go, but now that's clearly not the case. I didn't like how I felt around him. Especially right now.

I would show up, but let's be honest. I planned to enjoy hiking and the outdoors surrounding Sundance Resort.

He showed up. Shocker. Alright, I was sucking up my pride and ego. Here goes another shot and I couldn't believe I was trying again.

## Day 1

June/5 my bday , anniversary and 6/5- 65 Roses Day
(Kids have a hard time pronouncing cystic fibrosis so they are taught to say 65roses to help with the pronunciation)
We took the lift-Ray's lift (It reminded me of Raymond from Melody Ranch)and took two peaceful hikes.

1. Drybed loop
2. And a steeper one-Mandan summit

I was loving the names of the dried up ski runs.

"Top Gun," "Maverick," and "Wedding Ring."

Green grass lined the slopes and at the top of Mandan summit. We could see waterfalls. The Stewart Falls trail was closed.

Down below, a bride and groom were taking some pre-wedding photos under the "Wedding Ring" sign.

Would I still be wearing my wedding ring after this weekend?

Lawrence was present and respectful when he had to take a few calls.

The groom ran up the Mandan trail with his father to get a good look at the view we were taking in and she yelled at him to get back down the mountain to finish their photos. I was sliding down at a slow pace while he ran past us, flipped over and somehow missed a large boulder. He's so lucky.

I couldn't imagine him getting hurt on his wedding day.

As they were getting back on the lift to go down to Sundance Resort she said, "Don't get blood on my dress. Don't touch me."

So far it's been an amazing birthday morning. I hope it continues to be an amazing birthday weekend and retreat.

In marriage it requires two wanting and very willing partners to both be there together. I think it says a lot.

Are we healthy for each other?

Has too much damage been done?

Can we fully forgive? Fully change or is the damage that's been done irreparable?

The morning was over and it was time to head to the retreat.

The first day we got a ride from our Sundance resort room to a Sundance cabin just up the road on Timphaven. It was not too far up the road. We got out of the car and tipped the gentleman for the ride. I held my vase of red roses that Lawrence surprised me with for my birthday. Lawrence carried most of the luggage as I walked into the cabin with my red roses. I was not a huge flower person but roses were a symbol of Sixty-five roses—again what kids say instead of cystic fibrosis, so the one flower I liked was roses. How sweet of Lawrence to remember that. It was my birthday, anniversary and 6/5 roses day all on the same day.

As we entered the beautiful wooden luxury cabin just up the street from Sundance Resort, I felt safe. We were greeted by the retreat counselors and they told us to run around the cabin and choose a room. So we did. We ran downstairs and put our stuff in the downstairs room next to the movie theater. The temperature was cool downstairs, so I thought it was perfect for Lawrence. He got hot easily. I was okay bundling up in blankets. Bears were the theme of the three story cabin. In addition to six large rooms there was a hot tub on the deck, sauna, steam room and game loft with foosball.

This was going to be a great week. Not only was the cabin perfect for my needs and tastes, the Sundance Resort was just down the hill. I unpacked and quickly read my devotion and did a rewire. I was going to embrace this experience with a good attitude and open heart. I was here for a reason.

We were the second couple to arrive.

One couple sat on the couch. Durae was beautiful, with bright blue eyes. She retired after selling her furniture business. We exchanged smiles. We would be spending time together at meals and I sensed a nice warmth. Her husband Jim, a CEO of a software company, too was sweet and I was excited to get to know them better. They were from Arizona.

Lawrence and I then went out to the deck to meet two

other couples that had just arrived. One couple was re-tired doctors in their late 60s from Missouri and the other couple was the exact same age as us. The husband was a director at Disney and the wife ran a tattoo parlor in Los Angeles.

There were four couples and the two retreat leaders— a married couple of 45 years. I would doubt the retreat's credibility if the leaders were not married themselves.

The retreat was for any religion in which a moment of silence was taken before each meal to worship however you choose.

Three of the most important things I learned at the retreat.

Anyone can be married, but to have a healthy marriage

1. it takes two
2. center principles
3. belief in a higher power(GOD)

## Day 4-Last day of retreat

I sit here on this bench as the water flows in front of me. This was representative of the tears that flowed as well. The sun is beating on my neck. The Sundance mountains are be-hind me as well. I am tired and mentally exhausted. Should marriage be this hard? If I want an everlasting one, this part is hard. If I want a marriage for eternity it's going to take a lot of work. Marriages that go through so much pain and deep trust problems are very hard to repair but it can be done. Do I have what it takes? No, I just spent the week ana-lyzing myself and my marriage. I am very sensitive. My heart hurts because I am so exhausted. Lawrence and I went to lunch and we had nothing to say. We made commitments at the retreat. But will we follow through with them? No, of course not.

It really is over. Time for me to accept.

The retreat went terribly. We shared a town car to the Salt Lake City Airport. On the car ride we agreed to be done. We were both exhausted.

Lawrence flew from the retreat to Georgia to work on a new show. I hopped off the plane in San Diego and my brother picked me up. I was in tears yet again. I was done. So I did it. I called my lawyer and said I was ready. She was the best attorney in San Diego and reminded me I had already paid a retainer fee. There, of course, could be more costs depending on how amicable we stayed, but since the decision was mutual and we agreed to be friends, it should be a quick case.

I started filling out the paperwork needed to file.

Lawrence, who agreed to the divorce, was acting so strange.

He was in Georgia and I was in California taking care of the boys.

I could not help him. I was across the country.

# Episode 4

## THE CREEPY SHOW

**Soundtrack:**
**What Do You Want**
**(Jerrod Niemann)**

**Let Me Fall**
**(Juni Ata)**

He was now living in a six bedroom Georgia house working on a creepy Stephen King novel turned into a series.

He rented a big house in hopes of us coming out, but I was tired of fighting. He was arguing with me over silly things and yelling at me for not having the kids near their phones. Does he really expect Trent to answer the phone at soccer practice? Please.

He called me crying.

"What is your deal? We both agreed to this and we know it's best," I said, concerned. "We have been up and down for years and through all extremes, I can't physically handle this; put me out of my misery already."

"You did it, I can't believe you did it," he said

dramatically and frantically. "I am not doing well. I can't deal with this and work stress right now."

"Are you okay? You are scaring me. You do not sound okay. Who is the girl I hear in the background?" I paused for a few moments and seriously was super worried about him.

"That's Karey, my assistant, she is here helping me. I have been throwing up all night and just shaking from the anxiety of you moving forward with the divorce. I can't believe you really did it." He blamed me while crying.

I got on Instagram and messaged his assistant. I did not have her number, but we followed each other on Instagram. This girl had my credit card and I didn't even have her cell.

*ME: Something is not okay with Lawrence. I am worried.*

*KAREY: He is doing better. The news of the divorce really shocked him. The doctors are here. He is just really dehydrated and stressed, like a panic attack from it.*

*ME: "Do I need to fly out there? I am at Paradise Point for my kids' friend's birthday, but I can fly out if I need to, but not sure if that the best.*

*KAREY: He will be fine. I got it under control. He said he doesn't need your help.*

I felt bad not being there. We agreed to get a divorce, but I just wanted to help him. I needed to stop. My helping was not helping. He will be fine. He has an assistant and doctors. Sometimes helping is doing nothing apparently. I had to let him be. I had two boys right in front of me in San Diego that needed me so badly. They needed my love and I couldn't leave them. Okay. I would stay. I told myself I'd put a smile on my face and enjoy the party. I did. I was getting good at this. Trying to focus on what's right in front of me could be challenging and rewarding.

The next day I called the attorney's office and asked her to hold off on filing. Lawrence needed some time and was in no place to even have custody of the kids. I didn't want to tell them he was sick so I just said he was taking it hard and had a lot of work stress. I hated lying, but not everything in life is meant to be shared. I would explain later, but there is no way Lawrence was in any shape to go through a divorce. Okay, I was strong enough and would give him space and support at the same time. This was hard for me, but this was how I help. Let him live his own journey. If I didn't stay strong and take care of myself the kids would not have a mother or a father. I wanted someone to hold me. I was alone again.

# Episode 5

## Jet Lag and the Deal

**Soundtrack:**
**He Can**
**(Robbie Conrad)**

**Six Months Later...**

His Atlanta show ended and he flew home days later. I didn't know what to expect or what to say; I just knew he needed help. I got a personal trainer for me and scheduled yoga for Lawrence before my session. This worked a few times, but Lawrence was soon over it. He could barely hold himself up. I still loved this man and I couldn't save him. He was home in San Diego. I encouraged him to go to the beach. I wanted him to find the soul of the man that matched with mine that night, the first night we met. The surfer, the jokester and my best friend. I had been deprived of his support and reciprocation for quite some time. It was apparent. He couldn't help me or give me support. He needed to help himself. I was drowning again.

When Lawrence moved home the kids and I had

expectations of all this special family time, but our expectations were wrong. He was there in person, but not present.

"Lawrence, what is going on with you, you are home, but not happy. You have our boys, the beach and everything important to you and I am worried about you," I said as he lay on the couch. He lay there all day.

"It's just been a lot and the work stress is still coming even though I am here. I shouldn't have left Atlanta."

"Then go back. I got it. Go do what you need to do because the kids are asking why Dad is not the same, why Dad is sad?"

It's like the universe knew what we needed. The owners of our mansion decided to sell it. We had 30 days to be out. Luckily, I found a beautiful home for lease just two miles from the mansion and near my sister. She was always so supportive and we could help each other out even more and the cousins could have their cousins to ride bike to one another's houses. We would be downsizing in some eyes, but upgrading in my eyes. We were moving near a lake with fishing and boating. We could walk there. The mansion was fun, but I was getting tired of everyone thinking we were loaded, because we were not. Money flowed easily to us, but we helped it flow out to make memories and support causes dear to our hearts. Moving would save us $6000 a month. Why wouldn't we move? Would we have some new unexpected expenses? Lawrence, at one time, had all this money set aside for us, but it seemed to disappear. I was starting to regret not signing his dad's yolo pact.

Lawrence left and flew back to Atlanta to deal with the work stress. I could not have it in my home with my babies. I could not have it around me. I knew he was on his journey and I was on mine, but I was getting battle fatigue. It was time to revisit my self-help list and modify a little. I had failed to do it daily and I needed to be strict if I was going to survive this and be the best for my boys.

Every day I needed to:

- **Read my daily devotion-remember that Jesus was by my side holding my hand and no matter how alone I felt I had him to guide me. (believe in God)**
- **do some rewires(for example thank God for my past, remind myself that I know how to support my family, my favorite one was 'everything works out.' It does) I did four exercises with these rewires to help them sink into the subconscious. When you have battle fatigue you have to train your mind and keep it strong for yourself and your children.**
- **Work out-Tues/Thursday trainer**
- **Mon, Wed soccer**
- **Wed, Fri run**
- **Any other free time walk**
- **See Alma every week to clear head—life coach says combine her science with faith**
- **For example rewire: I am strong for my boys**
- **"Dear Lord, help me be strong for my boys. Take my burdens from me."**
- **With Alma, trainer Glenn, my friends and family I could do this.**

Days passed in Atlanta. I had not heard from Lawrence. I called and texted and finally got through to his assistant just to see if he was alive from whatever disease he had. Whatever it may be? I was starting to feel crazy. I didn't know what to think or believe anymore.

I wanted to give up and walk away, but my job was to

make sure the kids had a dad while allowing him to be on his own journey.

Whether I woke up to a good day or a bad day, I made sure I got in the car and went to Starbucks. It was my routine. Whether it was Ellen asking me if I was okay, she could always tell when I was struggling or Marc telling me I was beautiful, or Stella asking me about my kids, they were part of my battle training plan to keep me strong.

They had no idea that I woke up praying my kids would have a dad, but every day I was greeted with kindness and respect. I worked on the school foundation and would run into the moms at Starbucks. They asked me how I was doing? I always wanted to be real, but could you imagine me saying "Doing great, my husband is sick and I don't know if he will live or die." I helped plan the school auction and people thanked me for my help. God, if they only knew that planning this was giving me a bigger sense of purpose.

I ran into another mom at Starbucks. "I want your life," she said.

"You don't want my life," I replied.

"No, I do. I get jealous following you on Instagram and Facebook," she smiled. "You are always on amazing trips and at 5 star accommodations."

If she only knew, she would not want my life. She would want my incredible boys and trips, but definitely not all of my life.

So, yes, I didn't work for money, but working on myself and helping the school brought me the joy and peace I needed to stay strong. Giving time and money made me happy. Dealing with a loved one with addiction is like getting the shit kicked out of you every day mentally.

I did the move near my sister's family of six without Lawrence, Single moms move, why couldn't I? I hired a group of Marines that needed cash and they rocked it. I paid babysitters and friends to help me unpack and five days later we were fully moved in. Lawrence came back home, but was a mess. I even had people help me put my boys' beds together. My sister and family and friends all came together. Most didn't know my struggles. I just said Lawrence was working from home when he was lying in the guest room. I struggled daily about whether I was doing enough to help him. If he died would I hate myself forever? Was I in a nightmare? Was I in denial? I still had to keep it all quiet to protect my boys and for fear of his mortal struggle with addiction getting out into Hollywood. I wanted Lawrence to leave the industry on his terms, but he needed a break. If the truth got out, he would lose his job and we would lose his insurance. I needed to get a job just in case, I would continue to write. It was the only way to be there for the family.

I told myself to just keep going. During this period my kids spent a lot of time at my parents' house. My job was to keep them from seeing their dad in a bad place. I could not have a straight conversation with him to help him.

Ellen came over from Starbucks and helped me unpack too. She didn't want anything. Starbucks is more than a coffee; it's a community. This village was truly a village. She just said friends help friends out. God is good. Nobody really knew what I was going through except my family. I didn't really know what I was going through either. I just tried to survive one day at a time.

God is still good. In the new house, the kids were excited about their new rooms and new places they could ride their bikes to.

Lawrence tried to play with the kids but still was very stressed. There was just ongoing stress. Even though I thought he took care of it, it didn't stop. He was irrational, argumentative and I was helpless.

"Lawrence, can you tell work that you need to stop, you need to take care of yourself? I don't care if you have to lie and say you have cancer, but you need to take care of yourself."

"They don't understand. They just put me on a new show," he mumbled.

"Did you try to talk to them?" I pleaded.

"They offered to buy me out for the year. This is what I worked so hard for, so hard for I can't ask them for time now. I am signing the deal of a lifetime," he said falling over.

"You are not going to be here to have this deal of a lifetime if you don't take some time off," I cried.

"You don't get it, you never will. By the way, the studio will never understand. They keep sending me scripts for the next show," he yelled with bloodshot eyes.

"You are scaring me. You just got a huge box from them by the way."

"That's my wrap gift," he quickly opened it and put ten bottles of Grey Goose in a cabinet. "I needed to get that out of the house and quickly.

The next day I drove Trent to his soccer game in Del Mar at the polo fields and Lawrence met us there.

Lawrence could not find the field and missed almost half the game. This wasn't like him. He was not himself— who that was I did not know anymore. He was the chattiest I had ever seen, yet the sloppiest.

Is he buzzed at 8:00 a.m.? I knew he still struggled with alcohol sometimes, but in public? I thought he had cancer or a disease. Lord, help me. Was I in denial? I just wanted to snap my fingers and make it all go away. I wanted to wake up from this nightmare. What if people we know saw him like this? They would know he is not himself.

I was on my own journey. He was on his own journey. But what if he hurt himself or someone else? I would never forgive myself.

We left the field. I didn't want to be anywhere near him. I didn't want to make a scene. The next game he showed up and stood at the end of the field. This time he fell over and pretended to play with my nieces. Was he hammered? I didn't want to make a scene.

I drove home with my mom and Trent. Lawrence insisted he was not riding with us. Our oldest was at home. I did not want to make a huge scene, but after begging him to ride with us there was no point. I prayed to keep him safe.

Lawrence never made it home from the field. I sent my sister and her husband looking for him, but he was nowhere to be found.

I was afraid he was dead or possibly with somebody else, but thankfully he arrived home hours later.

"Where have you been?" I asked calmly trying not to escalate the situation.

"Oh, the time change from Atlanta, I fell asleep in my car."

I looked in the cupboard and four huge bottles of Grey Goose were gone. How is he still alive? Fuck. He is a functioning alcoholic and it has caught up with him. Everything started to make sense. I didn't want to accept it. This wasn't my life. This was not his life. This was not part of his plan. Our plan.

Our marriage or divorce was the least of our problems at this point.

I asked my parents to take the kids that night and of course they did.

I needed a miracle...

*"Dear Lord, I pray he will get better, I pray for you to*

*bring him back, the man I once knew. Every night I pray for a miracle. And every day I wake up and things don't change, I lose hope.*

*You want my burdens, well here they are. You can have them. All of them.*

*I feel angry, I feel sad, I feel hopeless, I feel helpless. I want my boys to have a dad. Is that too much to ask for them? I have one son with a disease and can't handle another. Why me?*

*Am I doing enough? I have been told the best I can do is be supportive and do nothing. Let him have his space, his own journey.*

*It doesn't feel right, what if he dies, and I didn't do enough?*

*Will you be there for me through that pain? Will you tell my kids and hold them when they cry day after day?*

*I was told people have to help themselves, is that true? Can you please help him? Amen. Get him to rehab and I will never stop believing in you."*

I stayed up all night praying and thinking how to get him to rehab. He was an alcoholic, maybe had a disease too. When it came to addiction I was naïve. I started reading about alcoholism. I started reading about functioning alcoholics. It all fully clicked. My mind went a million miles an hour. I had some clarity. Disease or alcoholism? Duh, that's what he was trying to tell me, **alcoholism is a disease that destroys** you. **HE IS BATTLING ALCOHOLISM.** Okay, what if I looked at alcoholism or alcohol use disorder, like another accepted disease-cancer? They destroy loved ones, leaving them hopeless. Survival rate for both vary. The main difference is that people would not judge you if you suffer from cancer, but if you struggle from alcoholism you sure are judged. I judged Lawrence. Nobody chooses cancer. Nobody chooses alcoholism. Nobody plans to get cancer and nobody plans to be an alcoholic. Yes, people choose to have a drink, but nobody plans to become addicted. Genetics can play a role in both. He was clearly battling addiction, but what if I talked to him as if he had cancer? Did he say disease instead of alcoholism because he feels powerless in his battle? Is he in denial about how bad it is? He seemed to admit that. After reading I came to the realization that alcoholism was a disease. Okay, I needed to think quick. The kids were out of the house and I did not have much time. Shit, all this time he was having an affair with vodka. I was accepting it for real this time. I was sad. I was angry. "Snap out of it, Reese." My boys needed a dad.

I woke up early while Lawrence was passed out on the couch and walked with my sister. I picked up Starbucks from Marc that morning and then met Makayla in the middle of our neighborhood loop. Marc could tell something was off.

"Makayla, I know he needs help or he for sure will kill himself or someone else, but I am still in shock. I have known it was a problem, but then he said it was a disease. I didn't realize how big of a problem it was. I have just been in denial and confused. Sterling has a disease; I don't know why he deserves to go through all this, but I do know I need to save his life and make sure he doesn't accidentally harm others."

"I think just go to him and tell him how worried you are," Makayla suggested. "You have nothing to lose, but he is so not well." This is truly what sisters are for.

"I seriously am afraid to ask him to go to rehab. I fear a fight, especially when he is past a point of reason. Everything I read says he has to hit rock bottom and he has to want to go. I hope this is his rock bottom."

"You have no other choice," she said. I felt bad I was putting my sister through this and adding worry to her life. I also knew I could trust her 100%.

I walked two miles, vanilla breve latte in hand, and then gained all the strength and calmness I needed to talk to Lawrence or the fragment that was left of him.

I walked in the house and there he lay in the guest room with a giant bottle of Vodka. Thank you for the wrap gift.

"Lawrence, about yesterday. I am worried about you. You do not look well. I want our boys to have a dad. If you want help I can get you help, but only if you want it." I prayed in my head. If there was a God this was his time to shine and I needed a miracle.

"I want help. I need help. I have been trying to tell you. Do you know what to do?" he asked, crying hysterically. I was shocked he agreed to go.

"I can get you help. If you want to go to rehab, I can take you today. There are some nice places here," I said calmly. The truth is I didn't have a place ready or even know what place was available because I didn't think the conversation would get this far. I thought he would tell me to fuck off and that he didn't have a problem. Think fast, I told myself. I only have a small window. **Miracles do happen!**

"Thank you, I don't deserve you, just leave me. What about Trent's soccer game?"

"The best thing you can do for your boys is to stay home. He is in the finals and Grandma will take him to warm ups. I will meet her there later at game time." I did not want anyone seeing him like this.

I called two places. One in La Jolla and they did not answer.

The next one I called was ten miles away. I left a message and five minutes later received a call.

# Episode 6

## Home Box Office and Lawrence's Angel

**Soundtrack: Getting Better
(Juni Ata)**

**Find Me I the River
(Cast of I Still Believe)**

"This is Steve; did you call?" a calm voice asked.

"Yes, for a family member, he needs help. It's alcohol. Just alcohol, I think. He is my husband and his name is Lawrence." Tears ran down my cheeks, again. This had been a long journey.

"I just ran home from church early because I forgot to put the groceries away and saw your call. I know this is probably overwhelming, but we can help him if he wants help. He will be okay. I promise."

I had 30 seconds to decide if I could trust this man with changing Lawrence's life. My gut said yes. I was getting better and better at trusting my gut. My gut had been telling me for years something was off. I just couldn't pinpoint it or accept it. The voices in my head said yes he is safe to trust. I think I found Lawrence's angel, because it couldn't be me anymore. I could not save him. It was not my job. I was not qualified. He was Lawrence's angel, but I knew he was our angel. It was time to heal myself too.

I sat there listening and just let the tears come down my face.

"Are you still there?" Steve asked.

"Yes, I am still here. Sorry, just overwhelmed. I am still processing everything. When can I bring him in? This is going to sound crazy, but my son is in soccer finals at the polo fields."

"Reese, it's going to be okay. I promise. I will help him. Let me get the team ready. If he is walking around, go to the game and bring him in after the game. I do need to talk to him." Steve was assuring and in that moment I mentally passed my fixer torch to him. I also just handed the rest to the Lord because I couldn't carry this burden anymore.

"Okay, yes he is walking around," I said looking at him.

"Can you get him on the phone?" Steve asked with calmness and security. He reminded me of my other angel, Brandon, the wedding angel. Okay, no time for fantasies, I needed to stay present. I wanted to escape this reality, but I had to face it.

"Yes, here he is." I handed Lawrence the phone.

Lawrence and Steve chatted for a minute and I knew it was going to be okay. Lawrence was slurring badly.

I got in the car with the biggest hat and glasses on and went to Trent's game in Del Mar. Trent played the best he had ever played. I continued to wipe tears streaming down my face during the medal ceremony and pretended I had a bug in my eye. I knew Lawrence would be okay, but it was a lot. My friend's brother helped me carry my chair and everything. It was like he knew I needed a boost, I needed some weight taken off me. The little things and the beauty they have in moments of need.

My mom took Trent to her house even though he begged to come with me. He could not go home and see his father in the state he was in. Sterling was with my dad and it needed to be this way until I could get Lawrence to rehab.

I got home and packed his suitcase with the list the nurse gave him over the phone. He couldn't write it down so I had to.

They had laundry facilities so he could wash clothes eventually.

- Sunscreen
- (5-7) changes of clothes
- Comfy/gym clothes
- Athletic shoes for trainer and yoga
- Hat
- Sunglasses
- Toiletries(I wasn't sure, but I packed anyway)
- I put Spike in there from our engagement day

They would go through whatever I packed.

Luckily, it was me packing so I filled up the suitcase with probably ten outfits. More than the norm.

I drove him to the address, trusting this team of people with the father of my children's life. This was my husband's life. I had never met these people, but knew I had to take a leap of faith. We pulled up to a mansion on a hill that over-looked the ocean. It was beautiful. I knew he was going to be okay, but I was scared.

I parked the car and got his suitcase out.

"I am scared," he cried. "Stay with me, don't leave me."

"I love you, but you have to do this on your own. I cannot

come, but I put someone in your suitcase, Spike, from the day you proposed. You are strong like a lion." I was crying now.

"Thank you." He started crying again. I hated seeing this tough man in this state. It ate at my heart and I felt like I was going to faint. I was numb.

It crushed me to see this 6 foot man, father, surfer, TV producer in this state, but I knew it could only get better. I knew I would get better too.

Could they save him? Could he save his career, the deal of his life that he just signed? I would do it. I would talk to his assistant. We could help save it.

We entered the mansion/rehab facility through the side door. We sat with the nurse for a while and took vitals as well as signed forms and answered questions. I hugged him and said goodbye.

### Rehab Diaries:
### DAY 1

Today was one of the hardest days of my life, but I do believe in miracles. I also felt a sense of peace as Lawrence agreed to check into rehab.

I didn't know how strong I was until today.

I was nervous making the call. I was nervous he would change his mind, but for the first time in years there was hope. Our boys will have a father. Steve promised me everything would be okay. I believed him.

We answered a million questions, got a tour and I said goodbye. As sad as this sounds. I said goodbye to our marriage and I said goodbye to our relationship. I couldn't mentally and physically handle any more. I needed to be strong for my boys and give Lawrence the space he needed. I needed to be held.

## DAY 2(day 1 detox)

I sat in the guestroom staring at the bed where I found him. The bed where I had the rehab conversation with him. I didn't plan on any new outcome that morning. Flashbacks started to swarm my mind, there was a glimpse of when I had suggested rehab in the past, begged him to go and he always denied there was a problem. I had asked him to get help, but he had told me I was crazy. I eventually just let it go. I drank with him at times. I denied it because it never did any good to fight him. He kept a great job and did all the fatherly things so I convinced myself there was no problem. So many flashbacks jolted my memory. I knew he needed it this time if he was going to live.

Hard tears flowed down my face as I stared at the bed. Tears were becoming my new look. There was a plushy I had made him for Father's Day. It was a stuffed body that you snuggle with, but to be funny I put the boys' pictures on the head so they could sleep with him while he was working out of town, a little snuggle buddy to remind him the boys were near. He clenched the plushy yesterday and I knew he wanted to live for them. Being away from the family all those times was probably part of the problem, but the pain he felt from the day Sterling was diagnosed was probably the root of it. Like I said. He was never the same after Sterling's diagnosis. It made sense. He poured alcohol in his wounds and could I blame him? He didn't plan on this outcome. It just seemed like temporary relief at the time that he grew to become dependent on.

More tears streamed down my face and I felt closure. I guess it was closure that I was in an unhealthy relationship for so long, but the right thing was to stay. My boys were my driving point. As many times as I wanted to leave our chaos

I wanted to make it work for them. I knew moving to San Diego would give me support if things hit the fan. Moving to San Diego gave them a bigger village and a chance at coming out of all of this. They may not have known what they were going through, but they did go through it.

Lawrence working out of town, I knew the kids could know their dad or what was left of his soul after the alcohol. It was the best of sad worlds.

He could be far away from us while he came to terms with his addiction, and the kids wouldn't be subject to it. I was in denial at times, but subconsciously knew what was best for them. I always had concerns, but did not truly believe he was a full blown functioning alcoholic. I hate labels. My mind had a weird way of dealing with it.

I did not realize the extreme of how much he consumed. I know it went in waves, but we had so many problems over and over and over. Everything I read said you can't have a marriage if you don't have a sober partner. I can't say I was always a sober partner either. I needed to work on this and if I couldn't I needed to check myself in too.

It had been a wild ride. Now it was time to take care of my boys and take care of myself.

I deserved love. I did what I had to do, but it was soon time to do what I need to do.

When he was better, when he was clean, it was time to say goodbye. My children would have a father a sober one. Time for me to heal. I needed someone to hold me right now.

I cried and cried and cried as I reflected on the times—the years when things didn't add up or make sense.

I know for part of it I was in denial. I knew I was. The more flashbacks I had, the more I knew I was. I was not perfect, but I was hard on myself.

I came from a family with parents that did not drink.

All the times he needed to go back to the hotel room, or back to the car, or when the neighbors questioned me about the ambulance. All the twists always made me think he was cheating on me. And he was cheating with a tall bottle of vodka. I knew there was some sort of affair. Should I have left? No. It had to happen like this. This is all part of God's plan. So I will not beat myself up. I did the best I could in each step of the journey until now. I would be compassionate to myself.

I will always love him. I will always be his friend, but it's time to do me. The best I am, the best I can be for my boys.

I don't want to be alone in a relationship anymore. I am proud of him.

I take no blame or responsibility for his addiction. I also don't know if he was struggling with this when we married. He was so good at hiding it.

When I checked him in he said he averaged at least 12 double shot mixed drinks a day.

He must've just added to everything he was drinking because I never realized it was that much. Yes, he took out the trash often, but I hated trying to keep track. It just caused stress.

———((●))———

Life has its own stress without career stress. I wonder how many people in the TV and film industry go to rehab? Wouldn't it be great if we could all support one another in those journeys and be proud of people for getting help? Could we get rid of the stigma, the judging when people are doing their best to get help?

Alma, my counselor, helped me see the big picture today. She came to my house.

My family is my rock. I am blessed. I believe in miracles.
I walked with my sis again.

## DAY 3

Mentally drained. Too tired to write much here.
Prayed he was okay at rehab.
I drove by the street where he was hoping to send good vibes.
Not his Pawn.
He tried to play me to get out of rehab. He said he needed to be right on the ocean, not a view.
Not happening.
It was hard to know what to believe in his head space. Was I talking to him? Was I talking to a disease?
I was wrong. Steve called and explained.
Lawrence just wanted more outside open air so Steve worked it out.
He decided to stay. No transfer to Passages in Malibu. So complicated.

## Day 4

Today I was angry. My mind felt out of control.
Yes, my goal in life was to save a life. I never thought it would be my husband's. I can't take credit. He saved himself with a little help from the man above.
There was so much chaos for so long. I fought for a marriage for years that couldn't be saved because, if your partner is an alcoholic, how can you work on your marriage until they get help? I did feel clarity. All the times I was angry because things did not add up. The lies.
I actually called his assistant to see if he was actually

cheating on me on top of the affair with vodka. My mind was all over the place. Why would she tell me if he was? I didn't hire her. He did.

I was going through finances to keep us on track and realized there were charges still happening while he was in rehab. Money didn't add up.

Then I realized it was charges going through later. Thank God. I couldn't handle any more surprises. There were numerous charges like from a perfume shop, in-home care(IVs), a lot of weird stuff.

It was sad- thousands of dollars of in-home care in Atlanta. All the nights he went too far.

I feel hurt that I allowed myself to be in an emotionally one-sided relationship in which he had nothing to give. I was happy he was getting help.

Now Lawrence is allowed to come home on the weekends after detox. I was taking the kids to Mammoth to get away in the mountains, my happy place. Now I needed to change plans so my parents offered to take the kids to Great Wolf Lodge. Lawrence wanted to see the kids. He was irritable and irrational for weeks so I don't think they had a desire to hang with him.

I don't like the fact that they are letting him call the shots at rehab. But the big picture is whether it helps him get better for the kids. Evan explained that being flexible was needed to keep him getting treatment. Evan explained he had a man wanting to live.

He may get sober, hallelujah, but he is still covered in terra-cotta and until he takes it off he has no love to give me. I appreciated him saying that I don't deserve this and he was sorry. Because I don't. I was proud of him aside from my pain. Proud he was willingly getting help.

I love him as the father of my children, but know I am definitely not his soul mate.

I have far outgrown my 21-year-old naive self and know what I want in a partner. A connection. Honesty. Trust.

This whole coming home thing at night stressed me out, I was not ready to have him home.

My sister helped me clear out the garage, backyard bar and kitchen from any booze.

All that was left were the huge Grey Goose bottles from his work. They could be used to give as great holiday gifts, although I struggled with putting alcohol in another home. I struggled regarding whether I will ever have another drink. I could donate the bottles to the school auction since it was off campus.

Rumor had spread at the studio that Lawrence was away to take care of our son with cystic fibrosis. Rumor had it that our son is not doing well.

We didn't start it. Telling someone their producer that handles multi-millions is in rehab can create a lot of doubt. If they could just understand his amazing potential sober.

I am staying off social media and need to keep an eye on the kids as well.

We cannot be seen having fun, etc. since everyone thinks it's serious with our son. It's not a lie we made up, but an assumption that turned into a rumor.

Everything works out.

So thankful for my family in all this.

### Day 5

Today I felt better. I worked out with Glenn. It's like God knew what was coming and set me up to survive it. I was in my village. My LA counselor was right. I would need family if things went sour. She knew it would. I had family around, I have Alma, I have a counselor. I have my devotional.

We have a beautiful safe home. I went to back-to-school night alone. No big deal. Lawrence couldn't always make these anyway. I had a moment where I read a poem Trent wrote. It was about the meaning of life and how sad he was when he saw people hurt others or themselves and when he saw people die. It was about world peace and it was beautiful.

He had artwork on the wall. His favorite possessions were our dogs-Lassie and Tucker. He's doing great in school. I sat there with the school foundation shirt on. If only they knew that the one who had rarely missed the foundation event planner and had raised a ton of money for the school was sitting here with a husband trying to get better in rehab. You never know what anyone is going through. And I don't like lies but sometimes they are needed. Trent thought his dad was on a business trip because knowing his dad is in rehab at ten is not going to help anyone. Same with Sterling. There would be a time for that and it was not yet. Lawrence and I could talk to them together when he got out.

They are both doing great! Sterling is on the middle school cross country team, and I am so proud of him. He was on honor roll all last year, but I think it's time to cut him some slack. He feels everything and knows something is off. We will talk to him as soon as Lawrence is ready.

Trent had soccer and hung with friends after. Sterling has Trevor over to hang out with.

When you are going through something actually hard, it's crazy how much little things do not matter—especially my boys' grades. They are bright. But I realize how little kind/positive things can carry so much good weight

Lawrence comes home tomorrow. The plan was to fully detox him and then he would spend every day at rehab for the next month, but nights he would be at home. I was angry at first, but he seems good. The program would not let him come home unless it was best for him and us. The program is working with us. The place on the hill might be a perfect safe haven in the future for other Hollywood actors and producers. It's so far off the radar who would know about it? There is a bigger picture and we can help so many more people.

He agreed to have me breathalyze him anytime at home. He said it was not necessary; he never wants to feel the way he felt during detox again. It sounds promising. I didn't want to be his mom, as I felt like I had been that for years. I was done. He was on his own journey and I was there to support. Could I?

I was praying he could stay strong because he has a long road ahead of him. I am grateful he is doing better, my sole purpose has been to make sure the kids have a dad, and now that the kids have a dad, they must also have a healthy dad. I could not imagine what Lawrence was going through to be sober.

My birthday wishes were always for him to be sober and Sterling to have a cure for CF.

At least one is coming true.

## Day 6 in rehab (day 5 of detox) (Friday)

He comes home today, we can do anything or go anywhere. I am happy, I am scared of the unknown. Everything works out. I got this.

We do need to stay away from crowds and can't run into anyone we know. Stymie Productions still thinks it's our son that is the medical emergency.

He wants the beach, the kids want Mammoth.

Does it work this way, at least a decade of a progressive

disease and five days to kill it? Well, there is still therapy and meetings to take away the terra cotta. Can he do it? I get it. Having a kid with CF with a shortened life expectancy is hard and horrible as a parent. I feel like it progressively got worse when our son was diagnosed, but I think there is more. He had a lot of struggles before our son so I think there is work stress to address and other wounds that were there when I met him. He was in good hands. Steve promised to never let go of his hands. I needed to let go.

Big and little lies were now my life for a while, well, our life to save his job, to save our insurance. This is why people lie at times. To protect the ones they love. It's wrong, but it can be necessary.

I picked him up. He was calm and relaxed and wanted to go shopping. He said he needed shoes and clothes. He also needed a Red Bull.

This was the first time in a long time that we were having a sober or non-irritable conversation.

It was nice. Did I know this man anymore? Is it going to be OK? I liked the stranger I was hanging out with. He was very nice. Pleasant, calm.

After shopping we came home and he made some comment about us having big marriage problems.

I straight up told him how upset I was with that because his behaviors had been contributing to our big marriage problems for years. After everything we'd been through this week he had the audacity to tell me that we had big marriage problems.

He finally admitted that he was the cause of many of his problems. I think that's what I wanted to hear because I bent over backwards to cover his ass all week, to do what was best for the kids and our family. I admitted that I didn't know if I was ready for him to come home. I was relieved,

I was happy, I was sad and I was angry. There were a lot of jumbled up emotions. I was honest that I was feeling all these things and I don't know if him coming home was the best thing. I wasn't sure if I could be that strong positive rock for him because I was just trying to be that for myself and the kids.

He said he was sorry. He said I didn't deserve any of it and he understood I was going to have all sorts of feelings and emotions and that was OK.

The thing he said that I will never forget...

"I am sorry, but ever since Sterling was born twelve years ago I have resented you. I have resented myself too. I didn't love myself and I didn't love you. I have resented you because you gave Sterling the cystic fibrosis. I did too, but that's why I have not been kind to you, basically our entire marriage."

"Thank you for being honest and thank you for making me strong," I said in tears. If I don't leave after that I don't love myself. I was already leaving, but thank you, God, for just making sure I never go back. Was Lawrence in a place that was truly making sense?

I explained that I didn't know if he was going to live or die numerous times. I explained that I never thought I'd be saving my husband's life and to hear him say that made me really sad. I got really angry and said the meanest things.

The worst is "I should have let you die." I will always regret taking the low road there. He hurt me one more time and I let him, but then I hurt him right back. No more. I was not good for him and his recovery. Could he please call his parents? I was not qualified anymore. I had no more compassion or empathy to give.

There's a part of me that wanted him to stay there and suffer being away from us. Would he think twice when hitting the bottle again? I shared with him that my heart took on a lot of pain over the last so many years and I don't think he realized that.

I would put a smile on my face until he finished rehab. I needed the kids to have a dad.

I cried to my sister. "How was this fair to me?"

"I don't know," she responded.

### Day 7(Sat)

Sober family BBQ with cousins at our home
Lawrence wanted to cook for everyone.
That was very kind.

### Day 8(Sunday)

10 mile walk (5 with Makayla and 5 with Lawrence)
Watched beach sunset
I was the paddle ball referee

### Day 9 (Monday) Labor Day

Brunch at my parents for my bros' birthday with our whole family
Shopping with mom and sisters

### Day 10

AA meeting
I talked to Alma as I felt angry again. We got to the root and sometimes feeling helpless makes me angry.

I felt helpless because he came home and I didn't know how to help.

There are situations in my life when I felt helpless.
As simple as playing the sax as a kid.

## Saturday-Sept 7th

We were not healthy for each other clearly...
Rewire-
Dear Lord, help me stay calm and hold a positive space for Lawrence.
Five things to remember to :

1. Get my own life
2. Use boundaries to detach with love, no more trying to fix people
3. love myself
4. check in constantly with my feelings
5. Allow people to have their own journeys.

The truth is I was in a toxic relationship for years.

I thought marriage was sacrificing for the man I loved. But it took me years to find myself, my identity, by doing charity events and living life for me. My joy didn't depend on his happiness. My happiness and peace should never depend on someone or something else. It all comes from within.

With the rehab I found myself being pulled into that place again. I wanted to make sure he was healthy and that's not my journey to live. That's his.

I helped get him there and now I needed to let him go. I needed to let the amazing team of people help him and focus on myself.

The kids have a dad, alive and well.

I have myself. In trying to help him through the rehab and be supportive it's easy to let the life get sucked out of myself again, but I won't. All this anger. Why am I being so mean? He doesn't deserve it. I don't deserve the pain he caused me, but I am better than this.

I need to read my devotional, work out, walk with my friends, drink my lattes, do my rewires and do me. Why is it that every time I help him I forget about me? Enough.

It's because I have battle fatigue and I need love, but I am worn down emotionally. I will keep fighting to be the best for myself and my kids. I can't get love from a man that can't love me.

I love myself, I don't need a relationship to feel loved.

I don't need a relationship to make me happy.

I love myself and I am proud.

I'm getting untangled, but this whole situation has been hard on the whole family.

When he was in rehab I thought wow, okay

30 days he works on himself, I work on mine, but then he came home and said he doesn't love me.

I need to be calm and I need to give space.

Fuck relationships!

I only want a healthy one.

I am fighting for love that isn't there, but fighting for space, but not sure how to do it.

Shell on the gas station it was the yellow shell from the Camino de Santiago. The yellow shells were placed so that we could follow them on the trail and I found my last yellow shell at the Shell gas station near our home. It was my sign after The Camino, that I was truly home.

### September 11(day 17 of rehab)...

I got busy working on myself and spending time with my boys....day 11-27. Too tired to share here.

## Day 28 (Lawrence was up for an Emmy)

This was his first day out of rehab.

This was the first time in our history of 16 years that we would be attending a party sober together.

Lawrence earned an Emmy nomination. We grabbed each other's hands and stepped out of the town car onto the first red carpet-we will call this drop-off red carpet, one of many carpets. Here we go.

# Episode 7

## FROM REHAB AND MEHAB TO THE EMMYS

**Soundtrack:**
**Broken Heart**
**(Eric Michael)**

I do not know what tomorrow brings, but what I did know was right now for the first time in my life I had Lawrence kind of back. That sounded good, but in honesty, I didn't know him. I didn't really know who he was, but I did know that I loved this man in front of me and would always care about him and want the best for him.

I looked at him and said, "Lawrence, you got this."

I also knew it would be the last Emmy party or Hollywood party that I ever attended. I went to support Lawrence and, of course, enjoy the Emmys.

In the chaos of cameras, people, champagne, and, of course, stars, I asked myself how I felt at the Emmys with Lawrence? That was something that was a new habit for me. How did I feel? Not how did he make me feel, but how did I feel? The Emmys were an adventure. Lawrence did not win, but from the second we stepped out of the town car it was an experience.

We walked about 400 yards through the Staple Center

that was converted to a cocktail setting. People dressed in black lined the walkway, handing out Altoids, Chapstick, lip gloss, and even hairspray. It was free shopping and I was thinking I could use these as stocking stuffers. After we walked 400 yards through the Staple Center we entered the red, well, wide purple carpet. The beginning was a sea of people with press present for another 100 yard walk. Eventually we made it to the thinner purple carpet lined by an audience for another 100 yards. I was an Emmy rookie and definitely had the wrong shoes on. It was 90 degrees while people walked under big fans to cool down. Water was tray passed to the guests and music played.

When Lawrence reached the purple carpet, I felt joy. Thirty days ago I didn't know if the kids would have a father or if he would have a job and here he was sober at the Emmys. I was proud of him. Miracles do exist. I was proud of myself. I felt I had helped him in his journey to get sober and get this far. Was it my journey to help with?

I also felt at peace. Although he was sober and we could try to build a life together, this calmness took over me and I said this was the last Emmy or Hollywood party I would ever go to because it was time for me to let Lawrence be on his own journey. My friend told me that I would have a moment when I just knew I was done but in a peaceful way. I had it. The complete feeling of peace that parting ways was the best and healthiest for us. The song by Salena Gomez, "Lose you to love me" was true for us. I loved myself but almost losing him made me realize that we aren't right for each other. As long as we stay in our marriage together I can't fully 100% love myself the way I should.

That's how I felt. I felt at peace, knowing I had made a decision in my heart and knew that it was best for us and knew he would agree with me.

I felt at peace knowing that I was ready, I was strong enough to let him go. For the first time I didn't care what my family thought, what my friends thought, or even what strangers thought, because I was listening to myself and that's the only way to peace, joy, happiness—all the natural highs that life brings. I was at peace even knowing that my boys were going to be great. In time they would be the best they could be and I couldn't guarantee that if I stayed in this marriage. That's when you know. When you don't care what anyone thinks. I did it. I stuck it out for my kids, for the vows and for all around me that supported us, but I didn't care about my vows anymore and I didn't stress about my children because I was at peace and if I was at peace, change would not break us. Peace within both of us was not possible in our toxicity. There was one last celebration we agreed to do together.

# Episode 8

## BEST FRIENDS

**Soundtrack:**
**Break Up in the End**
**(Cole Swindell)**

He made it to his 50th birthday
We rented him a beach house and he surrounded himself with everyone that had been part of his life.

He played O.A.R.'s "Peace," because it was what we both wanted for so long and we had it. We needed this peace to help us embrace the change that was coming because it's inevitable.

The kids ran around the beach playing like we did the night we met.

We were very different people 16 years later, and although the wrong things may have brought us together, we knew that they led us to right now where the right things would now keep us together for a lifetime. Our children. We would forever be a family.

Our wedding song.

"God blessed the broken road that led me straight to you." -right now in this moment.

We had a good love story, we had a crazy marriage, but the one thing we have are amazing children. He needed lots of space for himself and I started to go down that deep dark tunnel again. I wasn't going to do it this time. I had to put myself and the love I have for myself first. If I lost myself again I couldn't imagine all the journeys it would take to get out. This time I'm staying on my own Journey, my own path. I will always keep that space of hope of what we can be for the boys.

**I love myself so I will walk away** with my head held high, knowing that I gave everything, every ounce of my soul to make this love story turn out a different way. Time to write our own healthy journeys that will always be touched by our greatest gifts...our boys.

We will continue to follow the divorce vows:

1. Be 100% happy for each other
2. Celebrate what we have-our boys
3. Take 100% responsibility for my part in the divorce

We both had wounds and brought the worst out of those wounds. We both continue to work on those wounds so that we can be the best we can be for our children and the world around us.

I called the lawyer, asked her to file, and our divorce process was officially started. It may not have been a beautiful marriage, but I was inspired to someday have a beautiful friendship.

A few days later the lawyer emailed me proof that we were legally separated. I wasn't scared. I knew it would be okay. Lawrence would get better and so would I.

I got a text.

*RAE, ITS TINA. I JUST MOVED TO NASHVILLE COME VISIT ME.*

# Episode 9

## Running to Nashville

**Soundtrack: Halo**
**(Eric Michael)**

**Her World Or Mine**
**(Michael Ray)**

never imagined what I could feel until country music came into my life. The day I filed I got that message from an old LA friend.

*TINA: COME TO NASH, COME GET AWAY. I WILL BE YOUR TOUR GUIDE.*

*ME: OH, DO YOU KNOW WHAT'S GOING ON WITH US?*

*TINA: YES. I HEARD FROM P YOU ARE GETTING DIVORCED.*

*ME:WELL, I DIDN'T GET DIVORCED. I AM GOING THROUGH IT, BUT WE HAVE BEEN UP AND DOWN FOR YEARS. I REALLY COULD USE A POSITIVE DISTRACTION OR A GOOD FRIEND OUTSIDE MY SD BUBBLE. I THINK*

*IT'S HARD FOR MY FAMILY AND FRIENDS WHEN I VENT OR TALK ABOUT THE DIVORCE BECAUSE THEY ARE GRIEVING IT AND LOVE LAWRENCE TOO. IT'S JUST BEEN A LOT. I AM AT PEACE WITH IT. I CAN'T DO ANYTHING ELSE.*

*TRINA:YAY COME!!*

*ME: I DO NEED TO GET OUT OF SAN DIEGO FOR A BIT SO I AM GOING TO COME.*

*TRINA: WHEN YOU GET HERE, LET'S BUY COWBOY BOOTS SO DON'T PACK TOO MANY PAIRS OF SHOES.*

*ME:K I WILL BOOK A PLACE SO I CAN BRING MORE GIRLS WITH ME AND NOT DRIVE YOUR HUB CRAZY.*

I went online and booked an Airbnb in 12 South.
I went online and booked a flight.
I sent my girlfriends the address of my Airbnb and my flight itinerary. I was going regardless, but I would be happier if a few other girlfriends could join me. I would go there and write too.

I loved music so this was a perfect place for my well-being. I needed this. I looked at the rows of fancy shoes in my closet, I wasn't bringing any of them. Goodbye, fancy shoes, I am going to Nashville to buy some cowboy boots. I need a change.

I just wanted to have fun. I wanted to break some rules. I owed it to myself. I wanted to do whatever I wanted. I could. I was free.

Life was taking a toll on me and I needed to lift my spirits. My trainer was concerned I was becoming depressed with complaints of constant physical pain. I wasn't sleeping. I fought daily to keep a positive attitude and outlook. I barely ate.

Tina and I chatted daily about what we could see and do there.

I have to be honest I didn't love myself 17 years ago when I met Lawrence. I love myself so much now from all the work I've done and I feel love so much stronger than I've ever felt it.

I deserve it. And whatever comes out of this amazing trip. I'll have no regrets.

I set the divorce papers on the counter with certainty for Lawrence to indicate that he received.

Although our divorce isn't final, our love story ended a long time ago and I just had to love myself enough to admit it.

I don't regret believing that marriage is forever, because it has to be with the right person. I don't regret all the effort I spent trying to fix my marriage. If I could go back and give advice to the younger ones it would be not to fix others. It would be to allow people to have their own journeys. Work on your own heart. And you don't have to stay in a relationship to help someone over your own needs. It would be to trust my intuition more and not doubt myself so much. It would be to not ignore my gut and the strong feeling I felt when something was not right. I would listen to less people in my life telling me what I should do and what I shouldn't be doing. I would listen to myself more.

I guess I share this for you if you're reading this and you've got a chance to make some changes, then do it.

But like I said, for me, no regrets, because I wouldn't be sitting here right now packing my suitcase, about to explore the world of Country. I had to go through everything to feel at peace with my decision.

My goal was to stay present.

Hollywood, it's been fun but my heart belongs to Country...for now.

From red carpet to hay bales.

And from heels to cowboy boots.

God really gives you exactly what you need.

Thank you, God.

———— •(()•) ————

Nashville was a blast. I drank five days straight with Tina and my other girlfriends. My girlfriends rock for just being there for me, but this party scene life was not the life I needed. My friends were not even big drinkers, but partied with me through all my emotions. I asked them to just have a great time with me and they did. Hill from SD, Tina and Paulina from LA. Thank you for being there for me! Sorry you almost missed your flights from our party escapades at Winners and Losers. I will never forget stumbling next door to have ice shots together. I will never forget the falls, the spills, the laughs in midtown, on Broadway and in 12 South. Thank you for being a reckless 21-year-old with me. Shopping in the Gulch and wearing my new boots out with you girls will be something I cherish forever.

Self-reflection time, filling my voids and pain with alcohol was definitely not what I needed long term. That was the last time I drank. I didn't owe that to Lawrence, but I owed that to my kids and myself.

# Episode 10

## FOLLOWED MY SHELL HOME

Soundtrack:
**Whiskey & The Bible**
**(Eric Michael)**

**Marry Me (Train)**

Back in San Diego, Lawrence and I were still under the same roof and for some crazy reason I still loved him. We were not meant to be, but I still loved him. We had a five bedroom/five bath home, so we had plenty of our own space. I was on the left wing in the master and he was on the right wing in the guest room. We had downsized, but I still felt blessed with the amazing 4500 square foot one story on an acre lot. Wow, if this was downsizing, we were doing pretty well. We were having horrible fights. He felt I was spending too much money and locked me out of all our bank accounts. My debit card would not work. I could not take out cash. I was furious! I walked into the bank in tears. Seriously, after all I had been through with Lawrence, he was going to stop me from taking out cash and treat me like that. I apparently was worth nothing. I had to beg to get a credit card by using projected alimony. This is what I got for holding down the fort. All of our money was kept in the business account and like that he had me taken off. Talk about feeling hurt and sick to my stomach. I thought the wind was knocked out of me. Time to wake up from another bad dream. Dang, I couldn't wake up because it was my reality. How much pain could I endure? I called my lawyer. She was a rock and I knew I had no worries with her by my side. This is what lawyers are for—to defend you.

It didn't matter how big my house was, I needed to leave that night. I slept in my friend's (my friend who I called a sister) pool house. I cried myself to sleep thinking...what happened to our divorce vows?

The next day I returned home.

I walked into the house and saw Lawrence standing in the kitchen, "Mom, you and Dad are big fat liars," Trent screamed at us. I was not used to this side of Trent, our youngest, but I was proud he was using his voice to share his feelings.

"What do you mean?" I asked my sweet, but angry blue-eyed boy.

"You promised us you and dad would be friends. This is not a friendship. You barely talk. I don't want to be around either of you."

"Trent, you are right. What do you need?" I asked putting my arm around him.

"I want a family trip. Sterling is coughing, but you two are too busy fighting. I think Hawaii would be best for all of us. Sterling can clear up his cough and we can have a family vacation."

"Trent, you are absolutely right. Can your dad and I have some time to go outside and talk? Would that be okay with you?"

"Yes, please," he said desperately.

We walked outside. I sat on a lounger and he sat next to me on the other one. I turned to face him.

"Hey, I know we agreed to get divorced, but can we put pause on everything? Can you give me a chance to be the man that you deserve? I need time. Take the kids to Hawaii with me? Please? Let's go on a divorce moon. Either way I will always love you. Can we do one last trip as a family? Please."

I responded in anger with a dagger stare, "After everything we have been through, I am the mother of your children and you have treated me like shit. After everything!! The nerve. I can't help it if you resent me for giving Sterling CF. I had no control over that. We agreed to the divorce vows and to be kind to one another. I don't trust anything you say anymore."

"I'm sorry; I didn't mean it like that. I am still working on myself and I'm sorry for blaming you. I'm sober. I am trying to own everything, be aware and take personal inventory every second of the day, but I need some grace right now. Every day is a struggle for me right now."

"I will go to Hawaii for the kids. I will be your friend, that's the best I can do right now. I can't continue to love you at the expense of my mental health-this stress. Who is here for me through all this? I will go for the kids. I will put on a smiling face for our boys because I love them, and they deserve to see us amicable."

I did not want to go, but I had to go for my boys. We needed to put our egos and pride aside for our kids. If I couldn't have a blast in Hawaii, I needed to do more work on myself.

Lawrence had to scout a location in New York, so he met us on the big island. His sponsor flew to New York and then to Hawaii to keep him company.

Lawrence's parents gave him some birthday cash so when he arrived he asked me if I would blow it with him. He pulled out $10K.

We had the dolphin suite overlooking the dolphin lagoon. We spent the days walking and exploring with the kids. They found sea turtles that lay out on the beaches daily. They gave them names...

We did a helicopter ride over the volcano and eruption area. The coast was pushed out from the eruption and beachfront homes were no longer beachfront. We flew over villages, living off grid with no power and running water. That life seemed appealing to me.

We swam with manta rays in the dark. The black lights attracted them to the surface and their white undersides were illuminated.

We ziplined near waterfalls and screamed as we soared over deep valleys.

We also swam with the dolphins as a family. We were blessed. Our marriage was not intact, but I had the most amazing trip. I was at peace. Lawrence was at peace and so were our children.

Who was Lawrence? I was trying to get to know him and he was trying to get to know me. I was sober too.

We had to let the first marriage die.

We were redefining our relationship as parents and friends.

When we returned stateside, we attended Trent's talent show together and soccer games, we parented both Sterling and Trent with a united front. This was new for us. Our kids were asking what was wrong with us. "Why are you getting along? Why are you so united?" We were truly great friends with a great foundation. We were healthier than ever. We were better co-parents than when we were actual parents.

We were legally separated, but solid friends.

Both realized how being sober together was the best relationship possible. I stayed committed to giving up alcohol. Not for Lawrence, but for myself and my boys. I had already seen the damage it did to our marriage. I didn't want to be in a relationship with alcohol for me and my boys. They had seen enough of it. How could I continue to drink when they knew their father struggled with it? I would be lying if I said I hadn't struggled with it too. Clearly it was a nice numbing concoction when I was struggling.

It was a choice I decided to make.

Friends started coming to us for advice. We were getting along so well, and they wanted some of that. Our goal was to save marriages and help people work on themselves when they came to us.

Our lawyers were confused when we both asked to push our mediation date off for a bit. We said we needed more time to heal, which we did. Getting along was healing for not just us, but our boys. We both loved our lawyers and wanted to be as honest as possible.

**One year later we started secretly dating...We saw Steve once a week together. We saw Alma once a week together. Glenn also trained us once a week together. We chose not to drink together. We went to church one day— then every week together. We had to both fully forgive to make dating work. We had a date night once a week together.**

Lawrence landed a hit TV series focused on Navy Seals and all veterans. It was filming in Coronado, just 40 minutes from our house. God was giving us everything we needed. Lawrence could produce while coming home to the family every night. I was on my way to selling my first novel to Stymie Productions. I was hoping they would make it into a series.

There was so much good going on. Our son, Sterling, was now a healthy teenager and about to start the newest drug to improve his lung function 10-13% and increase his life expectancy. Thank God!! Will he live a full life without needing a lung transplant? He enjoyed riding all over town with his friends in between classes at Tempest Academy. He skied every chance he could in Mammoth.

Thank you, CF Foundation, and thank you, Vertex!! Thank you Lawrence for doing the blood work to prep for the new Trikafta!!

We are praying it works. Trent just performed his own dance in the talent show and did amazing. He was surrounded by love on both his football and soccer teams. Our boys are amazing. There is peace in our home.

If you have marriage problems and there are drugs or alcohol in your home, do me a favor and try getting rid of them first. See what happens to your marriage. It doesn't fix every problem, but we are actually able to work through problems now with two sober partners. If I had to diagnose myself I would say I definitely abused alcohol.

Lawrence wanted me to stay at rehab with him, but I needed to be home for my kids. I was able to do it on my own, mehab. Every holiday is a new day for us—sober. I am not saying all marriages with alcohol or drugs are doomed. I am saying if you are having problems in your marriage and there is alcohol, then try doing marriage without it and see. It was a problem for our marriage and a problem for our family, so I walked away from it. Our kids knew their father struggled with it, and so did I, so what good would it do to continue to drink in front of them? No good.

I had a dream about my wedding angel. I woke up wondering what I would say to him if I saw him again. I would thank him and hug him. I would ask him if he was happy. I hoped he was.

He had a special place in my heart. I prayed I would run into him again, so I could see him and say thank you for that critical night on my journey.

Unfortunately, days after this dream I was actually at a funeral with my sister a few minutes from our homes. Our friend from high school, her best high school guy friend, Cal, had passed away after a long battle with cancer. He was only 37. He was my date for a formal dance in high school and we had the best time. I asked him with a Pamela Anderson cutout. I covered her face with a picture of me and a sign in her hands, "Will you go to the dance with me?"

I think he said yes to be nice to my sister. I had a sparkly purple sequin tube top paired with a long purple skirt. I had great abs. He showed up in a cheetah print suit and I could not get enough of it. He was hilarious, and our dance photos were the best. After winter ball we met up with my sister and many friends in Green Valley for a party. I sat outside and randomly shared a bottle of vodka with Chris, a guy I just met through my sister. Last thing I remember was waking up to Cal giving me mouth to mouth. I was naked in the bath tub with cold water being poured on me. I never wanted my first kiss to be that way. That was the type of guy he was—always making sure everyone was okay. I didn't know him like my sister did, but I believe he saved my life that night, so I will call him my high school angel.

I can't believe he left us so soon. Maybe I was dreaming again, but I wasn't. I wish I was.

There at Cal's funeral I was in deep conversation with my friend's parents when a man walked up to me and gave me a huge hug. His blue eyes froze me, after all this time I could not get words out.

"And here we are," Brandon said, all smiles.

I couldn't talk. We just stood there looking at each other for a minute in silence. I had so much I wanted to say but couldn't and then he walked away. For eight years I had hoped to run into him and had even dreamt about him. I didn't want to run into him this way. I did nothing to stop him. I couldn't. So awkward.

My mind was in a weird, dark place, a different type of sad place. Cal died on Sterling's birthday at only 37 years of age battling cancer. Sterling continued to battle cystic fibrosis every day with pills and treatments, the median life expectancy being 37.5 years. I could not imagine Sterling leaving to heaven early. Lawrence himself was battling a disease. My mind was stuck on the thought of these three incredible men battling three different diseases and one losing his battle. When Brandon hugged me I felt a sense of security I felt that night at the wedding. His kiss on the cheek left me smelling like cardamom. It must have been his lip balm. I felt his heart belonged to someone else.

Brandon just lost his best friend and all I could get out as he walked away was, "We always meet under the most awkward circumstances."

He didn't hear me. So, I tried to yell, "I enjoy following your journey." I followed his company on IG. He turned around like he heard something but was confused and kept walking out to the parking lot.

I couldn't say anything and that's just how life is sometimes. Awkward. Everything happened for a reason and I will never see him again, but that was the beauty of life. Clearly, it does not always go as planned or hoped. I had Lawrence to focus on and for now he was winning his battle. Over one year sober. I was proud of him.

I heard on a TEDx Talks, Paul Churchill

"I've been duped by alcohol"-

Dr. David Nutt harm scored twenty of the world's most addictive drugs. Alcohol was found to be the most addictive drug. Alcohol kills more people each year than every other drug combined.

33% of all traffic fatalities are caused by alcohol.

3,000,000 this year worldwide will die from alcohol-related causes.

Other points that were eye-opening to me:

In sobriety, 5% will make it to 90 days, of those only 5% will make it to 2 years. That's 2.5 people out of 1000 that make it to sobriety after they make the decision to stop drinking.

Alcoholism is not an indication of weak morals.

It does not discriminate. Even CEOS. In 2016, the Surgeon General recognized addiction as a chronic disease of the brain worthy of compassion just like any other chronic disease like diabetes or heart disease.

The stigma keeps people from reaching out for help. If we got rid of the stigma, more people may get help and more addiction problems could be prevented.

Community is the best way to face this issue. It's time to shred the shame. This is a disease just like cancer. With alcoholism, we try to keep it a secret.

Don't keep it a secret. Reach out before it too late.

I also read on the National Institute on Alcohol Abuse and Alcoholism that:

Alcohol is the third leading cause of death in the United States.

In 2015, of the 78,529 liver disease deaths among individuals 12 and older, 47% involved alcohol.

Among cirrhosis deaths in 2013, 47.9% were alcohol-related.

Lawrence proposed on a hike around the lake.

Marry me. I want more kids with you.

You are my best friend.

We got married on Broad Beach in Malibu at Madeline's house-played by Reese Witherspoon, where they filmed "BIG Little lies." We said new vows right where her new, 2nd chance vows were said on the hit show.

Our friends gathered around. We were both sober, unlike our first wedding. I asked Kevin Richardson from the Backstreet Boys to sing "Have you ever seen the rain?" for our wedding song.

My dad played the guitar. It was simple. Our guests wore all white and everyone celebrated at the house after. Our boys were right by our side through our vows. I had never seen such big smiles. Among our friends was Lawrence's Angel, Steve. There was also Alma and Glenn. They were angels too. It took a team to put us back together and I will always be grateful for the people put in my life, including God.

Not all marriages get a second chance, or a third, or a fourth or a fifth or sixth... We let our first one die, it didn't work, but we did the work and with peace in my heart and the life I want, I am fulfilled.

Lawrence was without a doubt the man I wanted to continue to grow and heal with. He was now trustworthy. He was accountable and responsible for his actions and so was I. We attended church together as a family. We prayed together and got baptized together. We did not have this in our first marriage. We now had true faith. We both had a relationship with God and put him first. For us this was the only way we could work. We would live God's plan not ours.

We bought a 10 acre ranch with horses and goats in San Diego. We decided to build a retreat. We decided it was our mission to help save marriages and help those with addiction. The retreat also included a program to support families that have children with diseases. Oh, and Starbucks agreed to a coffee shop at our center.

We named it "S.A.G. Ranch of Light" because anyone can be a light in darkness. (STEVE, ALMA, GLENN)

## 1 Corinthians 13:4-8 (NIV)

Love is patient, love is kind. It does not envy, it does not boast, it is not proud. It does not dishonor others, it is not self-seeking, it is not easily angered, it keeps no record of wrongs. Love does not delight in evil but rejoices with the truth. It always protects, always trusts, always hopes, always perseveres. Love never fails.

*TO LAWRENCE AND MY KIDS, I LOVE YOU.*

*TO THE HARDWORKING TV AND FILM CREWS OUT THERE, YOU ROCK. TO ALL THE CELEBRITIES, THANK YOU FOR DOING WHAT YOU DO, JUST MAKE SURE TO PRACTICE WHAT YOU PREACH OR DON'T PREACH AT ALL BECAUSE KIDS ARE LOOKING UP TO YOU. TO ALL THE PRODUCTION HUSBANDS OR WIVES, MAKE SURE YOU LIVE YOUR DREAMS TOO BECAUSE WE ARE MUCH MORE THAN OUR PARTNER'S BETTER HALVES.*

CPSIA information can be obtained
at www.ICGtesting.com
Printed in the USA
LVHW030548291220
675307LV00001B/27

9 781977 233110